"DON'T BE FRIGHTENED,"
MARC WHISPERED.
"YOU KNOW I WON'T HURT YOU."

"It's not that," Gaby said, trying to ease away from him, but his big hand caught her waist. The touch of his hand was such a dark pleasure that she couldn't move. His chest rose and fell and his black eyes searched hers, making her heart go crazy. She smelled him, breathed him, and her knees went weak.

"You used to love touching my chest," he murmured, his lips parting against her forehead, and she could hear his ragged breathing as both big hands drew her against him. "Do you remember? Every time we were alone you'd unbutton my shirt and lie against me . . ."

"No," she said with a moan, jerking away from him, her eyes wide and afraid. "No!"

"You haven't forgotten. And you haven't gotten over me. Not yet." His dark eyes raked her body with a look of bold possession. "Even today," he said triumphantly, "when I touch you, you're mine."

TANGLED DESTINIES

Diana Blayne

A Dell Book

Published by
Dell Publishing
a division of
Bantam Doubleday Dell Publishing Group, Inc.
666 Fifth Avenue
New York, New York 10103

The trademark Dell® is registered in the U.S. Patent and
Trademark Office.

ISBN: 0-440-20927-7

Printed in the United States of America

Published simultaneously in Canada

June 1991

10 9 8 7 6 5 4 3 2

RAD

August 8, 1990

Dear Readers:

Tangled Destinies is one of my favorite Dell titles, and I'm delighted to see it back in print again. This book was written while I was working for Dell Editor John Collins, one of my editors from the old MacFadden Paperback Romance line at the now-defunct Kim Publishing Corporation which gave me my start as a published writer.

John, along with then-Dell Ecstasy Editor Anne Gisonny, have been two of my staunchest supporters as I went from novice to professional romance novelist. It was their constant reinforcement of my confidence that got me where I am today, and I'll never forget either of them.

I always enjoyed working with both editors, but *Tangled Destinies* was solely mine and John's, and we had a ball working on it.

From the opening scene where Marc and Gaby meet to the dramatic confrontation with the hit man, this book was a real challenge to write. John and I felt that the prologue was the best way to set the stage for Gaby's vengeance against the man who sold her out for money. It was more than just a love story to me, it was a chance to show how two characters developed over a period of years and the hard lessons they learned from the past.

Marc is Italian, of course, and I have to admit that I find Italian men very appealing (as well as Latin men). There is something about the Italian temperament that blends passion with sensitivity. I loved that quality in Marc, and the way his stubborn pride played against Gaby's independence and sophistication. It was a delightful book to write. I hope you enjoy reading it as much as John and I enjoyed working on it. It remains one of my favorite novels.

Love,

Diana Blayne

Diana Blayne

PROLOGUE

She knew someone was following her. Icy dread numbed her throat. It was almost dark, and it didn't help to know that her own stupidity had put her in this particular neighborhood as darkness fell over New York City. She could have waited for the bus, but she'd been too impatient. It was spring, and the few trees along the streets were just budding. She hadn't thought what a long walk it would be from her piano teacher's home to her own.

Her auburn hair blew in wavy strands around her thin face, and her big green eyes swept restlessly along the deserted street. There wasn't a single person in sight. Clutching her cashmere sweater closer around her thin shoulders, she bit on her lower lip. She crushed her leather purse and sheet music against her small bosom as she held on to them like a life preserver. Stupid, she told herself. Stupid girl, wearing clothes that shouted money, walking through a neighborhood where you could be mugged for a dollar bill. Behind her, the footsteps suddenly grew quicker, more determined.

There were two sets of footsteps, Gaby realized suddenly as a feeling of panic came over her—one heavy, one lighter. She glanced nervously behind her as she turned the corner and quickly looked away again, her heart racing torturously. She'd caught a glimpse of them then, both ragged and greasy and mean-looking. Ahead were only alleys and dark buildings. She quickened her pace and noticed a garage a little farther down the street. If only it was still open.

She started toward it, but the footsteps were closer. They must be running, she thought. Would she be able to make it?

"No!" she cried, but it was too late. They reached her just as she was passing one of the alleys. The taller one caught her arm, and the shorter one tugged at her bag, sending her sheet music flying in all directions.

She held on to her purse with all her strength and tried to scream, but almost before she could utter a sound, one of them shoved her toward the alley, ignoring her furious attempts to fight back. If only she hadn't been wearing silly flat rubber-soled boots! She'd have given anything for spiked heels.

"Don't touch me!" she raged at them. Her hair came loose and flew around her shoulders as she struggled.

"Shut up, Red," the taller one laughed, holding her by the shoulders. "Get it, Terry!"

"Let go," the short one growled, tugging at the purse. "Come on, baby, you got all kinds of money, ain't you never heard of sharing?"

"Yeah, we ain't all rich, you know," the tall one mumbled.

"Whew!" The heavyset boy whistled as he studied the contents of her bag. "Five big ones." He held up the ten-dollar bills in his fist. "Not bad," he grumbled, digging further.

Gaby was terrified. She didn't care much about the money but wasn't sure what would happen next. She'd never felt so alone or helpless. Tears stung her eyes when she saw one of the boys grin at her lecherously. She backed away, preparing to defend herself from them, knowing exactly what was on their minds, but she tripped on something and fell heavily to the ground. She felt her back hit the hard concrete, saw them looming over her, felt hands at her blouse.

"What's going on here?" an unexpected deep voice demanded from the end of the blind alley.

The boys jerked up, staring toward the light. The figure blocking it looked massive, even at that distance. Very dark, wearing a white T-shirt and tight slacks that showed every bulging muscle. Even at this distance Gaby could see crisp, straight black hair and eyes so big and black that they deemphasized the formidable straight nose, square jaw, and leonine quality of the rough face.

"Hey, Marc," the shorter boy protested, hands palms upward. "Hey, no trouble, okay?"

11

The man he'd called Marc stared past him at the thin, disheveled redhead on the ground. "You okay, honey?" he asked her in a voice like deep, dark velvet.

She wanted to cry now that it was almost over, now that she had help. "Yes," she managed, but her voice sounded quavering. She scrambled to her feet, clutching her blouse.

"Come on over here, then," he coaxed. "You're fine now, they won't bother you again."

Once she was safe behind him, Marc took two quick steps forward. He landed a powerful blow to the taller boy's solar plexus, sending him crashing to the ground. Almost without pausing he spun around to Gaby's other attacker, who by now was cringing. A quick right hook sent the boy sprawling next to his friend.

"That make you feel any better, honey?" Marc asked with a chuckle.

"Thanks," she said, panting and holding tight to her open purse as she joined him. He looked good even close up, grease stains and all. His mouth was wide and had a chiseled look to it, and he was smiling mockingly.

"My pleasure. Terry and Gus aren't my favorite neighbors. They take any money?"

"A little," she said, glaring down at them. "Let them keep it. I don't want to soil my hands by touching it."

Marc scowled and moved forward again. He bent and jerked the ten-dollar bills from the grasp of the shorter boy, who was still groaning. "Forget it, Gus," he said tightly. "You're not getting paid to attack little girls. Stick your dirty nose in my neighborhood again and I'll cut it off even with your eyelashes. Understand?"

Gus swallowed. "Yeah. Sure, buddy." He looked nervous. "You, uh, you won't mention this around your uncle?"

"Uncle Michael wouldn't soil his hands on you." Marc laughed mirthlessly. "He's got too much pride to bother with garbage. Get out. Both of you."

As the boys edged past, the bigger one shot a regretful glance at Gaby and took off running. One of them made a gesture that caused her to blush, but Marc returned it with interest.

"Hotshots," he muttered, staring after them with his hands on his narrow hips. He looked down at the girl curiously, noticing her cashmere sweater, leather purse and boots, and real pearl earrings. Money, he thought. Not much to look at, poor little thing, all thin angles from her shoulders down to her feet. That wild auburn hair must look stylish to her own crowd, and her eyes are the biggest, greenest ones he'd ever seen. He cocked his head to study her. In a few years she might be something to look at, he concluded. And she had spirit, which appealed to him.

"Out of your league down here, aren't you?" he asked.

"I sure am," she agreed, brushing back her hair. "From now on it's karate lessons. I'm being wasted at music class."

He chuckled. "What's your name?"

13

"Gabrielle, but I'm called Gaby. Gaby Bennett. And you?"

"Marcus Stephano," he volunteered. His head jerked toward the garage down the street. "I own half of the neighborhood auto shop. God didn't think I should be rich, but he gave me good hands. I can fix anything short of broken hearts."

"You saved me," she offered. "Thanks." With a mischievous grin she gestured at herself. "It isn't much, but it's yours."

He smiled, a genuine smile. "You're not so bad, honey. I like your style, Gaby Bennett."

"I like yours, too, Mr. Stephano."

"Marc." He pursed his wide lips. "What are you doing down here."

"I walked home from piano class," she confessed. "Not my brightest idea so far, but it seemed like a good idea at the time."

"You must lead a sheltered life."

"Smothered, if you want to know," she blurted out.

"Rich kid?"

"I guess." She sighed, walking along beside him. He towered over her despite her above-average height. "My dad's an investment firm and my mother is a jewelry store."

"My dad was a petty criminal, and my mother wasn't much better," he said matter-of-factly.

Her breath caught, and he grinned.

"Yeah, that's right, you're in bad company, pet," he told her. "I'm a mean man. I come from a line of those swarthy gangster types your mama probably warned you about. My uncle's big-time stuff around here."

"You don't scare me, big man," she returned, smiling back. "I owe you my life, remember?"

"Not your life, exactly," he said, letting his darker-than-night eyes go slowly down her slender body. "Do you eat?"

"No, I live on pure oxygen and Bach concerts in the park. But if you like, I'll start sneaking cream cakes for breakfast."

"You do that. We Italians like a little meat on our women's bones."

She laughed and fell into step with him. It was spring, and suddenly the world was bright and beautiful and blazing with new color. Overhead, the streetlights took on a magical quality as she walked toward home with a stranger who was rapidly becoming a friend. . . .

CHAPTER ONE

"Great shots, Gaby," Harry Dean grinned as he helped her up from a lounging position on the hood of a rebuilt 1956 Chevrolet. "Motocraft, Inc., will love it! You'll sell auto parts by the barrelful."

"I'd better sell transmissions." She laughed, stretching lazily in the skimpy halter-and-shorts set she'd worn for the layout. They were white, and she was nicely tanned from her long auburn hair down to her pretty toes. Slender, green-eyed, and vivacious, Gaby Bennett was a top model and earned big money at her profession. This layout for Motocraft, Inc., had been one of her best jobs to date. She was rapidly becoming known as the First Lady of Parts, an in-joke with her modeling friends.

Apparently the executives of the auto parts and transmission specialists corporation had been very picky, because ten girls had been turned down before they had approached her agency about the layout. Gaby had been picked immediately. This was the first of a series of commercials she was shooting for them, and it might involve some travel if the commercials caught on.

A thin, dark-looking man had been watching the photographer shoot the stills, and now he came closer. He had dark hair and eyes, and he looked oddly nervous. Gaby frowned, wiping her perspiration away with a towel as she relaxed away from the brilliant lamps she'd been bathed in for the session. He looked so familiar . . . hadn't she seen him before?

"You're Gaby," the man said in a pleasant voice. His manner was hesitant, rather shy. She smiled because she liked that shyness. It was an unusual quality, making him seem very different from most of the men she'd known.

"Gaby Bennett," she agreed pleasantly. "Excuse me, but do I know you?" she asked. "I'm sure that sounds like a line, but you look familiar somehow."

"We've met, but it was a long time ago." He looked at her hesitantly, as if not sure whether or not to go on. "I'm Joe Stephano," he said, finally introducing himself. "I, uh, I'm the executive vice-president of Motocraft, Inc."

Gaby felt the blood draining from her face. No wonder he'd seemed familiar. She remembered him all too well, a shy, younger version of his big brother Marcus. Joe had always been nervous around her. They hadn't seen too much of each other during that brief period of her life, but she remembered him. He brought back memories that were unbearable nine years later, memories of his brother.

She hadn't connected Motocraft, Inc., with the Stephanos because the account had come through a Mr. Smith, an executive of the company. She hadn't realized that Marc had achieved such fame and fortune. So he was Motocraft, Inc. Suddenly she realized why she'd been given the account. Was he trying to make amends? Well, it was years too late!

"It's nice to see you again," she said, forcing herself to keep smiling and extending her hand. After all, what had happened wasn't Joe's fault. "Do I thank your brother for this job?" she asked bluntly.

He flushed. His hand felt a little limp in hers, and he quickly removed it. "Uh, actually, you can thank me. Marc didn't find out until it was too late. That is, he sort of wanted a blonde. . . ."

"You don't have to apologize, I'm just grateful for the work," she said gently. So Marc hadn't wanted her here. No doubt he wanted to forget her completely, since betraying her had gotten him so far in the world. Maybe his conscience still hurt him. She hoped it did.

He stuck his hands in his pockets and smiled shyly. "I hope you won't hold the past against me," he began. "Marc and I never got along real well, even back then. I'm sorry things didn't work out between you, but that was a long time ago."

The memories engulfed her all at once, and despite her twenty-six years and all of her acquired sophistication, she went beet-red.

Her eyes held his, cool, quiet, green glades of solitude. "How is your brother?" She didn't want to ask, but she had to know.

He shrugged. "Marc's okay, I guess," he said, as if he disliked discussing his older brother. "The business is his life."

She let her gaze drop to his collar, noticing a tiny spot on it, like catsup, and she almost smiled. He was boyish, and she liked his apparent lack of sophistication. She glanced back up again, studying him. "Marc isn't married?"

"They try," Joe offered, "but he always escapes the noose. Slippery fish, my brother." He cocked his head. "You married?"

"I can't stand men," she volunteered, and grinned.

He burst out laughing. "Hey, that's good. I like that." His warm, dark eyes slid over her slender, well-proportioned body. "You sure look good," he blurted out, and quickly cleared his throat before she could speak. "Uh, you thirsty?" he asked after a moment's hesitation.

She smiled. "I feel like I've been in the desert for a month! These lights are hot!"

"Would you . . . I could buy you a soda or a martini or something," he volunteered.

"Sure," she said easily. "Give me a minute to get dressed."

He took a deep breath. "Okay!"

She laughed as she went to get her clothes back on. He was a nice boy, she thought. A brotherly

' type, if ever there was one. So she owed the account to him. That was surprising. But he'd always seemed attracted to her, even in the days when she was dating Marc. She'd liked him the first time she ever saw him, in the apartment he shared with his older brother. He was a nice, unassuming boy with a reserve that she'd taken for coldness until she saw the lack of confidence it camouflaged. Then she began to talk to him. Like most people, he responded to her smiling cheerfulness and opened up. He'd been a lot of fun. Apparently the shyness hadn't abated in all those years, but she wondered if he was still the mischievous boy underneath. Or had a lifetime of living in Marc's shadow left him without joy?

Marc. She closed her eyes as she donned a pair of white slacks and a multicolored silk blouse. She'd deliberately kept busy so that she wouldn't have to think about him, to remember. And now Joe was here and bringing it all back. But despite her pain and the years of wounded pride, she couldn't resist the hunger for bits of information about him. Was he well, how did he look, was he happy, was there a special woman . . . so many questions that she shouldn't have wanted to ask. But her heart would feast on just such tidbits. And she was like a puppet on a string. She had to know. She had to hear that he was satisfied with what he had, that giving her up had been worth the profit it had gained him.

Joe took her to an elegant little restaurant less than a block away and persuaded her to have lunch as well as something to drink.

"You must be hungry," he coaxed, smiling. "Come on, have a salad at least. That won't put weight on you."

"All right." She gave in gracefully, smiling across the white linen tablecloth at him. "But if I gain one pound, my agent gets to park his car on your spine for an hour. Deal?"

He laughed, then folded his arms on the table and shook his head. "You're a funny lady. I remembered your sense of humor best of all. You used to make me feel really comfortable." He looked down at his hands, slender and tanned, sensitive hands. "I don't mix with people very well."

"Most of us don't, if you want the truth," she confided. "We learn to bluff. Put on a big smile and leap in with both feet. By the time people realize you're not a live-wire personality, you're talking to them and you forget how shy you are."

"Come on," he chided. "You're not shy."

"I certainly am!" she replied. She tucked a long strand of shimmering auburn hair behind one dainty ear. "I've been shy all my life. But I learned to act like an extrovert. Now everyone thinks I am one."

"Yeah, well that doesn't work for me," he said. He studied her face. "Are you always as happy as you look in those product ads you do?"

She looked down at the silverware, touching her knife gently with a long, red-polished fingernail. "Is anybody happy all the time? I have my problems and I get lonely. But I suppose I've learned to like my own company. At least, I've had to until this past year. My mother died of a heart attack, and I've moved back in with my father, to keep him company."

"I'm sorry about that," he said. "I guess it's hard to lose a mother."

She sighed. "Yes, I suppose it was. We never got along very well, but I cared about her. So did my father. God bless him, he went crazy when she died. Just went all to pieces. She was the guiding force, you see. Mother made the rules and he followed them. This is the first time in his life that he's had the freedom to do what he likes, and now he doesn't quite know what to do with it," she said, smiling tolerantly. "He's a character, my dad. A dreamer. If he hadn't inherited money, and had Mother show him how to make more, I suppose he'd been running an antique store and giving away his profits."

"Do you look like him?"

"Not really. I have his awful auburn hair and green eyes," she admitted. "But I have my mother's facial features." She studied him. "You look a lot like . . . like your brother."

"Yeah, most of the men in the Stephano family kind of look alike. Why, we have an uncle who looks like he could be Marc's and my father."

"Uncle Michael," she said suddenly, remembering Marc's deep, gravelly voice telling her about his uncle, a slightly shady character if she remembered correctly.

"That's right. Hey, girl, you've got a good memory."

"Too good, sometimes," she said with a wistful look in her eyes.

He started to speak, but the waiter came, and they paused to order. He took out a cigarette and glanced at her.

"It's okay," she said, "I'm used to people who smoke."

"I'm not quite as bad as Marc," he said, laughing. "He smokes like a furnace these days."

"Has he changed a lot?" she asked, and her eyes were wide and softer than she realized.

He leaned back in his chair and studied her carefully. "Oh, he's changed, all right. So much that I finally had to move out on my own. Well, not quite. I don't like my own company that much, I have a roommate. Nice guy. He sells real estate."

"Have you been out on your own long?"

"Three years," he confessed. "Marc lives in an apartment on the East Side, overlooking the river. He's got a great view. Mine's a little closer in, and it faces another building. Not much to look at unless you look up, but it's a place to sleep."

"I guess Marc travels a lot," she persisted.

"Not too much."

The waiter brought their orders, and she gave up asking about the man from her past long enough to eat. Coffee was served when they finished, and they lingered over it.

"What about the men in your life?" he asked. "I don't believe you're that much of a man-hater."

"Oh, I go out on the town once in a while," she said, "but I work hard, and the weekends are the only time I have free."

He looked at his coffee cup. "I'd like to take you out to dinner tonight," he told the coffee. "It's

Friday, and I know you probably already have a date. . . ."

"No," she said, watching him color. "Actually I don't."

"Oh. That's nice." He crossed his arms on the table again and glanced at her hesitantly. "Well, would you come? I know it's short notice, but I had to get introduced to you first, before I could ask, you know."

She smiled secretly at his shy manner. She liked his style. In a way he seemed a lot like her. She tossed back her hair. "Well . . ."

"Be a sport," he coaxed, brightening as he added, "I'll take you to a restaurant that has a fountain. I'll even let you swim in the fountain."

She laughed delightedly. "Is there a fountain, honestly?"

"No. But for you I'll build one," he promised. He cocked his head to one side, studying her. "Be a sport!"

Her green eyes began to shine with amusement, and her face became exquisite. He caught his breath looking at her. Why not? she asked herself. She didn't like the usual type of man who expected much more than a handshake at the end of the evening. She thought that Joe wouldn't be like that. He didn't seem to be looking for a serious relationship any more than she was. What would it hurt? It might even be a dig at Marc. Yes, perhaps it would anger him, after all these years, to know that she was seeing his brother. She'd never expected that she might feel vengeful; it was out of character. But the affair with Marc killed something in her, knowing how little he'd valued the love she'd offered him. It had damaged her in ways she didn't even like admitting to. And the love-hate she felt for him, even after nine years, demanded some sort of reckoning. Wouldn't this be a little recompense? It wasn't as if she were using Joe. Joe knew the score; he just wanted a friend. Why not? Only the two of them need ever know it was just friendship. But Marc wouldn't know it. He'd think she was leading Joe on, to get even. She could get to him without ever laying a hand on him.

"All right," she said. "I'll come out with you. But, Joe, I'm no good-time girl," she added, putting it plainly, her face solemn. "Friendship is all I'm offering. Okay?"

He shifted in his chair, and something touched his eyes for an instant. But he grinned. "Okay," he said on a laugh. "Friends forever."

"Uh, I hate to mention it," she said hesitantly, "but isn't this kind of fraternizing with the brass, so to speak?"

"Let me worry about that." His dark eyes narrowed. "You aren't carrying a torch for big brother after all these years, are you?" he asked abruptly.

She shook her head and felt her body going rigid with remembered pain. "Not on your life."

"Good." He stretched lazily. "Suppose I pick you up about six?" he asked.

"You don't know where I live," she faltered.

He chuckled. "No? I asked your agency. Since I'm the boss, sort of, they gave it to me."

"You sure are resourceful!" She laughed, wondering if she should be pleased that her agency had sold her out to a perfect stranger. She also couldn't help but wonder what would happen when she saw Marc again. But she gave in with a sigh. Maybe it was fate. She'd cope. Besides, she rather liked this young man. She didn't date a lot because she hated having to fight off men with ideas about quick relationships. Joe didn't seem like a rusher, and she looked forward to being able to go out without being harassed.

Her father was out when she got home. Her parents had fought her tooth and nail to keep her out of modeling. Her father had even gone behind her back and tried to persuade one agency head not to hire Gaby. But eventually she'd found an agency that was interested in her, and she'd started making a name for herself. Thanks to those years she'd spent at a prestigious New England boarding school, she had enough poise and grace of movement to make her a natural. Not that she'd been so enthused at the time, she reminded herself pointedly. Oh, no.

Marc. She could close her eyes, and there he'd be, big and strong and softly laughing as she responded wildly to his very adult passion. It had always been Marc who pulled away, not Gaby. From the first time she'd sneaked away from home to meet him, it had been Marc who kept things cool between them. Even now she could vividly remember his words.

"You're a baby," he'd teased, nibbling at her mouth. "You're not ready for love yet, little one. It would haunt me all my life."

"But, Marc, I love you so," she'd whispered back, openly pleading.

"But you're barely an adult." And he'd kissed her and held her. His hands had touched her young breasts for the first time. "Soft little buds," he'd breathed at her lips as he felt the rapid hardening of the tips under his gently caressing fingers.

He was an emotional man, all sensuous blatancy, Gaby remembered, never dressing up his language or his remarks. It was what had appealed most to her, with her too sheltered background.

She had clung to him that day as he'd eased her down into his arms in the deserted park under the big oak by the lake. He'd smiled reassuringly as he laid her back on the grass and slowly opened the top few buttons of her blouse.

Gaby shuddered, remembering her own words to Marc that day. "I want to be yours Marc," she'd whispered. She'd lain quietly, feeling the soft coolness of the grass at her back as he dealt with buttons and then lace and hooks. She arched her back as he peeled away the bra.

"So delicate," he'd whispered deeply, his voice shaded with tenderness and growing passion, his black eyes devouring her as he loomed over her prone body, his big hands on either side of her. "So virginal."

"I'd die before I'd let anyone else look at me this way," she'd told him feverishly, and her body had ached for sensations it had never before experienced.

"And suppose I want to touch you?" he'd asked,

lifting his eyes to her soft, flushed face. "What then?"

Her lips had parted on hungry thoughts. She'd reached down and slowly peeled the blouse and bra from her body, feeling her nipples go hard as he looked at them, as she arched them toward him.

"Have you ever done this with anyone?" he whispered.

"Not until now," she'd replied, swallowing hard. Her breath had come quickly, like gasps. "Marc . . . I want to feel your hands."

"Yes. I want to feel you too," he whispered back. He lifted one big, warm hand and put it slowly over a soft breast, watching her body jerk as it swallowed her up, and he felt the hard tip rubbing in the dampness of his palm. "You're so little, darling."

"Too little?" she managed, afraid that she'd failed him somehow.

"Oh, no," he whispered, smiling. "No." His big hands had caressed her stiff young body, and she'd moaned in a way that had excited him beyond bearing.

Outside the house, car horns blew, bringing Gaby coldly back to the present. But her body trembled as she remembered how it had felt that first time he'd touched her, remembered the soft suction of his open mouth on her breast. She looked wildly into the mirror as she stood there nude, fresh from her bath, and watched her body respond even now, years later, to the memory of how it had been. Never since, not even once, had she reacted that way to a man. Marc had owned her body and possessed her soul. Every time she'd tried to give herself to any other man, the memory had chilled her to the bone, so that she was cold, icy cold, with men. They called her frigid, but it was the heat of Marc's lovemaking that had taken all her warmth away. She'd never been cold with him.

She dressed in a fever, tugging on a pale green cocktail dress with shaking hands. The dress had a bodice with only a whisper of lace over the strapless shoulders. She wouldn't need a shawl or a jacket, because it was summer and already hot at night.

She left her hair long, letting it drift in auburn waves down over her shoulders. She'd developed since those sensual days with Marc. She'd gained weight, and her body had ripened. She had a perfect hourglass figure now, long slender legs, and an all-over tan, a body that men wanted. Marc had wanted it long before it flowered. But Marc had wanted money more. And Gaby knew, even if nobody else did, how he'd attained his huge empire. Knew, and hated him for it. She tried to put thoughts of Marc far from her mind as she got ready to meet Joe. There was no reason to have the ghosts of the past harm her tonight. She was going to have a good time.

Joe Stephano called for her promptly at six. He was leaning leisurely against the stone arch past the door when she answered the door bell. She and her father only had a daily housekeeper now, Mrs. Sims, a charming middle-aged woman who kept things going like clockwork while Gaby and her father pursued their respective careers. Mrs. Sims left at five-thirty usually, except when guests were expected for dinner, so there was only Gaby to answer the phone and the door after that time.

"Very nice," he said appreciatively, pursing his lips at the deep cleavage and the way the soft fabric clung to every line of her body. "You'll stop traffic."

"I do hope so," she murmured demurely. He was just about her height, very thin, and he looked oddly out of place in his dark evening clothes, but she took his arm and followed him out onto the busy street.

He was driving an expensive sports car, a black one with a white interior, and she was impressed with its gadgetry.

"I usually get cabs where I'm going," he remarked as they drove down the busy street, "but they're so hot at night. Besides, I wanted to show this car off. It's brand-new."

"It's a lot of car," she said, because she knew the list price. She'd wanted one herself but had been hesitant to spend that much on a car. She could have purchased a house in some parts of the country for less.

"I like expensive things," he remarked. Her eyes went to the Rolex watch on his wrist and the silk jacket he was wearing. Obviously he went in style.

She leaned her head back against the headrest with a weary smile. "It's been a long day," she said apologetically. "I hope I won't be a drag."

"Not you, Gaby." He said her name for the first time and smiled, as if it pleased him to use it. "Never you. I thought we'd go Chinese tonight, what do you say?"

"I love Chinese food," she said dreamily.

"Then Chinese it is!" he replied. He stepped on the gas. "Hold on."

She did, wondering at the reckless way he cut in and out of traffic. Very often a shy personality camouflaged a person who thrived on danger. Joe hadn't looked like a daredevil, but he was shaping up as one. She was ready to give thanks for survival when they arrived in the parking lot of an exclusive-looking Chinese restaurant.

"Here we are!" He grinned. He let the top up before he helped her out and locked the car. "Hey, you look shaky. I didn't scare you, did I?" he asked, as if it mattered.

"A little," she admitted, because her legs felt like rubber.

"Hey, I won't ever do it again, okay? I'm really sorry."

He was so apologetic that she felt guilty for mentioning it. She shook her head and slid her hand through the crook of his arm. "Forget it. Let's eat. I feel like sweet-and-sour pork tonight."

"Me too."

It was the first of many dates. They got along well together, and Gaby liked the fact that he left her at her door with a wink and a grin. She didn't have to fight him off, and she was delighted to have someone to go places with, someone who

31

didn't ask for more than she was able to give. She relaxed with him.

The only hard part was wondering about Marc, about his reaction to it. She was sure that Joe had told him. But Joe never mentioned his brother, and she'd long since given up probing. It did no good at all to ask about Marc; Joe gave answers in monosyllables and quickly changed the subject. And perhaps that was just as well. It wouldn't do for her to get too curious about Marc.

She hadn't told her father that she was seeing Joe. There hadn't been the opportunity, anyway. Her dad spent a lot of time at the office these days, getting his finances straightened out after the time he'd taken off to mourn his wife's death. He was only now becoming his old, cheery self again.

Gaby continued with the Motocraft ads, which had just appeared on television and were gaining her a national reputation as the Parts Girl. She took the kidding good-naturedly, because added exposure meant added security in her job. The money was good, too, and she liked being self-sufficient, depending on herself for her livelihood. She and Joe eased into a companionable friendship, and her life was on an even keel for the first time in quite a while. Then Joe took her by the company offices in downtown Manhattan to meet the executive who was in charge of the advertising. And she ran headlong into Marcus Stephano for the first time in nine years.

CHAPTER TWO

Gaby had just left the elevator on the twelfth floor of the office building where Motocraft, Inc., was located when she collided with something big and warm and solid.

She felt his hands before she looked up and saw his face. Big, warm, firm hands that kept her from pitching to the floor. Hands that her body remembered long before her eyes flooded with helpless memory.

"Gaby?" His deep voice ran through her like ripples on clear water, and her heart beat crazily as she straightened, drowning in the spicy scent of his cologne, a scent she'd associated with him all the long years.

Her wide green eyes searched his black ones, and all her resolutions to hate him, to wreak vengeance, went into stark eclipse. She'd heard of people being frozen in place, but until now she'd never actually experienced it. She didn't move. She hardly breathed. The world narrowed to Marcus Stephano's broad, dark face, and she looked and looked until her starving heart began to expand with feeling.

Older. He was older. There were streaks of gray in the thick, straight black hair that still fell onto his forehead in unruly strands. There were lines under his eyes, beside his chiseled, wide mouth. He was heavier than he used to be but was still all muscle: broad shoulders that strained against a beautifully tailored jacket, powerful legs that were barely encased in thin, close-fitting slacks. Under his brow his dark eyes narrowed and stared down at her unblinkingly, as if he, too, were comparing memory with reality.

It was too quick. She'd expected that she might see him, dreaded and anticipated it with wild abandon. But she hadn't expected that it would happen suddenly, like this, before she had time to prepare herself. It was like walking into a hole in a shallow creek.

"Marc," she said, her voice sounding ghostly, not its normal, sweet contralto.

His chest expanded with what looked like a deliberate breath, but his face showed nothing. Just like old times.

"Surely I haven't changed that much, honey?" he asked, nothing hostile in his tone. "You've grown up, little Gaby. I hardly recognized you."

Her nails gripped her small purse until she thought they might pierce the delicate leather. But somehow she smiled.

"I'm nine years older," she reminded him. "Twenty-six, my last birthday."

"Yes, I know." He let his eyes go slowly down her body. She felt almost as if he were touching her skin, and she trembled inside. Part of her was glad that she'd chosen to wear a silky, sleeveless beige dress that clung lovingly to her body and that she'd put her hair up into a sleek chignon. She looked elegant and sophisticated, and her eyes were triumphant when she saw the masculine appreciation in his hard face. "You were a bud then. You've blossomed."

"Quite," she said in a haughty tone.

He still didn't react. His eyes went past her to Joe, as if he'd only just realized that his brother was with her. Joe's face was an emotionless mask, and his hands were jammed deeply into his pockets.

"Ciao, mio fratello," Marc said in Italian, and smiled pleasantly at the younger man.

"Hi," Joe replied. "I thought Gaby might like to see the offices and meet David Smith, our vice-president in charge of advertising."

"Oh, yes," Marc said. He glanced at his watch and pulled a gold cigarette case from his inside pocket, his eyes steady and curious on Gaby's flushed face. "You're our new image, aren't you, Gaby?"

He seemed so condescending that she colored. So that was how he planned to play it. Very cool, she gave him that.

"We're lucky to get her," Joe broke in, sounding more belligerent than she'd ever heard him.

35

"Gaby's reached the point where she's turning down work these days."

"Yes, indeed," she agreed, laying it on thick as she peered up at the taller man and treated him to a flirtatious smile. "I'm in demand, as they say. My bankbook runneth over." Her eyes narrowed, and the smile iced over. "Sometimes I make more than five thousand a week."

She'd chosen the figure deliberately, and she watched it hit home, watched his expression freeze in place. He didn't move for a long moment.

"Nice for you," he said then, and the mask was in place again. It had hardly slipped at all.

"Nice for you, if this place is indicative of your empire, Mr. Stephano," she said, glancing around at furnishings that were obviously expensive and probably had been chosen by interior decorators. "Amazing how far you've come from that garage where you used to work when I knew you."

"I got lucky," he said through his teeth.

"Oh, didn't you just," she drawled, delighting at the fury that darkened his eyes.

Joe, standing to one side, frowned at the byplay, seemingly oblivious to the undercurrents.

"Shall we go?" Joe asked Gaby, holding out a hand.

"Whenever you're ready," she said lightly, and took the outstretched hand. She didn't miss Marc's reaction, and that pleased her too. "See you, big boss."

Joe seemed as triumphant as she felt, and she darted a glance at him. Well, there was no doubt that he'd grown up in Marc's shadow. Marc had had to be father and mother to the younger man, and she remembered vividly how Marc wielded that authority. He expected immediate obedience, no delays, no excuses. He'd been rigid, and she'd wondered even then if he hadn't been too tough on Joe. She'd even mentioned it once, only to have him lash out at her for trespassing in family matters.

"Do you work here too?" she asked Joe.

"Me? Nope." He shrugged it off. "I have an office at the main supply store. It's kind of my territory. Besides, Marc and I do better when we only see each other occasionally."

"I see."

"How was it, seeing him again after so long?" he asked, pausing at the door to an office that carried David Smith's name in gold letters.

She grimaced. "Not so bad, I guess."

"He went up in smoke, did you notice?" He laughed, as if that amused him. "I'll hear about this, you know. He'll be all over me. Fraternizing with the employees . . ."

"Joe, you won't get in trouble, will you?" she asked nervously. She didn't want to be the cause of an argument.

"Don't worry, I can take care of myself," he told her. "Let him rage. Besides," he added with a calculating stare at Gaby, "he's got his own problems. I hear his newest lovely is angling for matrimony."

"His newest?" she asked softly.

"Lana Moore. She's a British woman. Very

wealthy. Brains and beauty. He's been her lover for the past year. Who knows, he might settle down at last."

Gaby felt sick, unsteady on her feet. But she couldn't let it show; she couldn't let Joe see how that news affected her. She smiled and acted as if she were on stage. "Think so?" she teased. "What will we give him for a wedding present? How about the engine out of that fifty-six Chevy?"

He smiled and looked so relieved that she almost burst out laughing. "You're terrific," he said under his breath. "Class all the way. Me, I got so many rough edges, I look like a building under construction, but you're pure, smooth curves, Gaby."

"What rough edges?" she said, chiding.

His thin shoulders lifted and fell. "My background shows. So does Marc's, although he hides it well. It's hard to go from poverty to money. Hard to leave old friends behind because they can't share your new interests, can't keep up with the money. Hard to try to fit into the life-style of new acquaintances who have money as a common interest, but you can't relate to them as well as you can to the old friends. You never quite fit in, you know?"

She shook her head. "I came from money," she confessed. "I've always had it. I guess it would be hard, though. Like having a foot in two worlds."

"Well put. Come on, I'll introduce you to Dave."

He opened the door. A thin, nervous-looking man stood up, smiling at Joe. "Hi, son." He laughed. He was barely forty, but he must feel

38

fatherly. At least he looked it with his bald head and narrow amber eyes. "This must be Gaby. I recognize you from your photos. You're doing a great job. We're getting a lot of attention because of you."

"I'm very glad, Mr. Smith," she said, leaning forward to shake the clammy, outstretched hand. "Thank you for giving me the opportunity."

"We're happy to have you. Can I show you around?"

"We'll show her around," Joe said possessively, and winked as he took Gaby's arm.

They gave her the cook's tour, and at the end of it she had a vivid picture of the size of the company. It was monstrous, and she wondered how Marc, even with executives and a board of directors, kept track of all of it.

"The mind boggles," she told Joe on the way out, all the while glancing around as if she expected that Marc might bound out from hiding. "It's so . . . big! How do you keep track of everything?"

"Oh, we have enough employees," he said easily. "It's mostly bookkeeping, anyway."

"Some bookkeeping! I'd go blind staring at so many numbers."

"The auditors do, I think." He laughed. He studied her for a long moment as they went down in the elevator. "There's a party next Friday night at Marc's apartment. Come with me."

She felt herself go trembly. She wanted to go. She wanted to see Marc, just once more, to let her eyes have the freedom to look at him, to enjoy the sight and smell and reality of him after all this time. She'd thought that after all these years she'd gotten over him, but now, after seeing him just once, she wanted desperately to be near him again. It was so dangerous, though. The trap was there: she could fall in headfirst; she could give up her soul to him all over again. And this time it would be harder to let go. Despite his betrayal, despite the anguish, a part of her belonged to him and always would.

"I don't think so," she said quietly.

"Don't be afraid of him," Joe taunted lightly, touching her face. "I'll be right there with you. He won't bother you."

That's what you think, she thought. She looked up, her green eyes dominating her soft face. "Do you know how it ended between Marc and me?" she asked abruptly.

His eyebrows arched. "Sure. Your parents sent you away to school, to get you away from him."

She opened her mouth. "Almost," she told him. She and Joe were friends now, and she liked him. He felt like the brother she'd never had. And that being the case, she didn't want to hurt him, to disillusion him about Marc. She knew he still looked up to his older brother, and she couldn't destroy his dreams. She remembered how it had hurt when Marc destroyed hers.

She smiled faintly. "He told you, then?"

"Marc?" He stuck out his lower lip and laughed. "He never tells me anything. I just probed until I dragged that out of him. He wouldn't talk about you afterward. Not one word. I guess it stung, having you taken out of his life like that."

Sure it had stung, she thought, but the money had surely taken out the sting. He'd used it to good effect, too, she thought bitterly. She straightened. So he hadn't told Joe the truth. How odd. Perhaps he didn't want his younger brother to know what a cold-blooded, mercenary man he really was.

Her eyes grew cold as she relived it. "I'll go to the party with you," she said. "It will be an experience."

"You'll get to meet Lana," he remarked, watching closely for her reaction.

She didn't give him one. She'd learned to hide her feelings. "What a treat!" she said sarcastically.

He chuckled. "Stick with me, kid. I'll protect you."

Her eyes twinkled as she smiled back. He was really a nice man when he forgot his shyness. He did, with her. She seemed to bring out a new side of him. Interesting how that happened, she thought. Some people could draw out the darkness, others the light. She tucked her hand in his arm and let him lead her out of the building.

She almost looked back. But the trauma of seeing Marc again kept her eyes facing toward the street. Now that it had happened, it was over. She could be prepared for their next meeting. And no way was she going to miss that party now. She wanted to show him how little she cared for him. She wanted to dress to the teeth and show him exactly what he'd thrown away for money. The thought brightened her eyes, sharpened her smile. Joe, looking down, grinned. He could be forgiven for thinking he was the cause of her heightened color and being flattered by it.

CHAPTER THREE

Marc's apartment was luxurious, just as Gaby had
pictured it. From the thick pile of the gray carpet
to the charcoal, brown, and beige striped furniture and coordinating curtains, it was as striking as
the man who lived there. She had to admit that his
taste in furnishings was very good. If he'd had any
part in the decorating, she thought bitterly, when
she caught a glimpse of him with the beautiful
blonde on his arm.

So that was Lana Moore. She was wearing a
black shoulderless gown, and it emphasized her
very apparent femininity. Her hair was done Gre-
cian style, very flattering to her delicate features
and big blue eyes.

Gaby was wearing gold lamé, her sheath gown
also shoulderless and with a deep slit down the
front of the skirt, but her carriage had more pa-
nache than Ms. Moore. She had the modeling

background to wear anything with style and exquisite grace. She was very grateful for that fact tonight. She couldn't have borne coming off second best to Marc's new love.

She'd left her own hair long, so that it swirled like copper around her face and shoulders. The few tiny freckles across her nose had been carefully camouflaged with makeup. Joe, when he'd picked her up at her home, had just stood and stared and whistled fervently. She'd grinned at him, pleased that he liked her choice of gowns. Now she was hardly able to grin as he propelled her toward his brother and Lana Moore.

"We'll get this over first," he whispered, smiling. He looked good, too, in dark evening clothes, although to Gaby he was still only a shadow of Marc. The older man wore his own dinner jacket with careless elegance, and Gaby had to force herself not to stare at him. His face as dark as the beautiful, masculine hand that curved around Lana Moore's milky shoulders . . .

"Joseph," Marc said in greeting, turning with a smile that lasted only until he saw Gaby. "Miss Bennett," he emphasized, nodding politely, although his eyes possessed her, thrilling eyes that had once looked hungrily on her. Was he remembering that? she wondered. Gaby felt as if she could almost see the thought in his mind.

The blonde beside him smiled, too, and it was genuine. She wasn't at all what Gaby had expected.

"He won't introduce me, but I'm Lana Moore," the woman said gently. She looked about Gaby's

44

age, and her eyes were as warm as her smile. "He's my best friend."

"How do you do?" Gaby asked politely, feeling as if a knife turned in her heart as she returned the smile. "I'm Gaby Bennett. I'm sort of an employee," she added, glancing at Joe.

Joe chuckled, reaching out to take Lana's hand. "Hi. I'm the black sheep, remember me?" he asked. "Gaby, here, is our new commercial lady. She's making the transmission-and-parts business boom."

"No wonder you looked familiar!" Lana said. "I should have known straightaway. I've seen your commercials. You're even lovelier in person!"

How horrible it was, to be admired by the woman who'd replaced her in Marc's life, in Marc's heart. She had to act for all she was worth. "Thank you, but it's the quality of the merchandise selling itself," she replied. "I'm only the window dressing."

"More than that," Joe said under his breath, and tugged a lock of her hair affectionately. "She's the whole show."

"There's a buffet, if you'd like something," Marc told Joe and Gaby, and his arm drew Lana closer while she beamed up at him.

"All I'm allowed after meals is butterfly steak," Gaby murmured dryly. "But I'd love some coffee," she told Joe.

"Sure. Come on. See you," he called to Marc and Lana, and guided Gaby toward the buffet.

Her eyes, if he could have seen them, would have shocked him. The anguish in them would have melted steel. But she quickly erased it and clung to his arm.

"She's lovely," she said. "And she seems a wonderful person."

"She's a nice kid, all right," he agreed. "I hope he won't hurt her too badly. He's an iceberg, old Marc. He can't seem to give. His emotions are tied up in knots."

Not always, she wanted to tell him. There was a time, once, when he was as open and giving and loving as a man could possibly be. And with the memory tugging at her heart she turned and looked full into Marc's eyes across the room. Suddenly they were locked, mind and soul, for an instant that burned away time, that made her throb with remembered passion. His lips parted, and his dark eyes went down her body slowly with total possession. *Oh, Marc,* she thought miserably, *how did we ever come to this? Why wasn't I enough? Why did you want the money so much more than you wanted me?*

Tears stung her eyes, and she turned away before he could see what a fool she was making of herself. He liked her body, yes, he always had. She was unconsciously flaunting it tonight, to make him aware of her, of what he'd thrown away. And now she felt cheap and sick, after meeting Lana, after seeing how helplessly in love with him the British girl was—in love with him, as she'd been, so long ago. But that was the past. There was no going back, however much she might have liked a second chance. Marc was making it painfully obvious that he wanted no second chances. He'd gotten what he was after. He had money and power and a beautiful woman to share it with. He had the world. And Gaby had . . . what?

She sipped her coffee quietly.

Joe, watching, seemed to sense her sadness. "Does it hurt so much, seeing him with her?" he asked tersely.

Her eyes closed. "It was nine years ago," she shot back. "I'm over him."

"Are you?" He took a swallow from his glass of brandy. "It doesn't look it."

Her green eyes flashed as she looked up at him. "Don't. Don't put our friendship at risk. You're trespassing on memories you have no knowledge of."

"They must not have been good ones. He's forgotten easily enough," he added, gesturing toward Marc, who was nuzzling his dark face against Lana's hair as they spoke to another couple.

She bit her lower lip. "Stop it!"

He took a deep breath. "Look . . ."

"*You* look," she shot back, furious. "I'm going to get some air."

She put down her cup and went out onto the terrace, breathing in the soft, sultry night air, glancing down on the city and the gleaming silver ribbon of the river as it wound around toward the horizon.

Why couldn't Joe leave it alone? Why was he so angry about her relationship with Marc? They were only friends. And he'd better accept that fact or she was going to stop going around with him. He was nothing more than a friend—he never would be—and she'd made that clear to him over and over again. Yet here he was, behaving like a jealous lover. Her heart was too shattered ever to be put together again and risked with a man. She'd thought Joe understood that.

She turned, strolling aimlessly between the huge potted plants and stone benches, only vaguely aware that the others who had been on the patio had gone back inside, that she was alone.

"Quite a sight, isn't it?" Marc asked suddenly, coming up beside her with a smoking cigarette in his hand. He spared the skyline a glance before he turned to study Gaby, much more thoroughly this time. "You've changed."

"I'm older," she reminded him. She leaned back against the cool stone of the balcony, breathing deliberately to keep him from seeing how his unexpected appearance had disturbed her, set her to trembling. She searched his hard face for traces of the young man she'd once loved. "So are you."

"I had nine years on you, even then," he reminded her. He took a draw from the cigarette and dropped it to the floor to grind it under his heel. "I was twenty-six to your seventeen. Why are you dating my brother?" he threw at her without warning.

Just like old times, she thought. Marc always had been blunt. "Why shouldn't I?" she asked.

"You know damned well why not."

"You surely don't imagine I'm doing it for revenge?" she asked, laughing nervously.

"What other reason could you have?" he replied. "We both know Joe's not your style. He never would be. He's a marshmallow."

"And you're a knife," she shot back, staring at him blatantly. "You even cut like one. I like your brother. He's real. You never were. I only imagined you."

"That was nine years ago," he reminded her. "And it's over. It was over before it ever began."

"Do forgive me for trying to compromise you, Marc." She laughed lightly, her green eyes shooting sparks at him as she folded her arms over her breasts. "I was very naive, remember."

His face went harder. "Yeah."

She tilted her head back so that her soft hair fell like a waterfall down her back. "I'm not green anymore, though," she said softly. "So you don't have to worry about your little brother. I'll take good care of him."

He hadn't expected the frontal attack, and she caught the tiniest flicker of his eyelids. He reached for another cigarette. "There are plenty of other men in New York," he said shortly.

"I like Joe," she responded, hoping that her words would hurt Marc. She turned toward the apartment, but he caught her arm, holding her just in front of him. His palm against her skin was torment, bringing back memories of gentler touching, of silvery pleasure. His dark eyes stared angrily down into her shimmering green ones, and she had images of a dam held in tight control. She remembered all too well what he was like when that dam broke, how violent his passions were.

"Leave Joe alone, honey," he said softly, too softly. "He's not for you."

"What will you do if I don't, Marc?" she asked defiantly. "Send over some nocturnal visitors?"

"Nothing quite so permanent. I wouldn't like to see you hurt. Not that way." He reached up and caught her long hair, propelling her close against his massive body. He'd always been big, but now he felt like a mountain, and her body throbbed in instant response, a response she couldn't prevent.

"Don't," she protested.

"Aren't you curious?" he whispered, searching her face. "I am. I want to see if you've changed flavors, if you've aged, like good wine."

His wide, sexy mouth was poised just above hers, and she was blind and deaf and dumb to the whole world outside. She could breathe him, taste him, and the feel of his huge body was like a narcotic. Old memories came unbidden, washing over her like fire, making her ache with remembered passion.

"Soft," he breathed as his hands smoothed down her arms, coaxing her against his body. "You smell of roses in the darkness, just as you used to when you were a silky little virgin and I wanted to take you—"

"Well, don't expect me to fall at your feet these days, Mr. Stephano," she almost spat at him, using every ounce of her willpower to keep from throwing herself at him. He was the enemy. She had to remember that. She even managed a tight little smile as his mouth hovered over hers, tempting it.

"Can you keep it up?" he mocked, rubbing his

lips delicately against hers in a shiver of sensuous pressure. "Can you hold out against it? I remember that most of all, that your body belonged to me from the first moment I touched it. Do you remember when that happened, Gaby? In the park, under the old oak?" he whispered against her open lips.

"A hundred years ago," she retorted, jerking against his hold.

"At least." He was playing, toying with her; that cruel smile told her so. But her body began to ache at the sweet contact with his huge, hard-muscled torso, as it hadn't in many long years. If he kissed her now, she knew she'd melt onto the floor. She had to prevent him from doing that. She had to hold on to her sanity despite the fact that her knees were rubbery and her breath wouldn't come.

He trailed a long, lean finger down her throat. "If you don't leave Joe alone," he whispered huskily, "I'll come after you, Gaby. And he won't want what I leave behind."

"You don't even know what you left behind nine years ago, do you, Marc?" she taunted, feeling her anger come to her rescue. Her green eyes flashed as she arched her body away from contact with his and went rigid in his arms. "You threw me out like a used rag!"

His face went stone-cold at that accusation. He stared down into her eyes quietly, searchingly. His hands on her bare arms tightened, and she thought vaguely that she might have bruises if he didn't stop. . . .

"And for money," she continued, her eyes burning with unshed tears, the years of impotent rage all bursting behind a swell of emotion. "For five thousand dollars. That's all it took to buy you off!" His face had gone white, but she hardly registered it; she saw him only through a blur of fevered anger. "I loved you! I would have died for you! And you sold me out for money! You used me!"

"Gaby," he said hesitantly, as he slowly released her. "Gaby, you don't understand. You don't know how it was."

"I know," she scoffed, her voice breaking, and even then she smiled as she rubbed viciously at an escaped tear. "I know all too well. You were ambitious. You wanted to get up in the world. And you did. Don't you want to thank me for all this, Marc?" she asked, sweeping her arms around toward the opulent apartment. "I was the price you paid for it!"

"Your own parents sold you out, not me!" he returned hotly, dark eyes flashing, his face like stone.

Her lower lip trembled, and her eyes felt as if they had sand in them. Her throat was full of thorns. Beside her slender hips, her fists clenched. "I've hated you," she whispered. "For so many years I've hated you. I wouldn't even go down the street where you used to live, by the garage where you worked. I thought you loved me."

He seemed to have a hard time answering. He stared down at her, his dark eyes half hidden under his eyelids, his jaw taut. "You were just a kid," he said finally.

"Just a kid," she echoed. She drew in a steadying breath. "Yes, I was. Young and trusting and stupid." She glared at him. "I hear your new woman is loaded." She smiled slowly. "How much will she be worth when you throw her over?"

"Damn you!" he burst out, his face livid with anger, dangerous.

She avoided his sudden movement just as Joe came out onto the patio. Marc glanced at his brother with eyes that barely saw through their fury while Joe approached them, oblivious to the scene that had just transpired. Marc lit a cigarette and Gaby sat shakily on a stone bench a few feet away. Joe joined them with two glasses of champagne.

"Talking over old times?" Joe asked, a note of anger in his voice. He gave his brother a narrow glance before he sat down beside Gaby. "Here you go, love," he told her. "I'm sorry," he added softly.

"So am I," Gaby said, although only Joe understood the hidden meaning as she glanced past him at Marc. "Won't Miss Moore be missing you?"

He glared at her. "No doubt she will. Go easy on the sauce, Joe, you know how it hits you in the head," he said, cautioning his brother.

He turned and strode back inside, while Gaby sipped champagne as if she didn't have a care in the world. She was still shaking inside, but she didn't let on. She listened to Joe and answered his questions and put on the best act of her career.

But later, at home in the darkness, she relived her shame and guilt. How could she still feel desire for Marc after what he'd done to her? She'd have to keep him at a safe distance from now on. She wasn't giving up that contract, not even for him. And if he wanted her to stop seeing Joe, let him tell his brother the truth. Let him tell Joe that he'd allowed himself to be bought off, to give up the woman he'd sworn eternal devotion to. Let him show his only brother what an unscrupulous, conscienceless, mercenary man he really was. And on that thought Gaby cried herself to sleep.

Her father was at the breakfast table when she went down early the next morning, before she was to do the second set of stills for Motocraft, Inc.

"Fancy seeing me here!" Jack Bennett told his daughter with a grin. He was middle-aged now, balding, and a little overweight, but his eyes were as green as Gaby's. "I'm the other tenant, remember me? I live here occasionally."

She laughed. "Nice to have you home! Sorry I wasn't here when you got in. I went to a party." Gaby hesitated a moment before continuing. Should she tell her father that she had gone with Joe? Until now she had made it a point not to let him know she was once again in contact with the Stephanos.

"I . . . I went with Joe Stephano," she said at last.

He seemed to freeze. "Stephano?"

"Yes. He and big brother Marc own their own company now. Motocraft, Inc., the parts and transmission company that's been franchised. I'm doing all the publicity work for it. It was all decided before I knew who owned it, but it's too late for them to back out now."

"Stephano," her father repeated huskily. "I never dreamed he'd make it."

"He wouldn't have, if you and Mother hadn't bought him off," she said coldly, and stared into her scrambled eggs, missing the flash of his eyes. "Well, that's all water under the bridge now. You'd like his brother. Joe's nice."

"You're dating Joe?"

"Why not?" She laughed. "Marc hates it, of course, but Joe's a good guy, and I enjoy his company. Besides, he's sort of my boss."

"I never liked you becoming a model," her father began.

"Neither you nor Mother ever did, but I've proved that I'm capable of supporting myself, and now I want to go on doing it."

"What about marriage, children?" her father muttered.

"I don't want all that. My goodness, you know I'm not domestic. I can burn water."

"You wouldn't have to be domestic for some men. There's Peter. . . ."

"Peter Jackson is a very nice man, and he'll make some woman a wonderful husband," she said dryly. "But not me. I don't want to get married."

"Because of Stephano?" he demanded, lifting his head to stare at her. "Because of that childish affair?"

"You never would listen to me, would you?" she asked quietly. "I was in love with him."

He averted his eyes. "You were barely seventeen."

"Some women only love once. He was my world." She turned away and looked out the apartment window at the busy street below while her father stared blankly into his coffee. "There's never been anyone else, in any emotional sense. I don't think there ever will be."

"Only because it was unfinished, that's all," her father grumbled. "If the affair had gone on very long, you'd probably have tired of him."

"Think so?" She sipped her coffee. "Oddly enough, I think I'd have been hooked for life, so it's just as well that we never became lovers."

"You expect me to believe he never touched you?" he scoffed.

"Of course he touched me. But he never seduced me," she returned, whirling. "He was too aware of my upbringing. He said it would kill my conscience, and he was probably right."

Jack looked pale. "I thought you were having an affair with him."

"No such luck." She laughed. "Oh, well, it's over, anyway, and just as well that nothing regretful happened. I have to run, I'm shooting a TV commercial this morning. Wish me luck. I've worked with this turkey before, and he had me do fifty-five takes on one sentence in the last commerical he filmed with me!"

"Yes," Jack said absently. "Yes, good luck."

She got her things together and started for the door.

"Gabrielle?" he called suddenly.

She turned, smiling. "Yes?"

"If things had been different," he said, "you'd have married that grease monkey?"

"Yes, even if I had to live in poverty above his garage and have ten kids." She smiled, remembering. "Who knows? See you later."

"Yes. Good-bye." He watched her go out the door, and then he slumped in his chair like an old man, staring around the empty room. Empty, like his life. Like Gaby's. All because he'd listened to his wife one time too many instead of following his instincts. He sighed wearily and finished his coffee while the lines of a song flashed through his brain. "What do I say, dear, after I say I'm sorry . . . ?" But it was years too late to say that. He got up and went to work.

Back at the studio, Joe was waiting for Gaby. He watched while they shot the commercial and then took her to a late lunch in a nearby restaurant.

"Poor baby," he commiserated as she sipped iced tea. "Thirty-five takes! Wow!"

"He's killed me," she murmured. "I'll have them put his name on my death certificate under 'cause of.' "

"Want me to get Uncle Michael to go visit him for you?" he whispered under his breath.

She laughed. "I'll bet Uncle Michael is four feet tall and wears red striped ties."

"He's nearly six feet tall, silver-haired, and wears a diamond stickpin," he corrected. "And, in his day he was what is known as a ladies' man."

"My, my, and here I am with you," she teased.

He laughed, delighted. He sat with his face propped in his hands, staring at her worshipfully. He had a pleasant face, Gaby thought. It wouldn't stop traffic, and it wasn't as hard and chiseled as Marc's, but it was nice all the same. He'd really blossomed in the few weeks she'd known him, and he hadn't acted jealous since the night of Marc's party. He kidded with her. He seemed to enjoy her company, but he'd apparently decided not to push their relationship any further than that. She was glad; she had nothing more to give him.

"Well, I'm no ladies' man," Joe confessed. "But I'm rich and good-lookin' and overstocked with charm."

"You forgot to mention how modest you are," she prompted.

"Yeah, that too. I'm extremely modest."

She burst out laughing. "You nice man, you."

"I try, I try. How about dinner tonight?"

She smiled at him. "Sure, but you've taken me out so many times already. Why don't you come to the house for dinner about five and you can meet my dad."

"Taking me home to the old man, huh? Well, I guess I can survive. Okay."

"You'll like Dad. He's nice too."

"He'd have to be, to have a lovely daughter like you." He chuckled at the face she made. "Five, then."

"I'll be ready," she promised, and wondered what Marc would have to say when Joe told him, as Joe certainly would.

Her father was more nervous than she'd ever

seen him that night when Joe arrived promptly at five.

"Hello, hello, so nice to meet you," he said, acting flustered and shaking hands with the younger man. "I'm glad you could come."

Gabrielle smoothed down her white sundress and studied her father with a frown, curious at his lack of poise, his red cheeks. It wasn't like him to be upset by company.

"What can I get you to drink?" he asked, leading them into the spacious living room.

"I'll just have some Perrier," Gabrielle said. "Joe?"

"Vodka and soda," Joe returned. He sat down beside her on the sofa while Jack Bennett poured their drinks. "You have a beautiful home," Joe remarked, glancing around the expensively furnished room.

"My wife's, not mine," Jack said, smiling as he dropped into an armchair across from them. "She was very talented."

"She died several months ago," Gabrielle volunteered, staring into her glass. She smiled. "She was quite a lady, wasn't she, Dad?"

He nodded, and the nervousness seemed to go as he sipped his own drink. "Yes, she was. A little naive in some ways but charming." He glanced at Gaby. "How's the modeling coming along?"

"Ask me," Joe said, chuckling. He winked at Gaby. "She's doing just great. We'll sell millions of dollars' worth of stuff, all because of Gaby. I couldn't be more pleased about having her represent us."

"Uh, how does your brother feel about it?" Jack asked suddenly.

Joe shrugged. "Marc doesn't bother to acquaint me with his feelings. He hasn't said a word about the ad campaign. Well, maybe one word," he added, and he looked guilty.

"He tried to have me thrown out, I imagine," Gaby said, taking a shot in the dark and watching Joe clear his throat as if he'd choked himself on his drink.

"It was nothing personal," he said quickly, his dark eyes apologetic. "He just thought we should have a blonde."

"I could always have dyed my hair," she reminded him, grinning.

"Of course."

Jack got up quickly and announced that dinner was waiting, as if he felt the sudden tension and was determined to obliterate it. They talked about politics and taxes all through the delicious meal Jack's cook had prepared, and what had begun as a trying evening became a jovial one.

"Come again anytime," Jack said when Joe was about to leave. "Glad to have you."

"Thanks," Joe replied, shaking hands at the door. "I enjoyed it."

"So did I. I'll say good night," he added with a grin, and went upstairs.

She walked out the door with Joe in silence, and he seemed to be brooding about something as they stood beside his Mercedes convertible on the street. "I wanted to ask you something," he began.

"Yes?" She smiled up at him.

"I wanted to invite you out to the Hamptons with me," he said. "We—the family, that is—have a beach house there. It's nice and private, and we're having a few people down for the July Fourth holidays. I'd like you to come as my guest."

Her heart stopped. "You and Marc, you mean," she asked bluntly.

"Yeah," he grumbled. He stuck his hands in his pockets with a rough sigh. "Don't worry. He wouldn't be around much," he added coaxingly. "And, besides, the place is huge. We could always keep out of his way."

Yes, and it would irritate him beyond bearing, Gaby thought. She hesitated but only for a minute. Marc would hate it. That appealed to her. It appealed a lot. Maybe she could even bear seeing him with Lana.

"Okay," she said. "I'd love to. What shall I pack?"

"Something cool." He chuckled. "And a couple of dresses. We'll go to one of the fish places to eat."

She searched his dark eyes and became serious. "Joe, I wouldn't want to lead you on," she began, her voice quiet. "I like you. But that's all it can ever be. I enjoy my independence." Her shoulders rose and fell. "Knowing that, I'll understand if you'd rather I didn't go with you."

He smiled slowly. "Thank God." He sighed. "A woman without marriage on the brain. I like you, too, sweetheart," he added, brushing his knuckles gently against her cheek. "And I'm no more in the mood for a passionate affair than you are. But I don't make friends easily, especially women friends, and I enjoy showing you off, taking you places. Sure, I want you to come. But Marc won't, and that's why you want to come, isn't it?" he asked shrewdly, watching her face color. He laughed wickedly. "That's another reason I invited you. Marc's been running my life for years. But I've got my fingers in some other pies now, and I have my own spending money. Having you on my arm would give him hell, wouldn't it?"

She began to realize that Joe had his own problems with Marc. Perhaps he'd deliberately pursued her to get back at his brother. She wasn't sure now that she wanted to go through with it. Her own revenge was one thing. Joe's was something else. Marc had put a lot of sacrifice into bringing up Joe. . . .

Listen to yourself, she thought, *you're going soft already.* She laughed. "Okay, I'll go. We'll put the thumbscrews on big brother together."

"That's my girl," he said. "See you tomorrow."

"Okay. Good night."

"Thanks for dinner," he called as he drove off. And with a wave of his hand and a flash of white teeth, he was gone.

Gaby went upstairs to her own room and gazed out the window. Was she doing the right thing? She thought back to her youth, to the heart Marc had broken, to the aching humiliation of their final meeting. Her eyes went hard. Yes, it was the right thing. It didn't matter what Joe's motives were; her own were the only ones that concerned her. She could needle Marc if she kept her head. She could make him feel the same torment he'd inflicted on her. And she ignored the tiny voice that argued that she was more vulnerable than he was. The sight of him would be bittersweet anguish. To see him, be with him again, even with Lana Moore between them . . . no, that wasn't why she was going, it wasn't! She turned abruptly from the window and went to bed.

CHAPTER FOUR

Gaby saw Joe frequently after that. She expected
Marc to try to put a stop to it, but she saw no
evidence of any interference. She was relieved,
but in a way it bothered her, too, because Gaby
hated thinking Marc didn't even care. She had to
admit that she preferred his antagonism to his in-
difference and she wanted to hurt him as much as
he'd hurt her.

Meanwhile Joe was good fun. He had excellent
manners and a dry sense of humor. He took her to
the most expensive, delightful kinds of places.
She'd been accustomed to high living all her life,
so she never questioned the kind of money Joe
had. Motocraft must really be an enterprise, Gaby
thought, because even a vice-president got rich at
it. But, then, Marc was Joe's brother, and she imagined Marc didn't mind sharing. He'd once seemed
the soul of generosity to her. Back in the days

before he began to worship money and would do anything for it.

Joe had more cars than anyone Gaby had ever known. He changed them almost daily, going from his Jaguar to a Mercedes to a Corvette and then to a renovated MG Midget. Gaby liked the Midget most of all, probably because it wasn't new and it seemed to have a personality all its own. They alternated between going to restaurants and Joe's apartment, where he had a giant screen for his VCR. There they could watch first-run movies with popcorn provided by the woman who cooked for Joe and his roommate, Bob Donalds. Bob often joined them for the movies. He was good company, too, a real estate agent with a live-wire personality, just the opposite of Joe. Bob never seemed to mind company, and he liked Gaby. He was tall and redheaded and teased Gaby about being some long-lost relative because their hair was the same shade.

Gaby had been with Joe almost every day for three weeks. He seemed to just hang around where she was working. She wondered if he was on vacation or if Marc paid him to stay away.

She teased him about that once, and he gave her a startled look. "Well, Marc pretty much lets me do what I please, you know," he mumbled, and quickly changed the subject. She shrugged it off, since he didn't seem inclined to talk about it. And she really wasn't interested in his business affairs. She enjoyed being around him.

They went dancing and out to eat and to movies whenever Gaby's busy schedule would allow. She ran her long legs off auditioning for jobs, posing for stills, and doing runway modeling. She was popular and made a lot of money. But it cost a lot to maintain her wardrobe and pay the bills.

Gaby didn't particularly enjoy the life-style that went with modeling, and before Joe came along, she'd avoided the crowd she worked with. But Joe, despite his shyness, seemed fascinated with her world, so she introduced him to it. There were show-business personalities, politicians, even millionaires who circulated at the exclusive parties Gaby and her friends were invited to. She often thought she knew people only invited her to these parties because of her looks and because she was becoming a well-known model. Because of that she seldom accepted invitations. But she went to humor Joe. Marc didn't approve, and that made Joe all the more determined to do it. That was the one thing she and Joe had in common. They both liked doing things to spite Marc, to antagonize him. The holidays were only a week away now, and Gaby had already packed. She'd been all over Europe with her family but, oddly enough, had rarely visited the Hamptons, which were only a few hours from New York City. She was looking forward to the break in her busy schedule, despite the fact that she was sure Joe had gloated over it to his brother by now. He hadn't mentioned Marc's reaction, and Gaby hadn't asked for it. She was going to go and enjoy herself and not worry. Let Marc smolder. Vaguely she remembered the threat he'd made, but she hadn't taken him seriously. He had Lana to occupy him. He would never put that relationship at risk just to irritate Gaby. She shook the thought from her head, forcing herself to dwell on happy thoughts instead.

Her mirror told her that she'd changed quite a bit from the young girl who'd worshiped Marcus Stephano. She was no longer the skinny, eager, very unsophisticated child who'd been such easy prey for his seductive ardor. Even nine years ago Marc had been an expert.

Despite all the time that had passed, the memories were indelible. She remembered the last time she'd been alone with Marc, that evening when it had almost gone too far. Her eyes closed and she sighed as the memories caressed her mind.

She and Marc had gone to a movie, she remembered. It was one of many times she'd had to sneak out of her house to keep her parents from knowing that she was seeing a boy from the wrong side of the tracks. It had been a late-afternoon matinee, because it was too difficult to get out at night. The racy movie, combined with the danger of discovery, had given Gaby an unfamiliar and delicious taste of intrigue. She'd watched the people on the screen and imagined that they were she and Marc, loving each other wildly. It had stirred her unbearably. When he suggested that they stop by his apartment for coffee on the way home, she hadn't questioned the uncharacteristic nature of the invitation. He'd been careful until then to make sure they were never completely alone.

But once in the apartment, he'd closed the door and locked it. And as he'd stood there, big and dark in his navy slacks and open-throated white shirt, her heart had begun to pound wildly. He was incredibly sensuous with his chiseled mouth, black eyes, and tanned, olive body that hinted of untold delights. The way he'd looked at Gaby that night told her graphically that coffee wasn't all he wanted.

Gaby trembled as she thought of that long-ago night. She'd wanted him so badly. All the stolen minutes, the hard kisses, the too quick touching of hands on forbidden skin. All of it had exploded in a tangible expression of longing that night.

He'd come toward her slowly, tugging her against his big body, his eyes already apologetic even as he bent and kissed her in a way he never had before. She felt his hard mouth tremble in a caress tender enough to make her shiver too. It was wildly erotic, his tongue forcing its way into her mouth, his hands low on her hips, moving her against him so that she could feel his arousal.

"Sleep with me," he'd whispered, his voice husky with passion. "Come into my bedroom and let me take off your clothes and make love to you completely."

"You said . . . we wouldn't," she'd whispered, wanting him but frightened and uncertain. "You said—"

"Yes, I know, and I should be shot," he'd replied, his face hard with desire. "But I need you so much, little one." His big hands had crushed her thighs against his, and his eyes had been hot with desire.

"Oh, Marc," she'd whispered at his mouth as he bent and took it again, with more insistence this time.

"Don't be afraid of me," he'd told her. "I'll take good care of you. I'll make it easy and slow and sweet for you. I'll take a long, long time, little Gaby. I'll take you right to heaven."

He'd lifted her, carried her into the bedroom, and closed the door behind them. The room was spartan, with old furniture and a double bed that had seen better days, its brass worn and flaked. But it felt like paradise when he laid her down on it and began to kiss her.

Gaby remembered how tense she'd been at first, until his soft, tender kisses had relaxed her, until he made her want his hands and his eyes. She'd let him undress her totally, lying under his strong, rough mechanic's hands like a young sacrifice, unafraid, wanting him obsessively.

She remembered the way he'd looked at her untouched body, his dark eyes hungry and oddly reverent as they studied her. Bending over her, smiling tenderly at her embarrassment, he'd seemed so adult, so masculine, with his shirt rumpled by her searching, fascinated hands, baring a chest dark with hair and exposure to the sun. His hair had been unruly and hung down over his broad forehead.

"Gaby," he'd whispered, "you even look virginal. White and chaste and delicate."

She'd stretched under his hot gaze, loving the feel of his eyes on her, the way he followed the movement, watching it lift her taut breasts, stretch her long legs, her slender hips.

"Do you want to close your eyes, honey?" he

asked gently, standing. "Or do you want to watch me undress?"

Her body tingled even now as she remembered his question. She'd never really thought about how it would be until then. And as she looked at him she knew that she had to see him. She told him so and saw the desire in his eyes.

"I'm not as pretty as you are," he'd whispered. But as the clothing came away from his powerful, dark body with its rough hair and smooth muscle, she could have argued with him. Nude, he was the most exquisite masculine thing she'd ever seen. Her eyes dropped and lingered, fascinated.

"Come here," he'd whispered, watching her move to her knees on the bed in front of him.

And then he'd taken her hands to him, showing her how to touch him, how to drive him mad. And he'd laughed even through the shudders at her rapt fascination to the reactions he was unable to hide from her.

He'd touched her and teased her, giving her the most exquisite pleasure she'd ever experienced. She remembered writhing wildly on the white sheets, moaning in sweet anguish as he did the most shockingly delicious things to her body.

"You like that, huh?" he'd whispered, lifting his head to see her face. "Yes, I like it, too. I like making you scream."

"I'll . . . die," she threatened as he bent again, her voice breaking.

"Not yet," he whispered with a soft, wicked laugh. "Not for a long time yet."

Over and over again he'd taken her on the roller

coaster of sensation, teaching her things about her body that all the romances she'd read in her young life had ill prepared her for. By the time he finally moved over her, parting her thighs unresistingly with a hard knee, she would have done anything he'd asked of her. Even this. Especially this.

A shudder went through Gaby as she recalled how desperately she had desired Marc that day, how much she had wanted to give herself to him. But then they had heard the front door suddenly slam. Marc had groaned in agony, and his eyes had been terrible as he managed to drag his body away from her. He'd stumbled to the door, furious when he reached it, just in time to keep his brother from opening it.

"I'm busy!" he called through it. "Go away!"

"Oops," Joe had replied amusedly. "Sorry, big brother. I'll run around the block a time or two!"

And he'd gone quickly away. But the spell had been broken. Gaby remembered how she had crawled back into her clothes, feeling soiled and vaguely ashamed, and she hadn't been able to look at Marc. Finally he'd stumbled into the bathroom, leaving her there alone. A long time later he came back, dressed himself, and lit a cigarette.

"Are you all right?" he asked, and even now she remembered the concern in his dark eyes.

"Yes," she'd replied, her voice choked, her fingers clasped together. "Yes, I'm . . . fine." Her eyes had closed with embarrassment and shame. "I'd like to go home."

"Yeah. Sure. I'll walk you."

He did, in a silence that was cold and somehow

71

final. He'd left her at her door with darkness falling around them, and he'd touched her hair gently, hesitantly, looking for words that wouldn't come. She'd looked up at him with her heart in her eyes, but he'd only smiled faintly, and then he'd turned and walked quickly away. She remembered watching him, aching for words that would tell her that he loved her, that he was sorry, that he wanted her for his wife. But he'd never spoken one word of love. Not one.

She wondered now why she had never realized that her parents could see them from the window. She hadn't even considered that they might find out about her mysterious romance. Marc hadn't called her after that. He hadn't come to see her. And several days later, after Gaby had gone out of her mind worrying and missing him and hurting with guilt and neglect, her mother had called her into the living room and told her quietly and tersely that they knew about Marc. And then she told her that they'd given him money in return for cutting Gaby out of his life.

She'd gone straight to her father in tears, and he'd looked guilty and sick, but he hadn't denied it. Especially not with her mother standing rigid and unbending at the doorway. Even then Gaby hadn't believed it. Marc loved her. He wouldn't have taken a bribe! She'd tried to see Marc, to ask if it was true. He wouldn't talk to her, not on the phone, not even when she tried to see him at the garage in person. Finally he gave in to her persistence and went out to the front of the garage.

"What do you want?" he'd demanded.

"I want to know if you took money to leave me alone," she'd asked quietly.

"What did you expect, that I'd refuse?" he'd shot at her, his face emotionless, his hands clenched, his white T-shirt stained with grease, like his hands. "I wasn't born with a silver spoon, little lady. I have to work for my living. Yes, I took it! You didn't really think I'd prefer you to easy street?" he added, taunting her.

She hadn't answered. She'd been too shocked and hurt to utter a sound.

That had angered him, she recalled, as if her silence was in some way more difficult to bear than her anger would have been. "Get out of my life," he'd yelled at her. "I don't want you, little rich girl. You were just a novelty in the first place, until you became a gold mine. So get lost, will you?"

"Sure," she'd replied, shaking. "My mistake, Mr. Stephano, I thought you loved me."

"Did I ever say so?" he'd scoffed, laughing. "Don't you know when a man's got the hots for you?"

"I do now, don't I?" she'd replied, although something inside her had died when he laughed at her. "I won't bother you again."

She had run. It was the only time she could remember running from a problem, but she'd run all the way home, sobbing wildly. And it had taken her two days to get over it. By then her parents were determined to get her out of town, to keep her from being tempted into seeing him again. They sent her to an exclusive boarding school in

73

western Massachusetts where she learned to live again. And now that expensive upbringing was paying off. Now she had the poise to take on Marc Stephano and pay off a very old, very bitter debt.

CHAPTER FIVE

The Stephanos' summer home was located between Southampton and Easthampton, situated near enough to Mecox Bay that it had a glorious view of the bay as well as the Atlantic Ocean, which it faced. It was a long drive from New York City, but the Stephanos' helicopter made it there in no time at all. Gaby and Joe went alone with the pilot early Friday morning. Gaby hadn't had any pressing assignments, so she'd taken the day off. Marc and Lana and the Smiths wouldn't arrive until that night, Joe told her smugly. They'd have the whole house to themselves until the others showed up. Since the Fourth of July wasn't until the following week, it would be a very long holiday indeed. Gaby felt she could use it. She'd worked steadily since her mother's heart attack, trying to put it out of her mind. Despite the fact that she and her mother hadn't been very close, it was difficult to accept. There were still times when she felt near tears.

She was glad the others wouldn't already be in residence. She'd have time to relax and steel herself for another confrontation with Marc. That would help.

"You're gonna love this place," Joe told her when the chopper touched down on the heliport beside the house. "Marc really fought to get it, but he loved the look of it."

She was still catching her breath from her first glimpse of the property. It was worth fighting for, she thought. The house itself was unique, very Mediterranean in design, with heavy white stucco and a red roof and a high wall that enclosed it from prying eyes. Secluded patios led off each bedroom, overlooking the bay on one side and the Atlantic on the other. The property had its own private pier and dock and a deliciously large ocean frontage with a private, very white beach. Gaby immediately fell in love with both the house and ocean views. And although she'd spent a good portion of her life vacationing on beaches all over the world, this was different. The house was isolated, and there weren't any close neighbors. Just behind the house there was a tiered swimming pool with a patio, which had plush lawn furniture and a cabana. The cabana shielded the house from prying eyes, so that the pool area could be quite secluded. Off the master bedroom there was a walled patio that contained a hydro spa.

The beach had high walls at both property boundaries so that the occupants of the house could sunbathe without being observed, except possibly from the air or from passing ships. It was a haven of privacy all around. Inside, the bedrooms were widely separated and had exquisite bathrooms of marble and lots of glass. Gaby's was on the bay side of the house, and it had a bed with curtains all the way around that drew together. The bedroom was decorated in pastels and was beautiful. It was fit for a princess.

"There's a private wing for staff as well," Joe told her, smiling. "We have to bring Carla with us when we come down here, because we don't cook and Lana can't. Carla is a jewel. Very Italian. You'll like her."

"I already have visions of gaining twenty pounds before I leave here," she kidded.

"On you it would look good," he decided.

"It would cost me my career too." She laughed. "Oh, Joe, it's a dream of a house!"

"I'm glad you like it," he said. "Go ahead and unpack, put on a bathing suit, and meet me at the ocean. We'll swim until dinner."

"Wonderful!"

She rushed to get into her black designer swimsuit. It had straps that crisscrossed in back, and it was cut high at the hips. She didn't like bikinis, and this suited her sleek body without being overstated. She pinned up her hair and ran to find Joe.

He didn't look all that bad in black swimming trunks, but Gaby couldn't help but compare him to Marc, whose big, husky body she remembered so well without the civilizing veneer of clothing. Joe was slightly built, had no body hair at all, and was rather pale. But she had no interest in his body, anyway. Only his friendship appealed to her, and she hoped he understood that.

He let out a long, slow whistle. "My, my, what a dish," he said, smiling sheepishly. He'd come out of his shell a lot, but he still seemed a little uneasy when he flirted with her, as if it came hard to him.

"You're not bad, either," she said, laughing. "Race you!"

She took off running toward the crashing surf, with Joe right behind her, and dived in headfirst. The water felt wonderful. Gulls cried overhead, and she felt alive and on fire with a sense of adventure. Marc wouldn't want her here, and it would be hard watching him with Lana. Yet she felt real for the first time in nine years. It was as if her heart had been given massive doses of novocaine and had only just regained its ability to feel. Just to have Marc back in her life, even on the fringe of it, was a pleasure beyond bearing. She laughed and played like an otter in the water, and Joe watched her without really comprehending why she seemed so radiant.

"Having fun?" he called above the crash of the waves.

"Glorious!" she returned. "Isn't it beautiful here?"

"You're beautiful, all right."

"You're a flirt," she accused, and shot water at him from behind her uplifted palm.

He started to retaliate just as the helicopter returned. His face fell as he looked up.

78

"Will the chopper hold all of them at once?" she asked quietly.

He shook his head. "The Smiths were driving up, so they could do some sight-seeing. That will be Marc and Lana."

She felt her heart sink. Well, she'd asked for it, hadn't she? "You did tell him I was coming?" she asked, hesitating, her eyes big and green and questioning.

"Sure."

"Did he go through the ceiling?"

"Right through it to the roof," he replied. "But he gave in."

"I don't want to cause trouble for you," she said.

"You won't. We'll just steer clear of them. He and Lana keep to themselves most of the time, anyway."

She touched the foaming surf. "People in love usually do," she said.

"Lana's the one in love. I doubt that Marc is, though. But I have to say that she must be something, to have lasted a year."

Gaby frowned. She truly wanted to dislike Lana, but the English woman had such a sweet personality. Why couldn't she have been a scheming witch? Why did she have to be a nice person?

"You're sure you're over him?" Joe asked gently, his dark eyes narrow and searching.

"Of course. It's been nine years," she replied, a little too sharply.

"Yeah"—he laughed self-consciously—"I guess that would be stretching things, wouldn't it, for you to carry a torch that long?"

"It would indeed." Especially, she added silently, after the circumstances under which they'd parted. Her heart might be vulnerable to Marc, but her mind wasn't. It had vivid, total recall when it came to the past.

"Want to go meet them?" Joe asked.

"No, but you go ahead," she said quickly.

"Alone?" He gasped theatrically. "And watch Lana drool all over him? Never! Race you down to the wall!"

And he dived in headfirst, leaving her to catch up.

The helicopter took off again, and they swam for a while and then moved back up to the secluded swimming pool where Carla served iced drinks and dainty sandwiches and cakes. The Italian woman was huge and merry and middle-aged, and Gaby liked her on sight. The feeling must have been mutual, because Carla immediately adopted her and began to push food at her.

She refused gently, explaining that every ounce counted in her line of work.

"Better you get married," Carla chided. "Have babies. Work, what life is that for a young woman, hah?"

And delivering that bit of wisdom she turned and ambled back into the house.

"I guess she told you, huh?" Joe said teasingly. He'd pulled on a shirt and looked as relaxed as Gaby did in her short white beach robe. She'd loosened her hair and let the breeze catch it, blowing it around her face as she sipped a cooling citrus drink. She seldom drank. She'd seen too many young lives ruined by it in the circles she frequented.

Joe seemed to be just the opposite. He put it away with enthusiasm, never seeming to show intoxication. She wondered how long it had taken him to reach that immunity and worried about the next few days. Well, if it got rough, she could always go home.

She glanced toward the house. She wanted to go in and change, but she was having the most vivid, painful images of Lana and Marc together inside, and she couldn't have borne accidentally seeing or hearing something private between them. It had seemed like a good idea to come here and show Marc that she was over him. But now it was backfiring. She wasn't even sure anymore, herself, that she was over him now. Perhaps she'd only been fooling herself.

As if he sensed her thoughts, the patio door suddenly opened and Marc came out to join them. He looked as if he'd just had a shower, and he was dressed neatly in white slacks and an open white-and-red patterned shirt. Gray hairs mingled with the black ones on his bronzed, muscular chest. He looked as fit as he had in his twenties, when Gaby had first known him.

She lifted her face bravely, determined not to back down. Had he been making love to Lana, was that why he'd showered? Had he showered with her? The thought tormented her.

"So you came," he said to Gaby, his face giving nothing away even as his eyes narrowed and stared at her.

"I was invited," she said.

He laughed coolly. "So I understand. Well, I don't mind showing the hired help a good time if it doesn't become a habit."

"Hey, Marc . . . !" Joe began hotly, half rising out of his chaise lounge.

"Don't start World War Three on my account, Joe," Gaby told Joe. She leaned back, stretched, and smiled at Marc. "You and I understand each other very well. Don't we, Marcus?"

"Do we?" he returned.

"I can think of five thousand reasons that we should," she said sweetly, and watched his eyelids flicker with understanding. It made him even more rigid.

Joe frowned. "What is going on between you two?" he demanded.

"Mutual aid," Gaby said innocently. "If Marc will mind his manners, I'll mind mine."

Marc looked near an explosion. He'd only started to speak when Lana came out the door, looking exquisite in a floral print sundress. She stretched, ruffling her long blond hair. "Hi, everyone," she called gaily, smiling at all three of them. "Oh, what a gorgeous place! Don't you love it, Gaby?"

"It's beautiful," Gaby agreed, holding her tongue. "Joe and I have been swimming already."

"You'll have to try the seafood at La Mer, down the road," Lana continued, dropping down onto a lounge. "They have it fresh daily. And there are truck farms galore. Historical points of interest

. . . Joe will have to show you around, it's just magic here."

"Yes, I'm looking forward to seeing it," she replied, forcing a smile of her own. "You look very pretty."

"The dress is old," Lana confided. "I bought it in London last year, but it wears so well that I can't bear to part with it."

Gaby did laugh then, despite herself. "I know what you mean. I have a pair of jeans that I've worn to death, but I've only just got them broken in."

"Isn't it just awful, trying to make things stretch enough?" Lana sighed, glancing at her full hips and rather wide thighs. "I guess you'll never have that problem, you're so delightfully thin—"

"I like you the way you are, baby," Marc interrupted, and bent his dark head to brush his lips across the blonde's open mouth.

Gaby felt as if she'd been stripped of her skin, and she quickly turned away. Joe saw that, and his face went hard. He got up abruptly and held out his hand.

"Come on, Gaby, let's get changed and go out to dinner!" he said enthusiastically. "You two don't mind?" He glanced from Marc to Lana.

"Not at all," Marc said just as Lana was saying, "But, couldn't we come too?"

Marc shook his head. "We have to wait for the Smiths," he said sharply. "They're due any minute."

"Oh." Lana sighed. "All right, then. It's lovely

here, I do love it, but the restaurants are so delightful. Lots of people."

"Lana likes a crowd," Joe said, smiling at the blonde. "She'd die if Marc kept her here more than a week."

"Hadn't you better get going?" Marc demanded, even his stance belligerent.

"Sure. Come on." Joe took Gaby's arm and drew her into the house with him. "See you, people."

Gaby was grateful for the opportunity to escape. She clung to Joe's arm as if it were a life preserver during the walk down the long hall to her room.

"Keep your chin up," he said quietly, seeing far too much in her paleness. "Don't let him know he bothers you. He'll take you apart if he thinks you and I have anything going together. He's ruthless. More ruthless than he ever was when you knew him before. Don't dare give him any openings."

She stared up at him, feeling vulnerable. "It's only a residue," she whispered. "Just . . . leftover emotion, ashes. I'll get used to being around him and he won't bother me. Honest."

He searched her eyes for a long moment. "Okay," he said then, and smiled crookedly. "Get your glad rags on and we'll go eat fish until we grow fins."

"I don't want to turn into a shark," she muttered.

"Dolphins have fins," he reminded her.

"Fair enough. I'll be ready in thirty minutes."

"I'll time you."

Gaby stuck her tongue out at him and closed her bedroom door. She tried not to think about Marc as she took her shower, dried her hair, and put on delicate mauve silk and lace lingerie that matched her new dress. But all she could think of was Marc with Lana. She felt a deep, tearing sadness, a resentment that ate at her. All those long years she'd wondered about him, dreamed dreams that someday they might meet again. That he might tell her it was all a terrible mistake and he really loved her. And now she had to face reality. Nothing had changed. He was still the man who'd thrown her out of his life for money. She had to remember that during moments when the exhilaration of being near him got through her defenses. She had to remember what Joe had said about his ruthlessness. Remembering was her only salvation.

She brushed her long hair and glanced into the mirror, liking the way she looked in the sweet little mauve teddy with its delicate lace trim. It had a plunging neckline and high-cut legs, and it made her look like a doll.

She was smiling at her reflection when her door suddenly opened and Marc came into the room. He slammed the door behind him.

He stood just inside the room, glaring at her from under scowling brows, his face belligerent, his stance threatening. But as he looked at her in the thin garment that concealed very little, he seemed to forget for a moment why he'd invaded her privacy.

His chest rose and fell slowly. "Nine years," he said softly, "and you look as young and innocent as you did at seventeen."

She didn't flinch or try to cover herself. Model-

85

ing had given her poise and removed her self-consciousness around men. His gaze was steady and intimate, but she managed to ignore it as she went unhurriedly to the bed, picked up her dress, and eased it down over her head. It swirled around her legs, and she fastened the belt without looking at him.

"You must be used to men in your bedroom," he remarked, lighting a cigarette. "It doesn't bother you, being stared at, does it?"

"I'm a model. I get paid to let men stare at me," she reminded him. She sat down at the vanity and began to brush her hair again. "I assume you have a reason for storming in here?"

"I want to know what your game is," he said simply. "You aren't dying of passion for my brother. So why are you hanging out with him?"

"Simply because I like him," she said honestly, and turned on the bench to look at him. "He's a nice, quiet, easygoing man with a gentle personality."

He blinked. "Are we talking about my hot-headed younger brother, who bends the law to suit him?" he asked bluntly.

Her eyebrows arched. "Joe?"

He leaned back against the doorjamb with a heavy sigh. "There are a lot of things you don't know. About him. About me."

"He's a nice man. He doesn't make demands on me. He's good company, and I enjoy being with him." She put down the brush. "Shall we try a little honesty? I still sting, remembering what happened when we broke up. But I don't use people,

Marc, least of all people I like. I'd have to be pretty low to do that to Joe, in some vague, belated vendetta against you." She searched his steady, curious eyes. "Despite what I said at your party, I'm not eaten up with a lust for revenge. I have a successful career, I make plenty of money, and I have a father who loves me. I don't need or want anything more."

He was frowning now. One big hand went into his pocket, jiggling keys, and the other brought his cigarette to his wide, chiseled mouth. "A father who loves you . . . what about your mother?"

"My mother died of a heart attack a few months ago," she replied.

"I didn't know. I'm sorry," he said.

"We all die," she said emotionlessly. She stood up, straightening her skirt. "I won't get in your way. I just want to enjoy the solitude here and keep Joe company. Okay?"

"Joe drinks. A lot," he said pointedly, staring at her. "Especially since he started going around with you. He never used to do it so much."

She felt the guilt, as he meant her to. "Yes, I've noticed it," she replied quietly, avoiding his eyes. "I try to slow him down, but it doesn't always work. At least I make sure I drive when we go places."

"Smart girl." He was a little more relaxed now, a little less wary. His dark eyes wandered slowly over her face. "Oh, you're lovely, Gaby," he said with obvious reluctance. "Like a walking painting. I thought time and life would age you, but you look just as you did then. All big green eyes and black eyelashes that looked too long to be real, and a body so soft and sweet that it made mine ache just to touch you."

She yearned to respond to his words but knew she couldn't trust him. "I was just a novelty, remember?" she said, using the very words he'd used that last time they met.

His chest expanded with a slow, heavy breath. "Oh, I remember," he replied. "I remember too much sometimes."

"Don't tell me you have a conscience?" She laughed, turning away. "I wouldn't believe that. Surely it's a liability in business."

"Not in honest business," he returned. "There are guys who make a living stealing cars and ripping off the parts for resale, but I never indulged. My company is legit, right from the floor up."

"I wasn't insinuating that it wasn't," she said, her voice and face revealing shock.

His broad shoulders shifted against the doorjamb. "I'm touchy about that," he said. "We were actually accused of pirating parts a few months back, until I got my lawyer on it and made the accuser look at my books. God knows why he accused Motocraft. I make enough money on the up-and-up without risking prison to supplement my income. I guess he just couldn't get satisfaction from the police when his car was stolen and he wanted someone to blame."

"I suppose a parts company was a logical choice of victim," she said.

"I suppose." He took another draw from the

cigarette. "Our main warehouse is near his home. It was convenient."

"He should have looked for a car-theft ring," she suggested.

"There are plenty of those," he agreed. "Parts are big business these days. Uncle Michael says it's gotten so specialized that hoods these days only steal the parts they've got orders for. That's a far cry from stealing the whole car and stripping it."

"New demands, new methods," she said, but her mind wasn't on parts; it was on Marc's face, on the subtle changes age had made, on the masculine beauty of it. A sculptor would have loved him as a subject, with his Roman nose and chiseled features.

His lips parted as she studied him blatantly, and he seemed to return that hungry appraisal for an instant.

He averted his eyes suddenly, finishing his cigarette. "Okay, as long as you're just here to enjoy the holidays and I don't have to worry about you hurting Joe in any way, you're welcome. I won't spoil it for you."

"Thanks. I really needed some time away from work," she confided.

"Is it so hard, standing in front of a camera?" he asked.

"The lights get hot. The positions you have to hold are uncomfortable. The hours are long, and you have no free time during the week. You're on call for trunk shows and commercials, and if you get a picky director, you can do the same take fifty times before you please him. Backstage at shows you've got hotheaded designers who pin you up like the tail on the donkey, and you've got men forever and always trying to put the make on you. If you make it to the top, as I have, you've got the competition hot at your heels, and you have to work harder than ever to be the best. Hard work? Yes. I earn my living."

"It sounds like it, all right." He moved toward the dresser to put out his cigarette, coming closer than she wanted him to. He leaned past her, and the spicy scent of his body overwhelmed her. His broad chest was close enough to touch.

"You smell of gardenias," he said near her ear, his voice as deep and gravelly as she remembered it in passion. He touched her hair, just at her throat, and she jumped, gasped.

"Don't be so frightened of me," he whispered, half amused. "You know I won't hurt you."

"It wasn't that." She tried to ease away from him, but his big hand caught her waist, and his fingers dug in, holding her in front of him. The touch of his hand was such a dark pleasure that she couldn't move.

His chest rose and fell with quickly caught breaths, and the black eyes searching hers so closely made her heart go crazy. She smelled him, breathed him, and her knees went weak.

"You used to love touching my chest," he whispered. His lips parted against her forehead, and she could hear his ragged breathing as both big hands drew her gently against him. "Do you remember? Everytime we were alone you'd unbutton my shirt and lie against me, and your hands would play like crazy in the hair. . . ."

"No," she said with a moan. She started to push him away, and her hands encountered that thick growth of hair, feeling it wiry between her fingers. "No!"

"You haven't forgotten," he said against her forehead. "You haven't gotten over me, not yet. Even today, when I touch you, you're mine."

It was the sound of triumph in his deep voice that saved her. He was showing her that he could own her, that she could become property all over again. But it wasn't going to happen. Not again.

With a rough moan she jerked away from him and moved to the other side of the vanity stool, her eyes wide and half afraid, dark green with emotion as she faced him. "No," she repeated. "Not ever again, Marc. I don't repeat my mistakes."

"Why not?" he asked, and there was a roughness in his voice that was unfamiliar. His dark eyes went down her body with a look of bold possession. "You're no innocent child now. We could enjoy each other."

"You have Lana," she said. "You don't need me."

His shoulders lifted as he put his hands in his pockets. "Lana is just another link in a chain of women who like what I can give them. She isn't tied to me."

"Isn't she?" she challenged. "She adores you."

"So?" he asked indifferently. "If it wasn't me, it would be some other man. She's a nice girl, but she's got a cash register inside. She adds up presents and gives sex as change."

"I don't think that's all of it," she said. She folded her arms over her swollen, aching breasts. "Anyway, that's none of my business. I came here with Joe, to partner him in every way except in bed. I don't sleep around. Least of all with ghosts from my own past."

"And I don't believe in fairy tales," he returned blithely. "There's no way I'll believe that. Unless," he added with pursed lips and narrowed eyes, his gaze sliding sideways to the bed, "you'd like to offer proof . . . ?"

"Hold your breath, Mr. Stephano," she said sweetly.

"We almost made love once," he replied bluntly, watching the color come into her cheeks, bringing her hidden freckles out of hiding. "In my own bed."

"Joe saved me, thank God," she shot back. "He saved you, too, remember. Wouldn't it have been a joke if you'd gotten me pregnant before you took your infamous bribe?"

His face changed, darkened. He stared at her intently. "Yes," he said huskily. "Some joke."

"I'd like to finish dressing if you're through talking?" she added.

He sighed. "I suppose I am. Lana wants to go for a midnight swim." He took the doorknob in his hand and looked back at her. "I won't make love to her with you in the house."

"What . . . what business of mine is it?"

"All the same, I won't," he said, and went out while she was foundering in a swell of questions. He knew, she thought, he knew that it bothered her! But why make such a statement? Hating her as he did, as he must, wouldn't it have pleased him to make her worry and wonder about it? She finished her makeup without really seeing what she was doing. She was too confused to care.

CHAPTER SIX

Gaby had wondered how they were going to get to the seafood place until Joe led her to the garage. A classic Volkswagen convertible was parked there, shiny and white, alongside a dune buggy.

"These are our runabouts," he told her. "We use the beach house often, so we keep transportation here. Take your pick."

"The VW," she said immediately. "I love it!"

"We'll leave the top down, since it doesn't look like rain. Climb aboard!"

She jumped in beside Joe, who pulled out of the garage, and they took off in a roar.

It was wonderful to feel the sea breeze in her hair as they sped down the darkened road. If it had been Marc seated beside her, instead of Joe, her life would have been too full for words, Gaby realized. Odd, how indelibly Marc was painted on her memory. Nine years hadn't erased the intensity of

94

their relationship, the way they'd seemed to fit together in every single way. They liked the same things: they enjoyed just walking together, being outdoors, doing simple things. Although she tried to put him out of her mind, she couldn't help wondering if Marc still enjoyed window-shopping, if he liked long walks as much or even had time for them. She wanted to ask him so many questions about his life now. The biggest one would have been: Had it been worth it? Had that five-thousand-dollar check really been worth her betrayal? She laughed bitterly to herself. No doubt he'd have said it was. After all, he had everything now, including a gorgeous woman who loved him.

The seafood restaurant was made of weather-beaten cedar, and there were all kinds of marine artifacts around it. A rusting anchor, a pilot's wheel, ropes, compasses, and nets. It was a charming place, and the seafood was just delicious. She ate more than she meant to and topped it all off with a strawberry pie that tasted like heaven. Joe seemed to enjoy himself as well, and by the time they returned to the house, she was lazy and half asleep. He drank little that night, so she felt safe letting him drive.

When he pulled into the garage, Joe found that his spot had been appropriated by a white car.

"The Smiths," Joe said with a grin. "He always steals my spot. Wait until you meet Dave's wife, Steffie. She's a character."

"Is that good or not?" she asked.

He got out and opened her door for her, smiling at her windblown hair. "She drinks a bit too

95

much," he volunteered, oblivious to Gaby's ironic look. "And she likes the good life. But she's not altogether bad, I guess. Dave seems to worship her."

She found that out firsthand inside the luxuriant living room with its horseshoe-shaped plush white sofa, gray carpet, and huge stone fireplace. The room was exquisite, and Gaby sighed as she sank into the delicious depths of the sofa next to Joe.

"Hi, Dave, Steffie," Joe greeted the couple as they came into the room with Marc and Lana.

Dave's wife was a slinky blonde, her hair a little lighter than Lana's. She had restless brown eyes and a smile as false as her eyelashes.

"Nice to meet you," she said languidly, and dropped into a plush chair across the room. "Get me a gin and tonic, Dave," she told her husband.

"Sure, honey," he said, and rushed to get it for her. He was a good twenty years her senior, Gaby noticed, and as infatuated as a boy. Obviously she liked that, because she seemed amused and bored by his rapt attentions.

"They've only been married for a year," Joe said in a stage whisper. "They're practically newly-weds."

"Newlyweds," Steffie scoffed. "My God, at our ages? Well, at his age especially," she added, accepting the drink from her husband without even a thank-you. "Why, Dave's actually going bald. I do wish he'd see about getting a hair replacement."

Dave flushed. "Well, I had thought—"

"I know a man who does it," Steffie said. "But

Dave won't go to see him. Isn't there any nightlife around here?" she asked, glancing flirtatiously at Marc.

"My thoughts exactly," Lana said enthusiastically. "Isn't there a nightclub?"

"There's a country club, remember," Dave ventured. "I meant to buy a membership. . . ."

"I have one," Marc said easily. "If that's what you'd like to do, pile in the car and we'll go. Joe, Gaby . . . ?"

"Great," Joe exclaimed.

But Gaby hesitated. "I'm sorry, but I'm a little tired. I think I'll have an early night, if it's all right."

Marc searched her eyes, understanding her hesitation. He seemed as unenthusiastic as she felt, and she wondered if he didn't share her distaste for nightlife.

"Oh, come on, honey, you'll enjoy it," Lana coaxed.

Gaby shook her head. "No, really. I've had a long week."

"She works," Steffie noted. "I'm glad I don't have to any more."

"Gaby doesn't have to," Marc said unexpectedly, pulling his cigarette case from his pocket. "She chooses to work."

Steffie stared at her with new interest.

"I like earning what I have," Gaby stated quietly.

Marc stiffened, and Steffie stretched lazily, looking up at Dave speculatively. "I earn what I have, don't I, sweetie?" she asked with pouting lips. And

97

Dave went red again as her meaning became obvious.

Gaby stood up. "Have a good time," she told Joe. "I'm really tired."

He shrugged. "Okay. See you on the beach in the morning."

"Okay." She winked at him and smiled. "Good night, everyone," she added without looking again at Marc.

She heard them leave and went out onto the patio to breathe in the sea air. Carla was standing there with two full ashtrays in one hand. She looked at the younger woman disapprovingly.

"You not go with them?" she chided. "For shame, beautiful girl like you staying here all alone!"

"I don't like nightlife," she confided. "I'd just be dull company."

Carla pursed her lips and then smiled. "You nice girl. Lucky Mr. Joe."

"Joe's just my friend," she confided. "But I like him very much."

"Nice boy, a little wild. Mr. Marc . . . ah"—she sighed—"much, much man. He is wasted on that blonde, you know, Miss. He should marry, have children." She shrugged. "But, what do I know, hah? Nobody gets married anymore."

"It seems that way sometimes," Gaby said with a grin. "Isn't it beautiful here?" She closed her eyes and smelled the air with its floral scent from the gardens. "I'd love to sleep on the beach."

"Sure, and the tide would carry you to Bermuda." Carla laughed. "Come. I make you hot chocolate."

"How did you know I liked it?"

"Mr. Joe told me," she said. "It will help you to sleep."

"I don't need much help," she replied, following the buxom housekeeper back inside. "It really has been a long week."

The days passed lazily with the Smiths keeping mostly to themselves. Unfortunately Lana liked Gaby, and more often than not, the sight-seeing and dining out included both couples. Joe seemed irritated by his brother's constant company. He became moody. And Gaby became more nervous by the minute, having to see Marc constantly with the blonde, having to realize that there was a relationship between them. She stuck to Joe like glue, but it didn't help. The past was there all the time, and she knew that Marc was aware of the undercurrents. He couldn't help it.

The night before the Fourth, they went to the country club, and Joe and Gaby danced almost every dance. When he wasn't dancing, however, Joe spent his time at the bar. It was the first time Gaby had seen him drink a great deal too much, and it bothered her. To her embarrassment he eventually passed out in her arms on the dance floor.

The Smiths offered to take him home, but Marc wouldn't let them leave. Lana didn't volunteer to come with them, muttering something about men who couldn't hold their liquor, and then quickly apologizing, but not before Marc got a glimpse of her true opinion of his brother. He got Joe into the car, and Gaby sat beside him, taciturn and uncommunicative.

"I suppose he's done this with you a lot?" Marc said on the way back to the beach house in the little VW.

"No."

"He likes booze," he said, lighting a cigarette while he drove. The night seemed sultry and quiet to Gaby as they wound along the beach, past the beach houses toward their own. "He always has. He'll go on the wagon for a while, then he'll fall off it." He glanced her way. "He's vulnerable with you. When you ignore him, he hits the sauce. If you care anything about him, you'll stop bouncing him around."

She caught her breath. "Bouncing him around? For heaven's sake, I'm with him from dawn until midnight every day. I try to keep him cheered up!"

"Not in bed."

She glared at him. "What I do in bed is none of your business."

"I thought you said you didn't sleep around," he said chidingly.

"I don't," she said.

"Anyway, you can't be blind enough not to see that you're a bad influence on him. He's deteriorating day by day. I'm becoming very worried about him."

"You spend your whole life trying to protect him from the world, don't you, Marc? That's half his problem now. As to my part in it, what do you want me to do, stop seeing him?"

He just stared at her. "I wonder if that would solve anything?" He sighed. He shook his head. "It was an unlucky day when you walked into his life."

"At least Joe doesn't seem to think so," she said tersely.

She jerked her head back toward the ocean and kept it there until he parked in the garage.

He picked up Joe, as if the younger man weighed nothing, and carried him to bed. Gaby went into the living room while Marc undressed his brother and put him in bed. She was standing at the picture window that overlooked the ocean when he joined her.

"He'll be all right," Marc said. "A good night's sleep is all he needs, but he won't be up early. None of them will, after what they've put away tonight." He lit another cigarette. "I've noticed that you hardly ever drink. Why?"

"My mother used to do enough for both of us," she said tersely.

He stared out the window at a patch of white, foaming surf illuminated by a light from the house. "I never liked your mother," he said curtly. "She and I would have bumped heads if I'd been around her very much."

Her face tightened. "You only saw her once, didn't you? When she paid you off?"

His eyes burned down into hers. "You'll throw that in my face one time too many. Okay, so I took a bribe. Did anybody ever tell you that I paid the money back?"

Her legs shifted. "No," she said after a long pause.

"Well, I did. With interest." He turned away, dark and exquisitely masculine, and the scent of him caught in her nostrils, seducing her. She closed her eyes against it.

"You might have told me," she said, feeling very unsure of herself.

"Why bother? You and I are a dead item. I've got a woman now, haven't you noticed?"

"She's hard to miss, Marc, since she clings like glue to your arm," Gaby said as sweetly as she could.

"Wishing you were in her place?" he said, taunting her. "In my arms in bed at night?"

"Damn you!"

He liked that reaction. He laughed softly, his eyes shining with triumph. "Jealous, aren't you, even now?"

"Don't get a big head," she said hotly. "You're assuming too much. I'm here with Joe, not you."

"You wouldn't be here with Joe except that it gets you near me," he accused. "You haven't forgotten what it was like that last time we were together. You were crazy with it, begging me."

"You conceited ass," she burst out. "I was a child! Don't expect that you'd ever get that far again."

"You shouldn't challenge me like that, Gaby. I might decide to prove you wrong."

"I wouldn't hold my breath," she shot back. "And shouldn't you be getting back to Lana? She might get the wrong idea if you hang around here with me!"

"Lana doesn't own me. No woman ever will."

"I believe that. Love is the only way one person can own another, and you're immune. How well I know!"

"Say whatever you want. But if I offered you a night in my arms, I'd lay odds that you'd come running."

She well might, but he wasn't going to know it. "Really?"

"We'll see, won't we?" he asked musingly. "Good night, honey. Sleep well."

That was funny. She watched him leave, aching as she thought of him with Lana. She took two aspirin, went to bed, and surprised herself by going straight to sleep.

The next morning she was aware of surf crashing when she awoke barely after dawn. She smiled without opening her eyes as the sound seemed to come closer and closer. She stretched, her body bare except for her sheer, lacy nightgown, feeling the sea breeze like a sweet caress. She didn't care for air conditioning, so she'd turned it off and opened the patio door the night before to let the sea breeze cool her heated skin. Now it felt like heaven whispering over her.

She moved, enjoying the feeling of lying bare on the crisp, clean sheets, when she became aware of a movement.

Her eyes opened, and Marc was there in the doorway of the patio, wearing white swimming trunks, his chest and bronzed shoulders bare and gleaming with water. He looked at her, as if he could hardly believe what he was seeing.

She sat up, drawing the sheet up with her. "What are you doing here?" she managed to ask, her voice a frightened whisper.

"It isn't wise to leave the patio door open at night. We're not that safe here," he said. "There are some wild people on this stretch of beach occasionally, and they've been known to trespass."

"I didn't know," she said. "I'll keep the door locked from now on. I just liked the sound of the sea, and it was hot."

"Use the air conditioner," he suggested.

"I don't like air conditioning." She shifted, disliking the way her body reacted to that pointed stare where she was clutching the sheet against her breasts. "I'll open a window instead."

But he didn't leave. He simply stared at her hungrily, with an expression she remembered all too well.

"Won't Lana miss you?" she asked, trying to sound as sharp as possible.

"Lana, like the rest of my guests, is still asleep. What's wrong, Gaby, afraid of me?" he asked on a laugh, moving into the room, all sensuous grace and raw power in his hair-roughened near nudity. "You shouldn't have thrown out that challenge last night, you know. It was damned near irresistible."

"You'll manage to resist it," she said with a real lack of confidence, her heart beating wildly as he approached the bed. "You always did."

"Ah, but you were a baby then," he replied. He stood beside the bed, hands on his lean hips, his legs slightly apart in a stance that promised trouble. His face was an arrogant mask, so dark that it

104

was like a bronzed sculpture. "You're not that little girl anymore."

Her nails dug into the sheet. "I came here with Joe," she reminded him, desperate for a verbal weapon. His intent was all too obvious.

"Sure you did. To get at me. Both of you, using each other to get at me, and I don't like it. You're no more in love with Joe than a clam is."

"I'm not trying to get at you!" she screamed, defending herself. Her green eyes widened. "Why can't you get it through your thick, egotistical head that I'm not in love with you? It's been too many years to hold a grudge!"

He shook his head very slowly. "No, it hasn't. Not considering that we started something explosive and never finished it. We wanted each other. And that, at least, hasn't changed."

"I don't want you," she lied in a husky whisper.

"Like hell you don't." He moved unexpectedly and ripped the sheet out of her hands.

For a moment he stood transfixed, not even noticing her hands fighting him for her cover, her face burning.

"Stop, Marc!" she pleaded.

"Oh, no. Not now." He reached down and scooped her up into his hard arms, drawing her close against the warmth of his broad chest, crushing her breasts softly against him. His breathing sounded ragged, and her heart must have stopped because she lay there defenselessly, staring dazedly up into his face.

"What . . . where are you taking me?" she protested, but he barely noticed her efforts to resist him.

Marc laughed roughly, staring straight ahead as he strode out onto the patio, into the sultry breeze and sunlight, and started toward the crashing surf. "Stop twisting against me, Gaby, or I'll throw you down on the beach and show you what you've just done to me."

That made her stop, because she could feel the thunder of his heart against her breasts.

"Nobody can see us down here unless they come out of the house. And it's nearly dawn. They'll be sleeping off what they drank, so don't expect to be rescued. Not now."

He put her on her feet and stared at her body, which was barely concealed by the flimsy night-gown. "Yes," he whispered, drawing in a heavy breath as his eyes devoured her body. "Yes, you'd bring a man to his knees posing like that for a camera."

"Let me go back to the house. I want to go!" She whirled, but he caught her, holding her against him, shuddering with the warm, soft contact of her body.

His hands tangled in her hair, and he bent slowly to put his mouth against hers. "Gaby," he breathed, opening her lips with such tenderness that he knocked the fight right out of her. "Gaby, open your mouth and give me what we both want. It's been so long!"

Too long. Years too long. Tears stung her eyes as she closed them and let him have her mouth. She felt the petal-soft contact of his hard mouth, wondering at the restraint, at the warm caress of his hands as they cupped her flushed face and held it up to his. Why was he suddenly being so gentle with her?

His breathing changed. Roughened. He made a sound deep in his throat and slowly increased the pressure of his lips, opening hers under their expert caress, tilting her head back to give him more access. A breathless whimper forced its way out of her throat at the exquisite pleasure of being like this in his arms, feeling the warmth of his body and the delicious freedom of the breeze on her skin, the surf crashing around them. Her nails bit into his ribs as she touched him.

He eased her nightgown down over her shoulders. Gaby gasped when her breasts were suddenly exposed to his touch.

"Here," he whispered harshly, moving her hands to his swimming trunks.

"No . . ."

"Do it," he ordered, and then his tongue plunged into the sweet darkness, touching hers, fencing with it. His hips moved against her body, letting her feel him, making her aware of his desire for her.

"It's wrong," she moaned, trying to pull away.

"It's right," he amended. "It always was right with us. Take off my trunks, Gaby, and we'll lie in the surf and make love."

"I can't." His hands were moving down her body. They touched her breasts with soft reverence. He drew back to look down at them, to savor their high, firm perfection with his eyes.

107

"You're so beautiful," he whispered, taking the soft weight in his palms, loving the firm warmth of her. "I could get drunk just doing this. You always liked me to touch you this way, didn't you, honey? All those years ago you'd lie in my arms and moan when I put my lips here and tasted them, and your body would arch up and beg for more."

"I was . . . only seventeen," she said. It was hard to talk. His hands were magic, warm and big, and she looked down because she wanted to see them touching her, dark against even her tan.

"This, with you, is as exciting as sex. You always loved making out with me. You never held back, not ever."

"I was on fire for you." She laughed tearfully. "I loved you crazily. I would have slept with you anytime you asked, that's how out of my head I was!" She tried to push him away, but he caught her hands and pressed them against his chest.

He drew her fingers closer, raking them against the roughness of his skin. "Never like this, never with anyone, this magic we make when we touch. We'd die if we had sex, Gaby." His deep voice shook with feeling. "We'd die trying to get enough, to bear the pleasure."

"Marc, please, I wasn't lying," she said, forcing her lips to work. Her throat was dry; her body hurt with need. "I'm still . . . a virgin."

"Go ahead, pretend, it's all right," he whispered, bending to her breasts. He nuzzled them tenderly, making her wild when his teeth drew against her in slow, aching loveplay. His hands

108

were on her hips now, forcing them against the tautness of his own.

"Marc . . ." She shuddered.

"Shhhh," he whispered tenderly. His mouth covered hers. She felt him release her and then realized when he drew her against him again that he was nude.

"Oh, Marc," she whimpered, and she pressed against him willingly, her nails biting into the hard, bronzed muscles of his back. She smelled the salt of the sea on his body as her mouth opened, and she tasted his throat, his shoulders, with lips that trembled. She felt barely strong enough to stand.

"Oh, Gaby," he whispered with tender, unsteady words. He moved, easing her down into the surf. He knelt above her, letting her look at him. His hands eased the nightgown off her completely and then touched her thighs, teasing them like the foaming surf that teased her back, her legs, her feet as she stared up into his dark face helplessly.

His eyes searched her body, worshiping its slender, tanned perfection, its perfectly proportioned curves. "Dreams," he said huskily. "I've lived on dreams for so long. And now here you are. And I can hold you and touch you. . . ."

He slid alongside her in the surf, holding her eyes as his strong hands held her waist. "Shhh," he whispered when her hips jerked as he put the whole weight of his body over hers. "Don't rush it," he murmured, misunderstanding the movement. "We'll just lie together like this for a little bit; we'll feel each other. You're so soft, honey. It's like lying on velvet. Kiss me, Gaby. Remember how we used to do it and you'd start trembling when the kisses got deep and slow?"

His mouth was on hers. She felt his chest crushing her breasts even though his elbows caught the brunt of his formidable weight. The hair that covered him was sweetly abrasive on her skin, and she felt the surf under them and the glory of being allowed to feel him this way after the years of aching hunger. Her hands smoothed down his back, worshiping the hard muscle and rough skin.

He was shuddering, and she began to tremble. It was as if they were the only two people on earth. Around them the surf was storming onto the grainy sand, and she never noticed its watery roar or the discomfort of the fine, wet sand against her bare back. Marc was loving her, and she was lost in the delight of his warm, strong body as it curved down against hers.

She opened her eyes and looked into the black, passion-glazed depths of his. Her hands touched his hard cheeks, smoothing into the silvery hair at his temples as she felt his body tremble against the soft, involuntary movements of her hips and legs.

"Before we go crazy," he whispered unsteadily, "we'd better agree on who's responsible here. Once I rouse you and start taking you, I won't be able to think, you know."

Her mind felt blank. His legs were strong and warm over hers, and she felt the shuddering urgency of his need.

"Responsible?" she echoed blankly.

"I don't have anything with me," he whispered. "Should I worry?"

She swallowed. She was drowning in desire. She wanted him and was barely sane enough to comprehend the risk she was taking. Finally she managed to say, "Yes." Her voice faltered.

"Damn, damn, damn," he cursed. His hands hurt her as his body moved restlessly against hers, and she wondered if he might risk it in his hunger as he strained at calming breaths.

"I didn't even think. I don't—" He broke off, glancing down at her, watching her expression change as the hunger drained out of it.

Embarrassed and confused, Gaby averted her eyes from his body because she couldn't look at him. She jerked away and sat up, a slender, tanned ball with her knees drawn up, shaking.

He ran a rough hand through his hair, cursing softly. He was furious and it showed. He got to his feet unsteadily and dragged his swimming trunks back on. He stood trembling and, almost as an afterthought, scooped up the towel he'd used earlier and threw it at her without a word.

She moved enough to get the huge white towel with his monogrammed initial in gold all the way around her. She got to her feet shakily, avoiding his dark eyes. Then she picked up her soaking nightgown and rolled it into a ball.

Her hair was wet in back, and she smoothed a hand over it as she glared at him. "Doesn't Lana satisfy you?" she asked numbly. "Or was it revenge for what I said last night?"

"Maybe it was a lot of things," he snapped, suddenly angry again. "Does Joe know how hot you get for other men? Can't he satisfy you?"

"I don't sleep with Joe," she said simply. "I never have."

He simply stared at her.

"Do you really think I could ever love a man again after what you did to me?" she asked softly, watching his face go hard, his eyes darken. "I haven't offered myself to a man once, in all these years, because the memory of what happened always makes me go cold. It's pretty demeaning to find out what the man you love really thinks of you."

His face darkened with anger. "You were a kid."

"I was a woman," she replied hotly, glaring at him. "I loved you!"

He started to speak and then abruptly turned away, staring out over the ocean. "Some great love affair," he said coldly. "I was a greasy mechanic and you were a schoolgirl. What a future we'd have had."

She studied his broad back, the thickness of his shaggy black hair gleaming in the sunlight, and loved him still, despite everything. "I would have been happy just to be with you," she said wistfully. "Too bad you didn't consider the alternative. If you'd married me, you would have gotten a lot more than five thousand dollars. You'd have had it all. And I was so besotted that I wouldn't even have realized why you'd married me. You killed the golden goose. Tough luck."

"It wasn't like that," he said in a deep, haunted tone. He turned, and for an instant he let her see the depths of his emotion. An emotion so violent that it frightened her. "It was never like that. Do you want to know why I did it? Do you want the truth?"

"No," she said abruptly, lowering her eyes. "No. It doesn't matter anymore." She sighed wearily and shifted her legs. "Marc, don't make passes at me anymore, will you? Let me enjoy being with Joe, and don't complicate things. I won't hurt him."

"Why do you give in to me?" he asked pointedly, his gaze searching, curious. "Why do you let me make love to you if Joe's so important in your life? Why can I get that kind of response out of you if you don't care about me?"

"Maybe the memories got to me," she grumbled. "You left some scars that may never be healed, Marc."

He simply stared at her, as if he were turning her words over in his mind.

"Was that what you meant when you said you couldn't love? That you couldn't love . . . physically?" he asked.

"Any way at all," she returned. She was tired of it. All of it. She turned away. "Just please leave me alone. I'm sorry I came here. I don't even understand why I did it now. I guess I just wanted to needle you, to get back at you because I knew you didn't like me dating Joe."

His breathing was audible, even above the surf, and she realized why when his big warm hands held her shoulders from close behind.

"I was your friend once," he said softly. "I wish I

113

could turn time back and erase the hurt, Gaby. I'm sorry I hurt you so badly. I guess I didn't realize how deep your feelings went. I did what I had to do. For me and for Joe. And I didn't have a choice."

The wording was odd, but she didn't question it. She was too torn up emotionally.

"Turn around, Gaby."

She wouldn't. His hands turned her slowly so that she faced his wet, hair-roughened chest, and she watched the muscles ripple as his hands moved up to cup her face and lift it to his probing eyes.

"Such big, sad green eyes," he remarked. "Listen, pet, we can't wipe out the past. But couldn't we put it to one side for a while and get to know each other all over again?"

She swallowed. "Marc, I don't want—"

"Yeah, I know," he said, interrupting her and touching her lips with his fingers. "I just want to be friends, little Gaby. If you're going to be hanging around Joe, I guess we'll have to try to get along, right?"

She was wary of this new approach, and her face betrayed it.

"I know you don't trust me," he said. "That's okay. Just stop throwing off sparks and chewing on my pride for a while and treat me like a new acquaintance. Can you do that?"

"I don't know," she said, faltering.

He glanced toward the surf and watched her color. "Is that the problem, what we just did together?" He let his hands slide down to her shoulders and rest there. "It was natural and beautiful, that sweet passion we shared, Gaby. I'm not ashamed of it, and I don't want you to be. It was a moment out of time, when two almost-lovers relived the past. I won't do it again if you don't want me to. Hands off. I promise."

It was such a sudden change in attitude that she studied his broad, dark face suspiciously.

"Didn't you enjoy it, little one?" he asked in a deep, soft tone as he held her eyes.

"It's unfair to . . . to Lana . . ." she began.

"Lana has other men, Gaby. It's a very loose relationship. No commitment. I wasn't going to tell you, but we aren't even sharing a bedroom this trip. She's just along for fun."

Her eyes widened in surprise.

"I don't have to have a woman every night of my life," he said with a chuckle, and brushed the hair away from her face. "It looks like neither of us is committed. So who does it hurt if we make a little love on an early-morning beach?"

She couldn't manage an answer to that. Especially not when she looked into his dark eyes, eyes that for the first time lacked the cynicism she'd come to expect from him.

"You're beautiful without your clothes, little Gaby," he said, bending. "And I go all trembly like a young boy when I touch you. . . ."

He kissed her gently and slid his warm, searching hands under the towel. She gasped.

"Gaby," he groaned, increasing the pressure. "Gaby . . . !"

His voice broke as he suddenly lifted her off the ground and bruised her mouth with a kiss so intimate and hungry that it blinded her to the rest of the world. She slid her arms around his neck and gave in willingly, letting him have the softness of her body without protest. At that moment, if he'd wanted to crush her down into the sand and take her, she would have let him.

"Now you give in," he whispered shakily against her lips. "Now, when the others will be pouring out of their rooms any minute." He lifted his head and let her slide down to the ground, letting her feel his instant response to her closeness. "Listen, Gaby," he said huskily, staring straight into her eyes, if I take full responsibility for not getting you pregnant, will you come to my room with me right now? Will you lie in my arms again and let me love you the way you should be loved?"

His words stopped her heart. She looked up at him helplessly. It sounded so simple, so easy. He'd protect her. They could make love in his big bed, and she could let him give her ecstasy. Because it would be that. It would be a completion of a love that had never died. It would be fulfillment. She wanted him to the point of obsession. She knew that now. She'd never stopped loving him.

But afterward, what then? After he'd satisfied his passion for her what would he do? Would he walk away and go back to Lana? Would it be just an interlude, a prelude to parting? She couldn't trust him. He'd betrayed her once.

And what would it do to her? She'd never gotten

over him in nine years. If she let him make complete love to her, she never would. The memory of it would destroy her. It would haunt her every night of her life.

"No," she whispered, and it was the hardest single word she'd ever spoken. She pulled away from him with a tormented spirit and lowered her eyes to the beach. "No. I don't ever want to know you . . . completely."

"You won't trust me?" he asked unsteadily.

She glanced back at him sadly. "It's only sex," she said. "You said so. I don't want an affair. I just want my career and a little happiness. And when you've had time to think about it, you'll realize that you don't really want me, either." While that was registering as shock in his dark eyes, she turned. She tugged the towel back into place and walked toward the beach house. At the moment she'd have given anything to be back in New York City working herself to death. Anything would be better than having to face Marc now, with the memory of this morning between them. She wanted him so much, loved him so much. And all he felt was lust. He couldn't have put it any plainer. Perhaps she should feel triumphant that she could still drive him crazy with desire for her. But she didn't. She felt cold and ashamed of her easy surrender. Most of all, she was sorry that she'd ever come here. Her reasons seemed silly now. She'd expected that her presence would disturb Marc, and he'd turned the tables on her. Now she was becoming the victim. And she had to get away before she succumbed to his ardor. He knew that he could have her. She was afraid that he wouldn't hold back anymore, despite her innocence. She had to get away before he destroyed her.

CHAPTER SEVEN

It was late morning before Joe dragged out of bed, looking half dead. Gaby had stayed close to Carla, watching with haunted eyes the way Lana ran to meet Marc out on the patio and clung to him as they walked down the beach. Gaby would never play with him like that, as they'd played in the old days when they were dating. It was all over. There was no going back and no future.

With a clear mind she now knew why he'd planned that seduction scene on the beach. He wanted to show her that he could give her what Joe couldn't, that he knew she had no real attachment to his brother. He was doing that and revenging himself for her assertion that she didn't want him. And that was all there had been to it, all mixed in with a little lingering lust. She felt like an idiot, a weak and stupid idiot, for succumbing so easily. She'd always be just a body he'd wanted and never had. He'd never be able to give her what she needed most in the world. Love.

"Hi," Joe said sheepishly, still tucking a brown shirt into his white slacks as he sat down at the table with her. "Sorry about last night. I got loaded, didn't I?"

"Just a bit," she returned, smiling at him. "No harm done."

"That's what you think." He laughed faintly. "Carla, how about some hot coffee? Very strong, very black."

"For the head?" Carla asked, shaking a finger at him before she winked and went off to fetch the coffee.

"Have you been up long?" Joe asked innocently.

Gaby managed not to blush. "Not long," she lied. "Lana and Marc are down on the beach. I haven't seen the Smiths."

"You'll see Dave long before you see Steffie, I imagine," Joe said ruefully. "She took on more than I did last night. Poor kid, she's the unhappiest woman I ever knew."

"Her husband is much older, isn't he?" she asked.

He waited for Carla to serve his coffee and thanked her before he replied. "Yes, about twenty-two years or so. She married him for his money, I think. God knows she's done enough to try to spend every penny of it."

"He must make good money working for your company," she said carelessly.

He looked uncomfortable. "Yeah, he makes

120

good money," he replied, and concentrated on his coffee.

She shrugged and moved on to other topics of conversation. A little later he went to put on his swimming trunks, and she started out to the front to sit on the deck facing the ocean when she heard a voice.

She stopped in the hallway, trying to figure out where it was coming from.

". . . have to be more careful!" The voice was Dave Smith's, and it sounded frantic. "What if he checks the books? Lay off until the heat dies down. It's suicide to start it up again so soon! . . . Yes. Yes, that's what I said! . . . No, he's still in bed, I guess. . . . No. I'll call you when I get back!"

She moved out of sight, behind a door, as he hung up violently and came storming back down the hall. He was flushed, and she wondered if she'd overheard him blowing up at some unfortunate subordinate. What an odd conversation. Perhaps she should have made her presence known, but it would have only embarrassed him.

Lana and Marc stayed in the shade of the little cabana on the beach after they swam, and Gaby was careful not to go down there. She said she didn't want to intrude on their privacy and preferred being with Joe, anyway. That flattered him and didn't arouse his suspicions.

She mentioned the overheard conversation to him after Dave and a yawning, bored Steffie Smith had gone down the road to buy some beer. Joe stared at her for a moment without speaking, as if he were lost for words.

121

"Oh, it was probably a labor dispute," he said then, his face red. "Dave's good at handling them. Don't . . . mention it to Marc, okay?" he added then, watching her closely. "Let's not upset him. He doesn't get many holidays."

"I won't mention it," she promised. She smiled to cover her suspicions. But something was going on, she'd have bet on it. Joe didn't lie well. He always turned red.

As the day wore on it became almost impossible to avoid seeing Marc, especially at the table when they ate. But Gaby was careful not to let him catch her eye, and she kept her distance. He noticed it. He couldn't help but notice it, and it seemed to irritate him greatly. Once in the hall he started to speak to her, and she brushed past him, ignoring him when he called after her. It was unbearable, having to face him after what happened on the beach. The more she recalled it, the more it embarrassed her. How could she have allowed him such intimacy? How could she, knowing how he felt about her, knowing it was only a ploy to separate her from Joe, to play on her emotions?

His maneuvering was all so clear. She realized that he had never believed her assertion that she and Joe were only friends, that she wasn't leading him on. Marc was out to separate the two of them. It was so obvious now, she was shocked that she hadn't realized it sooner. If only she had. If only she'd resisted him. But it had been so sweet, so unbearably sweet holding him, being loved by him, kissed by him, wanted by him. She knew she'd never forget it, no matter how long she lived. But now she had to get away before he pressed his advantage. And she couldn't let him close again.

He and Lana went out that evening, but later they rejoined the others for the Fourth of July Eve celebration at the club, which included fireworks. She noticed that the Smiths kept to themselves, and Dave Smith seemed to watch her curiously. That disturbed her, and she began to suspect that Joe might have said something to him about what she had overheard.

Gaby felt cold chills down her spine, but she tried to laugh it off and went around with Joe, meeting people, enjoying the music of the live band and the spirit of camaraderie. Everybody seemed to be having a wonderful time, and Gaby was looking forward to the fireworks. She got into the spirit of the evening and danced until she thought she would collapse. She was having the time of her life when Marc came up and claimed her without a word as the band played a sultry, bluesy tune.

"You've been avoiding me since this morning," he said quietly, his eyes dark and steady on her face as he pulled her up against him. He was wearing a white dinner jacket with a red boutonniere and dark slacks, and he looked so handsome that she trembled with pleasure.

"Have I?" she hedged. She touched the boutonniere. "You look very handsome."

"You look very lovely," he replied. His hand tightened on hers, his fingers locking with her own as they circled the floor. "Joe's glaring at me," he said with a chuckle, glancing over her head. "Maybe he senses something, hmmm?"

"There's nothing to sense." She smelled his spicy cologne and remembered so many times going to bed with the scent still lingering on her skin after he'd kissed her good-bye. She closed her eyes and let herself drift. "He doesn't have any reason to be jealous of me. He's just my friend."

"That isn't how he tells it," he said softly. "He's crazy about you."

"You're imagining things."

"Am I? He's as much as told me to keep my hands off you."

She looked up. "This morning. He didn't see . . . ?"

"What an expression," he whispered, smiling. "No. No one saw us. Imagine how it would have shocked them? Me, kneeling over you like that. . . ."

Her face burned. She buried her hot cheek against his shoulder and felt his big arm pull her so close that she could feel the powerful muscles of his thighs. She moved away a little, and he just brought her back again.

"Stay where you were," he ordered. "I like feeling your legs against mine. What's so shocking? You know I want you, so why hide from the evidence?"

"Leave me alone," she moaned.

"No can do, honey," he replied. His breathing was audible. Deep and unsteady. He turned quickly so that she was intimately close to him for a blazing second. "You can't leave me alone, either."

"I'm going home tomorrow," she said, choking.

"Running?" he said, taunting her. His fingers moved against hers, slow and caressing. "Will it help? Won't it be worse, not seeing me every day?"

"Damn you, Marc," she whispered tearfully.

"Why don't you give up this farce with Joe?" he asked, his voice low and coaxing. "You and I would be so good together, Gaby. Stop seeing my brother and I'll teach you things you never dreamed. I'll let you sleep with me every night until we go blind making love to each other."

She felt her blood go cold. So that was his game. That was why he'd gone headlong toward her this morning. He was still playing the overprotective big brother. He really believed that she was leading Joe on in some way, that she was going to hurt his brother. And he was ready to sacrifice himself to save Joe. He was willing to give her what he imagined she was angling for—his exclusive attention. Dear, self-sacrificing man, he was going to make her a gift of his body! What devotion!

She pulled away a little, her green eyes sparkling with temper and black amusement. "Now that's what I call an interesting proposition. And I do mean proposition. You'll trade me your body for Joe's freedom." She smiled at the blank look on his face. "Why don't you try offering me money, Marc? For five thousand dollars maybe I'd make the same deal you did. I'd rather have the money than your body. I'm sure you understand, being a veteran of a similar offer yourself?"

He seemed to freeze. His eyelids came down, shuttering his black eyes. He stopped dancing to stare at her, as if he couldn't believe what he was hearing.

She threw back her head and laughed, as if she couldn't have been more amused, as if her heart weren't breaking in half. She pulled away, shaking her head. "Oh, Marc, you're priceless, really you are. Thanks, but no thanks. I'm in my right mind now. You won't find me such an easy mark again."

She moved away from him in the middle of the dance floor and went back to Joe, who got up from his seat, beaming.

"What did you say to him?" he asked, nodding toward Marc, who was striding toward the bar.

"Some very naughty things," she whispered, leaning toward him. "Say, can we go home tomorrow? I know it's the Fourth and all, but I've got so many irons in the fire. Would you mind?"

"Not one bit," he said. He grinned. "I'll have the chopper here by eight A.M. How's that for service?"

"Very nice," she said, resting her chin in her hands as she smiled dreamily at him. Wouldn't this put a thorn in Marc's ego?

For the rest of the evening she stuck to Joe, flirting with him, watching him open up to her. He was a nice man, she decided. He surely understood why she was flirting with him, because he ate it up and returned it. And Marc simmered,

126

with a puzzled Lana dancing stiffly in his arms the whole evening.

The Smiths left early, and during a brief visit to the ladies' room Gaby ran into Lana and found out why the couple had vanished.

"Steffie got quite smashed." Lana sighed as she touched up her lipstick in the mirror. "Poor little fish, she thought Dave was Midas, and now she's found out that he can't keep her in proper style. I think she'd like to leave him, but he keeps promising her more and more."

"Does Marc pay him that well?" Gaby probed delicately.

"I don't know." Lana shrugged. "He doesn't talk about salaries, but I got a peek at the annual report and figured it out once. He makes about the same as Joe—enough to live well but not extravagantly. Joe must really stretch his budget, what with the Mercedes and the other cars he runs. To say nothing of his clothes! Marc thinks he must be in debt up to his eyebrows. Oh, well, it's not my problem. Say, did you see that cute little Arab with the red bow tie? Isn't he adorable? He's a prince or some such thing. He just invited me to be part of his harem." She laughed gaily. "I think I'll say yes and see what Marc says. He's been broody all night, ever since you left him in the middle of the dance floor. Say, honey, did you have a fight over Joe?" she asked curiously.

"Yes," Gaby lied, to avoid any further questions.

Lana shrugged and winked at her. "Don't worry, he'll blow over. He loves Joe. He'll give in. Must run. Ta, darling."

Gaby stared after her curiously. If Joe didn't make a great deal of money, how did he stretch it to cover his luxuries? Now she was more curious than ever.

She didn't see Marc again that evening. He and Lana left before she and Joe did, and tonight Joe kept away from the liquor. She got to bed fairly early and was up by seven the next morning. When she got into the dining room, it was to find Dave Smith awake and dressed, too, and apparently in the middle of a furious argument with Joe. They were speaking in hushed whispers, but they stopped in mid-sentence when Gaby walked in.

She hesitated. "Am I interrupting something?" she asked innocently. "I just wanted some coffee."

"No, no, you're not interrupting anything," Dave said, smiling a little too brightly. "Excuse me, I've got to see about Steffie. She wasn't feeling well this morning."

"She never feels well," Joe said loudly, watching the older man leave. "She's a lush!"

"Joe!" she whispered, shocked, as Smith turned around and glared before vanishing down the hall.

"I'm sorry," Joe grumbled. "She's got a big mouth. He needs to . . ." He seemed to realize what he was saying and flushed. "Nothing. Come on, we'll have breakfast and then we'll get going."

"Is anyone else going with us?"

"Not likely." He laughed. "Lana and Marc are off somewhere together, and the Smiths will spend what's left of the day fighting, as usual. We won't be missed."

Gaby's mind had frozen on that remark about

Lana and Marc, and her face gave away her torment. Joe smiled grimly to himself and offered her some coffee. An hour later Marc and Lana had not turned up, and Gaby's pride was devastated.

She and Joe flew back to New York City. It was the end of the holiday. And the end of her dreams about Marc.

Gaby went back to work on the Motocraft account just after the holidays, but she felt a sadness that had nothing to do with working again. She was strung out emotionally from the strain of being around Marc and knowing what he really thought of her. She couldn't understand why he was so adamant that she stay away from Joe.

On the other hand, Joe was rapidly becoming her biggest problem. He began to hang around the studio all day while she was shooting. He was at her apartment every night without fail, and when he wasn't there, he was phoning. He sulked if she talked to other men. He began to change from the pleasant, nice man she'd known, to a brooding, secretive man with a possessiveness that bordered on obsession. He drank more and more. And she found herself becoming actually afraid of him.

"What's wrong with you?" she asked one morning when he waylaid her at the studio. "I feel like you're trying to smother me, Joe."

He stared at her. "What do you mean, smother you? I'm just hanging around like I always have. Feeding on crumbs." He laughed coldly. His dark eyes ran over her like hungry hands. "Boy, you're something, Gaby. My girl."

"Listen, we've had this argument a hundred times," she said gently. "I'm not anybody's girl."

"Not even Marc's?" he asked sarcastically. He cocked his head and stuffed his hands into his pockets, watching her color. "You're in love with him. A blind man could see that. But he's got Lana, and you'll never get him back, Gaby. He's a lost cause. So it looks like you'll have to settle for me."

"I don't love Marc," she lied.

"I saw how you looked at him when we were at the beach," he shot back. "You practically drooled every time he walked past you. What went on behind my back, hmmm? What did you and my big brother do together that made fires leap between you every time you looked at each other?"

"Nothing!"

"He hates you, did you know?" he asked cuttingly. "He thinks you're a tramp, Gaby."

Her eyes closed. "Look, I have to work. . . ."

"He told me so," he continued, his eyes hot and wild and unexpectedly cruel. "He doesn't like me seeing you, and it isn't because he's jealous. He thinks you're a bad influence. He thinks you're leading me to hell."

"But I'm not!" she said, confused. "You know I'm not!"

He shrugged. "God knows how he got the idea. He wants me to stay away from you. He says you're no good for me. But I told him we were in love."

Her face went paper white. "You told him that?"

"Well, maybe not in so many words. But Marc had always been one to jump to conclusions."

"I'm not going to marry you," she said, trying to make a joke of it. "Stop teasing."

"You think it's teasing?" He blinked and laughed oddly. "I . . . I'm sorry Gaby. I was out of line. Sometimes lately I say the weirdest things. Even I don't know why I say them. Forgive me. You look tired lately. Let's go out to dinner tonight."

She wanted to refuse but then thought better of it. She didn't want to be serious. She only felt friendship for him, he knew that, but he was acting wildly. Anyway, going out with him was better than having him hang around the house constantly. Her father's patience was wearing out; he complained that he never had a moment's peace lately. And neither did Gaby. She had to put a stop to this. She felt sorry for Joe; he was beginning to look really bad. Drawn and pale and thin. But pity wasn't going to help him in the long run, and she couldn't let him own her because she felt sorry for him. She'd have to find some way to let him down easy.

"Okay. Pick me up about six," she said. "And now, how about going to your own job and letting me work?" she added firmly.

He hesitated. "Well, I guess I could go see how the auditors are doing," he said reluctantly. He laughed, his eyes far away and bitter. "See how deep they're digging my grave."

"What are you talking about?"

"Nothing," he muttered. "Anyway, it was worth it. I got you."

He turned and walked away, leaving her gaping

after him, curious and nervous and just a little apprehensive about how he was going to react when she told him tonight that she wouldn't see him again.

CHAPTER EIGHT

"I'm going to become permanently attached to this thing eventually, you realize," Gaby told the newest photographer, Ed Reddy, as he finished shooting the last of the Motocraft, Inc., still photos she was under contract to do. All the commercials had finally been shot.

She stretched on the hood of the 1956 blue-and-white Chevrolet and laid back lazily, smiling brilliantly at him as he took her picture over and over again. Her long hair cascaded over the fender, her black-and-white bikini giving her an exotic look.

"Nice, nice. That's great. Smile, look at me, wet your lips, that's it, that's it," he rattled off, moving, weaving, shooting. And then he was through. "Okay, got it!" he said finally, standing erect, a rakish grin on his face.

"Thank goodness." She sighed. "I was beginning

133

to feel like part of this glorious thing. Who owns it, anyway?"

"I do."

The deep, gravelly voice was unmistakable. She sat up quickly, hating the racing of her heart as Marc came out from behind the lights with a smoking cigarette in his big hand. She hadn't seen him since the holidays at the beach house in the Hamptons, and the very sight of him made her blood run hot and wild. He looked gloriously tan, his hair neatly trimmed. He was dressed in a navy blue suit that had probably cost the earth, with a white shirt that emphasized his darkness and a tie that had a multicolored stripe. He looked devastating, and she wished that he could have grown fat and bald with age, so that she could wonder what she'd ever seen in him.

"Neat car." Ed grinned. "Trade you my motorcycle for it."

"Sorry," Marc returned. "It's been in the family too long."

"I'm going for coffee. Can I bring you back a cup?"

Marc shook his head, a smile on his face, but his eyes were cold and hard and staring at Gaby.

"Gaby?" Ed asked.

"Yes, please. Black, no cream. Thanks," she managed to say.

"No problem. Back in a few."

Ed went out and closed the door of the studio, leaving Gaby alone with Marc. A feeling of dread overcame Gaby. Judging by the grim look in Marc's eyes, she knew he was out for blood. Gaby swallowed her fear, determined not to show it. If he'd listen, perhaps she could confide in him, tell him how worried she was about Joe.

He moved closer, touching the fender beside her leg. "You don't remember it, do you, Gaby?" he asked without looking at her.

"Should I?"

"It was in the garage. I never took you riding in it; there was never time. But you saw it. It was red then. All red."

She did remember it, but she didn't want him to know that. She started to slide off the car, and he kept her in place with a bold, careless hand on her upper thigh.

"Stop that," she said in a faltering voice.

He moved his hand, but she didn't like the look in his eyes. She didn't understand the anger and contempt in them. "You can drop the puritan act now. And don't get your hopes up, honey."

She glared at him. "Well, I know you're not here to pat me on the back, so you might as well get it out of your system. It's what Joe told you about me, isn't it?"

He cocked his dark head warily. "Why else would I come to see you?" he asked. "Look Joe's been acting strangely lately, and I'm worried about him. My guess is that his problems have something to do with you, so I'm going to put it to you bluntly. If you like working, you'll stop seeing him."

"Don't you think I can see that something's wrong with Joe. He looks bad and even acts irrationally at times. But it's not my fault. It's not anything I'm doing." He looked bad that was true, but Gaby couldn't help it. Joe seemed almost to be living in a fantasy world, and many of his fantasies seemed to have to do with her. He wouldn't talk about Marc, he brooded about his job, and he'd tried every way possible to deepen his relationship with Gaby. He couldn't seem to accept the fact that she didn't have any romantic interest in him. He wouldn't listen.

There was something disquieting about Joe lately, about the way he behaved. She sensed that something had gone wrong in his life, something besides his failing friendship with her. She had a feeling that it had to do with Dave Smith, and she almost mentioned it to Marc. What a pity they weren't on better terms. She had begun to suspect that Joe was mixed up in things that weren't quite legitimate.

Marc's eyes probed hers relentlessly. "You'd better not be taking him for a ride, Gaby."

Her face registered surprise. "I've told you—"

"And I didn't believe you," he said, interrupting. He took a draw from the cigarette. "You lied to me."

She stared at him blankly. "What?"

"I told you in the beginning not to get mixed up with Joe," he said coldly. "I told you!"

"Yes, you told me, just like you tell everybody," she returned fiercely. "Just like you told Joe, all his life, every single move to make!"

"I had to! I was all he had, in case you've forgotten," he shot at her. "I raised him. I brought him

136

up by myself. Of course I ordered him around! Without a firm hand he'd have gone wild!"

"Would he? Or did you just want complete control over him?" she returned. "I remember when we were dating, you were always calling to check on him, talking to his friends to make sure he was where he said he'd be. You wouldn't let him breathe without instruction!"

"You don't understand," he said hotly. He moved closer. "Listen, there's more to it than that."

"So you keep saying." She drew in a weary breath. "Look, boss, it's late, I'm tired, and I'd just love to go home and sleep for a year or so. Today I officially finished this account," she added. "So you won't have to suffer my presence anymore. That should make your day."

"It will more likely make yours," he returned grimly. "You've dodged me for two weeks. Ever since we made love."

"We never made love!" she replied, her voice shaking. "You tried to seduce me. What were you going to do, Marc, seduce me and then tell Joe about it in detail?"

He glared at her with eyes that grew more fierce by the second. "What an opinion you have of me these days," he said. "Is that what you think? That I would do that to a brother I love, even to save him from the likes of you?"

"What do you mean, the likes of me?" she replied furiously.

"A model. A high roller," he forged ahead, forgetting the cigarette between his fingers. "It's clear that Joe's been acting wilder and wilder since he started seeing you. You and he have been seen together at the parties. Just what he needs, with a drinking problem, being dragged around to social water holes with you!"

"I didn't drag him—"

"I'll bet!" he said, cutting her off, his face hard with temper. "He told me he wouldn't have done it, but you insisted. He said you liked showing him off to your friends."

Her jaw dropped. Joe wouldn't have said that. He wouldn't have!

"Surprised that he told me?" he asked. "He told me a lot of stuff about you. Including the fact that you're sleeping with him. So there was never any need to lie."

She could hardly breathe. Surely Joe wouldn't have lied so completely about their relationship.

"It's just as well that this is your last day, Gaby," he said coldly, and she saw the arrogance back in his eyes full force, the contempt. He looked at her as if he hated her. "Because I'd have moved heaven and earth to break that contract. It looks to me like you're the worst thing that ever happened to Joe. And I swear, if he gets hurt because of you, I'll break you into little pieces!"

The words stung. She stared at him helplessly. "Joe told you . . . all that?" Her voice faltered.

"We're brothers," he said. "Blood goes deeper than lust. You didn't count on him telling me, did you? Swearing you were a virgin, baiting me with it. I shouldn't have stopped that morning, Gaby," he added cuttingly. "I should have kept on and found out the truth for myself. Maybe that would have been the best way to get you out of my life and Joe's."

"I'd have hated you even more than I already do!" she said, raging.

"You don't hate me," he said with a mirthless laugh. "You're as hot for me now as you were at seventeen. That gives me satisfaction. It makes me feel just great, knowing that you want me and all you can have is Joe. I hope you think about how it could have been with me when you're in his arms, Gaby. I hope you burn and keep on burning. Because you'll never have me now. I don't want my brother's leavings, any more than he would have wanted mine."

"You conceited animal!" she screamed.

"Oh, my, what a temper." He laughed at her. "Didn't your plans for revenge work out the way you wanted? You came back into my life a famous model, a woman desired by thousands of men. But I still don't want you, despite your new look, and that hurts, doesn't it?"

"You want me," she said, staring straight at him. "You may not like me or love me, but you want me!"

"I want ice cream, too, but I can live without it. Besides, honey, Lana's all you never could be. Maybe you satisfy Joe. But you'd never satisfy me."

She glared at him through tears, her face pale, her body taut.

"I'm not sleeping with Joe," she whispered huskily. "I never have!"

He gave her a look that spoke volumes, that

insulted without words. "I might have had some respect for you if you could have told the truth. I did the right thing nine years ago when I took a payoff instead of you. I got the best of that deal, even with having to pay the money back!"

Blinded by tears, she scrambled off the hood with a broken sob without seeing where she was going and ran into her dressing room. There was no door, no lock. She pulled the curtains and stood crying huge, hot, silent tears, feeling them run down her cheeks. How could he! How could he believe Joe? Why had Joe told him those lies about her?

She heard a door open and close, and voices. Marc's was close, and she knew that he'd been coming after her, probably to start all over again. Thank God, Ed had come back. The voices merged, one called good-bye, and the door closed.

"Hey, here's your coffee, doll face!" Ed said good-humoredly.

Gaby wiped her eyes on a towel that was hanging beside her neat suit on its hanger. "I'll be right there!" she told him loudly, and paused to fix her makeup before she dressed and ventured back out. Marc was gone. At least for the time being. She took the coffee with her and left quickly, saying good-bye to Ed and Motocraft, Inc., in the same breath. Not if she was starving to death would she ever accept another contract for the parts company. She wanted to forget that she'd ever heard of Marc Stephano.

Joe called for her at six. Gaby had almost decided not to go out with him. She was furious about the lies he'd told Marc. But when she opened the door and he smiled sheepishly at her and started apologizing for his behavior, she melted. He was the old Joe again. Her friend. Maybe he did have an explanation for it. Anyway, if she went, she might get him to explain why he had lied to his brother.

He looked bad. Every time she saw him he was thinner and more drawn. His eyes looked sunken, as if he didn't even sleep.

"You look terrible," she remarked at the restaurant, torn between wanting vengeance for the lies he'd told Marc and feeling pity for him.

"I feel terrible," he said under his breath as he finished one whiskey and ordered another. "Those damned outside auditors!"

"I guess you'll be glad when they leave," she said absently.

"Will I? I may be up to my neck in trouble when they leave," he muttered darkly.

She frowned, put down her drink, and touched his arm. "Joe, what's going on? Are you in some kind of trouble?"

"I was born in some kind of trouble," he grumbled. He looked at her, his eyes dark and wild. "Marc's smothered me all my life. If he'd given me half a chance, I could have made something out of myself. But he kept on and kept on, forcing me into the company, forcing me to work for him. I didn't want that. I hated it from the beginning. But he got his way, like he always does."

141

"You could have said no, Joe," she replied. "You had a choice."

"I never had a choice!" He seemed to be sweating a lot, and his collar bothered him. "Why is it so hot in here?" He sipped some of his drink and took a deep breath. "What was I talking about?" He laughed blankly, and when he looked at her, she noticed that he seemed to be staring beyond her.

"Joe, are you on something?" Gaby asked hesitantly.

"On something?" He took another sip of the drink. "I'm on booze, I guess. It sure does seem to affect me in the oddest way, you know? Lately my mind goes on vacation. I think it's that superpowered booze of Dave Smith's that's doing it. I'm just going to stay away from old Dave."

Joe rambled on, not really making much sense. Gaby began to get worried, wondering what could have caused him to become so confused and excited. Finally he seemed to come full circle and begin talking about Dave Smith again.

"Dave's getting too careless, too greedy," Joe said, and Gaby wasn't certain if he was talking to himself or to her. "I told him I was going to tell Marc all about it. I really ought to tell Marc. It's not right, what we've been doing, Dave and me. I kept thinking Marc owed me something. I mean, he had you, didn't he? Once, anyway. I guess he still could, if he tried." He stared at her, frowning. "You know he was crazy about you back when you left, don't you? Blind crazy. I just mentioned your name once, and he actually teared up. Marc, can you believe it? He'd have died for you. And for me."

She let him talk, not knowing what else to do.

"Marc was more a father than a brother to me." He sipped his drink and smiled vacantly. "Great guy. He fought my battles for me, he paved the way, gave me money . . . I got in trouble and he got me out. My whole life he's been my safety valve, my feather pillow. But, now"—he frowned —"I don't know. Now I want to stand on my own, but I don't think I can. I don't know how."

"Joe, something's wrong with you," she began, her anger gone, replaced by concern.

"I'm crazy about you, Gaby," he said abruptly. "We'll be so happy when we get married. I told Marc we were getting married, but he stormed off and wouldn't listen. He'll come to the wedding, though."

"Joe, we're not getting married," she said gently.

He blinked. "We're not?"

"We're friends, Joe," she said, her tone soft and quiet. "Just friends."

"Oh, that's what they all say, right, baby?" He laughed drunkenly. The liquor was making him worse. He started swaying a little, his voice slurring. "I got Dave to hire you for the Motocraft account, did I ever tell you? He owed me a favor. A lot of favors. I always liked you, Gaby. You made me feel like somebody. Not like Marc's shadow, like somebody." His voice broke. "Oh, Gaby, why did I do it to Marc? I stole from him. I helped Dave steal from him. My brother, my own brother, I stole from him. He's been so good to me, and I never gave him anything but trouble. And the auditors are going to find it, Gaby. We couldn't buy them off. They'll find it any day now, and Marc will hate me when he finds out!"

"You and Smith stole what, Joe?" she probed, horrified at what she was hearing. No wonder he and Smith had been so secretive on vacation. It even explained why Joe was drinking so much. Did Marc even suspect?

"I can't tell you," he returned. He finished the drink. "I can't tell you, Gaby. Marc won't want you." He assured her, smiling. "I told him all kinds of lies. I had to, you see. You're my girl. We're going to be married. I'm crazy about you, Gaby."

"You're talking wild, Joe," she returned, hurting as she understood that he hadn't known what he was doing when he fed Marc those very believable lies. Marc would hate her, but hadn't he always? And Joe was in trouble. She had to help him somehow!

"No, I'm not." He leaned back in the chair. "Let's go to my place. You know you want to." He got up, staggering a little, and grabbed her by the arm. "Come on."

He was strong! More so than usual in this drunken state. She struggled, mindless of spectators. "Joe, stop it!"

"You're coming with me," he told her with eyes so wild, they frightened her. "You're mine now. Marc can't have you. Come on!"

She dragged her arm away from him and ran out of the restaurant. Luckily there was a cab nearby, and she got in before Joe could catch her. When she got home, she went upstairs to her room. She didn't understand what had gone wrong with Joe. He'd never acted like this before, and he frightened her terribly.

As she'd expected, he followed her. The door bell rang over and over again, but she wouldn't answer it. If only her father had been home! But he wasn't, and she couldn't stand it. A few minutes later Joe started calling up to her, telling her he wouldn't leave until she came downstairs and let him in. He kept on calling, declaring his love for her and telling her he wanted to get married.

In desperation she finally called the police. Minutes later they came and took a struggling, incoherent Joe off in a squad car. Gaby watched them go with eyes like death. Marc would find out. God knew what he'd do then. He already hated her. He'd believe every lie Joe told him, and he was capable of anything. And what about Joe? Poor Joe, who'd lived his whole life in the shadow of his brother. What would he do? In his present condition, anything was possible. She was in such a state of shock that what he had said about stealing from Marc barely registered. It had been wild talk, anyway, and she put it out of her mind.

Later that night her father found her huddled in a robe in the living room, looking sick and drawn.

"Hey, what's this?" he asked as she raced into his arms. "What's wrong?"

"Oh, Daddy," she said, weeping. She sat down beside him on the sofa and poured out the whole miserable story with a few embarrassing exceptions, ending with Joe's wild behavior.

"For Pete's sake." Her father whistled. He got up and paced. "Off his rocker, I'd say. Poor guy." He glanced at Gaby ruefully. "You've sure had your problems with the Stephano family, haven't you, little one?"

"Joe fed Marc a lot of lies, and he believed them, that's all," she said quietly, wiping away the tears. "I guess it's my fault, though. I started seeing Joe to get back at Marc, to irritate him. But I swear, I never expected Joe to behave like this. I thought we were friends. He was acting so strangely that I had to call the police . . . oh, Marc will really hate me now!"

"What else could you do?" he asked gently. He sat down beside her and patted her hands. "He was probably just drunk, you know. Marc will realize that. Maybe he'll realize it enough to get help for him. You did what you had to, Gaby. Don't condemn yourself."

She nodded and smiled. But she did condemn herself. Her thirst for revenge had started it, and Joe had suffered as a result. Now the fat was in the fire, and she couldn't stop it from burning up. She didn't know what to do.

The next day she called her agency and discovered that Marc had been in touch, trying to locate her. She knew why, so she didn't return the call. The Motocraft account was ended, and she had to forget that the Stephano brothers had ever existed.

And she might have. Except that when she

turned on the television, a picture of Joe Stephano flashed on the screen. And when she turned up the sound, it was to learn that he'd died the night before in a car crash, presumably from driving while intoxicated. She watched the screen go black and didn't realize until she hit the floor that it was because she was fainting.

CHAPTER NINE

"It's not your fault," Jack Bennett said gently.

But Gaby only dimly registered his words. She'd slept only briefly all night long. After coming out of her faint she'd tried to call Marc, but there hadn't been any answer at his apartment. It had probably been a bad mistake to phone, anyway, under the circumstances. She imagined that he was hurting too much to want to talk. Joe had been the only close family Marc had. Losing him would leave Marc alone in the world. She hated that this had happened to him. She also hated her part in it.

It seemed so odd that Joe would go crazy from alcohol, as he had the night before. His behavior had been so totally out of character that it still bothered her to remember it. He'd acted more like someone on drugs than someone who'd been drinking. She frowned, puzzled. Joe had never touched drugs; she was almost certain of that.

He'd often remarked that drugs were for losers, that you risked too much by messing with them. Alcohol, he'd told her jokingly, was less dangerous. At least when he woke up with a hangover, he still had a brain.

"He acted like he'd been doing drugs," Gaby mumbled. She lifted her bloodshot, shadowed eyes to her father's. "He acted crazy. But Joe never used drugs. I'm positive!"

"Alcohol can do it," her father said quietly. "Don't you remember how your mother used to get sometimes?"

"Not like this." She sat up, clutching the robe around her. "Dad, something's not right about this. Something's definitely not right."

"It's the shock," he said, trying to comfort her. "Gaby, darling, try to remember that people usually make their own hells. You can't be held responsible for what happened to Joe."

"He's dead," she whispered, and her eyes burned with tears that overflowed down her cheeks. "Regardless of what he became, he was my friend, Dad. I really did care about him. I felt like he was my brother."

She burst into tears. He drew her close, as he had when she was just a baby, and smoothed her hair gently.

"There, there, darling," he said soothingly, and kissed her hair. "There, there. Everything will be all right."

But Gaby's heart was broken. So much had gone wrong in her life. Sometimes she wondered if the sun would ever break through the storm clouds for her. Poor Joe. Poor, poor Joe. And Marc. His grief would be so much worse than her own. If only she had the right to go to him, to comfort him. Lana would be doing that. She cried even harder with the thought.

Later in the day she phoned Motocraft, Inc., and asked about the funeral arrangements. She was told that the funeral would be held the next day, a simple graveside service at a nearby cemetery.

She went walking that afternoon and took a long, long walk, so that she could think, get things into perspective. She would always feel guilty about Joe. She'd genuinely liked him, enjoyed his company at the beginning. He'd been a good friend, like a brother. Why hadn't she realized that he wanted more from her? Why hadn't she seen that at the outset? Marc had. He'd accused her of leading Joe on. He'd told her at the country club that Joe was crazy about her. And she hadn't listened. She'd thought it was a ruse to make her stop seeing Joe. She should have listened.

It didn't seem possible that Joe was dead. Looking down the streets, crowded with pedestrians, she could hardly believe that he wasn't around somewhere. They'd had such fun together. She remembered riding in the little white VW convertible with him, laughing as they sped along the beach. That was how she'd always remember Joe. Laughing, kidding, so much fun. Her eyes misted.

Without realizing it she'd gone toward a street she'd avoided all these years, since Marc had pushed her out of his life. She stopped, a vision in her blue sundress with its delicate white pattern, her auburn hair lighter in the sunlight, her face like a delicately carved bas-relief. She stared at the old garage, which looked nothing like the one she remembered. In place of the dilapidated building and pumps with faded lettering and grease, there was a huge modern garage with the Motocraft, Inc., name on it. It was a transmission shop now, and its red-and-black logo announced it to the world. This had been the first shop. This garage, where she'd come every afternoon to see Marc, to laugh with him as he worked, to watch the muscles bulge under his grimy white T-shirt, to watch his hands, deft and sure, on engines he was fixing. She'd handed him tools and they'd talk, and she'd loved him with her eyes.

She turned away. It hurt too much, seeing it, remembering. Even then Marc had been wrapped up in Joe's problems, although Gaby never knew what they were. He'd made the odd remark about Joe being in trouble, but she never found out what kind of trouble. She'd assumed after being around Joe in recent weeks that he'd straightened out with age. But now she wondered. Those hints he'd made about doing a favor for Dave Smith bothered her, especially after the strange things Joe had said when he had been out to dinner with her. He'd confessed to stealing from Marc, along with Dave Smith. What if it hadn't been wild talk? What if it were true? She remembered Dave's odd conversation on the phone in the Hamptons, his argument with Joe. Something about what the auditors might find. And there was Joe's wild, erratic behavior. It had to connect somehow, but what did it all mean? Perhaps if she mentioned it to Marc, if he'd listen, she might start him thinking. Marc had a sharper mind than she had. He might make some sense of it. And if there was something suspicious about Joe's death, Marc might discover what.

The more she thought about it, the faster she walked. It made sense. What if Joe had been involved in something illegal with Dave Smith, and Dave had been afraid that Joe was going to spill the beans? Joe had been worried about the auditors, but Joe was Marc's brother. If Joe had confessed to some illegal doings within the company, Marc would have protected him, but what about Smith? Smith would have had no such protection. And Smith had a wife who loved expensive living, a wife he'd have done anything to keep. If he got caught, he stood to lose his job, his income, and therefore his wife.

Who had called in outside auditors at Motocraft, Inc., and why? What favor had Joe done for Dave Smith? Could Dave possibly have a motive for doing away with Joe, and making it look like an accident?

She knew she might be completely wrong, but she had to tell Marc what she suspected.

When she got home, she tried again and again to call him, to say she was sorry about Joe and tell him her suspicions, but she was never able to find him home. She gave up late that night, and the next morning she forced herself to attend the funeral. Marc might not approve of her being there, but she felt she had to go.

She wore a powder-blue suit with her sleek hair under a pillbox hat, and she looked sedate and elegant as she walked toward the small gathering in the cemetery. The service hadn't started yet. The priest was speaking with someone, and Gaby saw Dave and Steffie Smith in the group. She frowned as she stared toward Dave, noticing that he looked nervous and a little preoccupied. *Good,* she thought, *I hope you squirm, because I think you had something to do with this, and I'm not letting you get away with it, you rat!*

As she approached the casket, covered with red roses, her steps faltered. She had to force herself to keep walking and noticed Marc staring at the ground. He was in black, his head bowed, his face drawn and pale. Lana was standing beside him, wearing black, too, and clinging to his arm. She touched him, nuzzled against him, and he didn't even seem to notice. But Gaby did, and despite herself, she ached to change places with the lovely British woman. But she didn't have that right. She'd been cheated out of it twice now. Once by Marc's greed and once by Joe's jealousy. Marc was lost to her forever. It might have been her heart in that casket about to be buried. She felt empty and alone.

Marc looked up suddenly and saw her. And what happened to his face was indescribable.

For a moment he simply stared at her, as if not fully understanding who she was. Then, what little color he had seemed to drain from his cheeks.

"You!" he burst out, jerking away from Lana,

startling everyone who saw the fury he directed straight at a shocked Gaby.

She clutched her small purse, hesitating on the perimeter of the group assembled around the gray metal casket. He looked as if he might attack her.

"You tramp!" he shouted. His face reddened with fury. He threw a hand up toward her. "You tramp! What do you want here, to see your handiwork? You killed him! You killed him! What do you want here?"

"No," she said, her voice shaking. "Marc, I didn't!"

"Marc, calm down," Lana coaxed, frowning as she tried to soothe him. "This won't help."

But he threw her off and drew a shuddering breath. His black eyes accused her, spat at her. "I told you to leave him alone, but you wouldn't. You wanted to get back at me because I threw you over!" Marc choked. "You led him on until he was out of his mind. They found drugs in his system. That's what caused him to crash his car. And Joe never touched drugs before he got involved with you! You teased until he went crazy. And then you had the police drag him away like a criminal when he tried to talk to you! What kind of monster are you? Damn you, Gaby Bennett, you killed my brother!"

He used guilt like a weapon. She felt it strike deep into her heart, tearing at her. She knew she'd helped Joe into that casket. And she didn't have the strength to deny Marc's allegations. She looked at the coffin, her vision clouded with tears, blind to the priest's restraining hand on Marc's big arm, which held him back when Marc started toward her. She sobbed and turned away. Behind her she heard Marc's voice, accusing.

She could have walked under a car, she felt so sick. But that wouldn't have solved anything at all. It would only make a bad situation worse. She went back home in tears and was pitifully grateful that her father had gone on to work. She didn't want company. She took aspirins for the headache she was getting and went to bed. Amazingly she slept until her father came home.

"Was the funeral bad?" Jack Bennett asked. He sat down in the chair by the bed, concerned as he studied her pale face.

"Yes. It was bad," she agreed, without going into details. It was better if he didn't know how bad it had been. "How was your day?"

"Hectic. I have to go to Belgium for a couple of weeks." He sighed and looked at her, a worried expression on his lined face. "I hate to leave you at a time like this, but it can't be helped. My company may depend on it."

"That bad, huh?" she asked gently.

"That bad. Don't worry, we've been through tough times before. And you're a big-time model. If I go bankrupt, you can support me," he told her with a grin.

She laughed. "I certainly will," she promised. "I'll even take you to Europe for a week and not to work."

"That's a nice thing to look forward to." He studied her closely. "Don't brood while I'm gone.

155

Get busy. That will keep you from dwelling on it. Worrying won't bring him back, you know."

"I know." It wouldn't bring Marc back, either, or make him forgive her for what Joe had told him she'd done. But talking about it wouldn't help. It would change nothing. "Have a good trip," she said with a brave smile. "I'll keep the home fires burning."

"Don't push me out the door." He chuckled. "I'm not leaving until morning."

"Oh. Well, in that case, I'll get up and keep you company."

"That's my daughter," he said proudly. "Come on. I'll cook supper tonight."

"You can't cook!" she said accusingly.

"I can so. You pick up the phone," he began as she pulled on her robe and joined him at the door, "call the deli, and have them bring over whatever you want!"

She pursed her lips. "Now I know why I'm not married."

"Why?"

"I wanted somebody like you, and when God made you, He broke the mold."

He smiled warmly. "I love you too," he said, and kissed her cheek. "Let's eat. I'm starving!"

Jack Bennett gave her no time to think about what had happened at the cemetery. He did his best to keep her amused and talking until bedtime. The next morning she felt rested and a little less raw. Her father left soon after breakfast, and Gaby went to call her agency. If she could find an

156

assignment, it would help take her mind off her troubles.

She was lucky. A commercial was being shot for a hosiery firm and a model who'd been hired had taken ill. Gaby was hired immediately for a small part in it. The commercial's producer seemed to like her work. But even while she was working Gaby couldn't make herself forget Marc's cutting words or the hatred in his deep voice. He hated her for no reason, she told herself, but she felt ill every time she thought about it.

This wouldn't do, she finally realized. She would never have any peace until she found out if there was any substance to her suspicions. She had to know if there was a chance Joe could have been killed, if there was any possibility that someone had given him the drugs that cost him his life.

The best place to start, she decided, was with Bob Donalds. His roommate had to know him pretty well. And, besides, she couldn't walk into Motocraft, Inc., and start asking questions. Hating her as he did, blaming her as he did, Marc would probably throw her out.

Late that afternoon, when she finished her day's work, she went straight to the apartment Joe had shared with Bob Donalds. She hadn't seen him at the funeral. And that was odd.

The doorman called up to the room, and minutes later she was getting off the elevator on the floor where Joe had lived. She rang the bell, and it was a strangely restless Bob Donalds who let her inside.

"This is unexpected," he said nervously. He

looked disheveled, and there were bruises on his handsome face. He was sweating. His red hair was damp, and his white shirt was rumpled and stained.

"You look terrible," she said abruptly.

"I feel terrible," he agreed. "Look, you shouldn't be here."

She stared at him, hesitating. "Are you alone?" she asked.

"Yes. Now I am," he added. He put his face in his hands. "Gaby, you shouldn't have come."

"It's something to do with Joe, isn't it?" she probed gently.

His head jerked up. His eyes were wild and frightened, and she knew immediately that he was involved. Somehow he was involved.

"You know something, don't you?" she persisted. "It wasn't an accident. Joe never used drugs, you know he didn't. But I got a copy of the paper that came out on the morning after Joe was killed, and it said he was on some kind of drug, just like Marc said. Bob, you know as well as I do that Joe never touched drugs!"

"Maybe he changed!" Bob got to his feet. He looked hunted and more than a little afraid. "Look, I hate to be rude, but I've got to go out of town for a few days. I was just packing when you came."

"How sudden," she said suspiciously. He knew something. He was afraid, and he was running. "Who threatened you, Bob?" she asked point-blank. "Who beat you up?"

His face went white, making the freckles on his

158

cheeks stand out like measles. "I don't know anything," he said sharply.

"You know something," she returned. "It was murder, wasn't it?" The expression on Bob's face told her she was right, so she pressed on. "Was Dave Smith involved?"

He actually flinched. He didn't say a word, but he didn't have to. She could see it in his eyes. She'd been right all along.

"Was Joe helping Smith to steal parts from the company?" she said, prodding.

"Gaby, shut up!"

"That has to be it," she whispered, horrified at what she was puzzling out for herself. "Joe had so much money, money he didn't earn working for Marc. And he said he'd done Smith a favor. . . . He and Smith were privately selling parts from Marc's own huge inventory, but they were pocketing the money. That would mean a discrepancy on the books, and outside auditors would discover that orders were being received and processed and that no money was changing hands. That's it, isn't it? And when the auditors came in, Joe got scared and threatened to tell Marc to save his own skin, but Smith realized that it would be the end for him, and he panicked and killed Joe!"

"If you tell that to a living soul, you'll be in trouble too," Bob whispered, glancing around the room restlessly. He took her by the shoulders and shook her gently. "Listen, girl, I stumbled on it by accident. Joe talked in his sleep. And I happened to mention it to Smith . . . oh, hell, I was going to squeeze a little money out of him, and he sent a

159

couple of his 'friends' over to explain the situation to me." He let her go, turning away from her shocked face. "So I like money," he grumbled. "The real estate business hasn't been working out lately. I made a mistake. But I'm getting out before I wind up like poor old Joe. And you'd better get amnesia fast or you could be in trouble yourself."

"We could go to the police . . ." she ventured.

"And implicate me in a blackmail scheme?" he burst out. "What a neat idea. Will you visit me in prison?"

"We don't have to tell them that!"

"It would come out." He opened his door and stood beside it, waiting for her to get the idea.

"Are you going to let him get away with it?" she challenged. Her green eyes sparkled as they searched his. "Or didn't he act alone?" she added.

"I never had anything to do with it," he said harshly. "It wasn't me, I swear. I liked him." He sighed. "I'm sorry, Gaby. I like living."

"Yes. I can understand that, but I can't let it drop. His brother thinks I'm responsible for his death. I can't live with that on my conscience."

"You might not live, period, if you don't forget everything we just said."

"I'll live," she returned. Her chin lifted. "I'll live, all right. And I'll clear Joe's name. Keep your eye on the papers, Bob, from wherever you go into hiding."

"And watch for what? Your obituary?" He laughed mirthlessly. He let her out and quickly closed the door behind her.

160

Determination lighting her eyes, she went toward the elevator. She was going to get Dave Smith and expose his whole filthy operation. And with that firmly in mind, disregarding the danger, she hailed a cab and went straight to the main offices of Motocraft, Inc.

CHAPTER TEN

Gaby had hoped that Marc's rage had been due to grief and that he would be more receptive to hearing her out now. But after his secretary asked her to sit in the waiting room, she knew it was going to be much more difficult than she'd expected. She saw the young woman at the desk speak into the phone, turn pale, glance nervously at Gaby, and murmur, "Yes, sir," into the intercom.

"I'm sorry, but Mr. Stephano is in conference," the secretary said with admirable aplomb, "and it's only fifteen minutes before quitting time. He said that he can't see you today."

"I can wait," Gaby said, trying to smile.

The girl cleared her throat. "Uh, miss . . . ?"

"Bennett," Gaby reminded her.

"Miss Bennett, I don't think it will do any good," she said honestly.

"I'll wait," she replied doggedly. "If it takes ten hours or ten days," she added under her breath.

A few minutes later the door to Marc's office opened, and a man left with a briefcase in his hand. Marc stood in the doorway, glaring at Gaby.

"I can't see you," he said in a tone that would have killed mice. "Isn't that plain?"

"You *are* seeing me, Mr. Stephano," she replied, rising gracefully, "and you're going to hear me, too, if I have to take out a full-page ad in *The New York Times* to get your attention."

"Be my guest." He turned and went back into his office and closed the door.

Gaby sat back down, smiled at the secretary again, opened a magazine, and began to read. Fifteen minutes later she watched the young woman glance at her apologetically as she called Marc to tell him she was leaving. Gaby couldn't hear the reply. The girl left, closing the door behind her, leaving the office in a funereal peace.

An hour passed, and Gaby felt more miserable by the second. She thought of storming into Marc's office, but she didn't relish the idea of being thrown out. It was all catching up to her, anyway, the grief and fear and nervous apprehension about laying her suspicions at his feet. He probably wouldn't believe her, anyway, but she had to try. It was killing her to have him hate her for something she hadn't done. She'd cared about Joe too. His death had hurt her too. But now she was sure that she understood a great deal more about the way he'd behaved at the end, about his wild delusions and outbursts. Somebody had been feeding

163

him drugs, and he probably hadn't even realized it. Joe had been, all his life, a victim.

Her back and her legs ached. She was tired and wanted to go home. She glared at her watch and Marc's closed door and felt like throwing things. She was near tears when the door suddenly was jerked open and he strode out.

But he didn't look at her. He went straight to the door and held it open.

"I'm locking up," he said abruptly. "Care to spend the night here alone?"

"I want to talk to you," she said, rising. "It's important."

"Want to feed me some more lies, honey?" he challenged, and the hatred in his eyes almost broke her spirit. "Joe's dead, thanks to you. All your lies won't bring him back."

He couldn't have known how that accusation hurt her. Why wouldn't he give her a chance to tell him the truth?

"Listen. Please listen to me!" she pleaded, moving close to him. Her eyes were wide with pain as she looked up into his unyielding face. "Joe was involved in some kind of theft at the company. He and Dave Smith. Joe never used drugs; he hated them! Somebody gave him something, and the only person it could have been is Smith! Smith had him killed because—"

"Can't you make up something better than that?" he spat, closing his mind to everything she said. "Get out of here! Let my brother rest in peace and get out of my sight. You make me sick!"

"Please!" she begged.

"Shall I call the police and have *you* taken off in a squad car?" he said, challenging with pure malice, and he looked as if that was the least dangerous thing he might do.

"It's not a lie, it's the truth!"

"You wouldn't know the truth if it sat on you." He moved her out of the way with an ungentle hand and quickly locked the door. Even as she tried to repeat what she'd already said, he turned his back on her and strode off down the hall without a backward glance. Before she could reach the elevator, he was in it and gone.

So. That was that. He really did hate her, all right, and now there was no one to tell. She couldn't go to the police; they'd need more than her suspicions to investigate. Marc wouldn't listen. Bob had skipped town by now. Defeated and tormented by what she knew and couldn't prove, she went back to her father's house and brooded for the rest of the evening.

She hardly slept that night, but her mind kept working on the problem, gnawing away at it. She was desperate to find someone to listen to her, so desperate that she finally considered going to Marc's uncle Michael. He was one person who might listen to her if he hadn't been warned off by Marc. He just might even believe her. After she had coffee and a piece of toast Gaby set off to a part of town she had never visited before, to an apartment on the top floor of a rundown building. A place she'd once gone with Joe, a place she'd seen only from the outside. Joe hadn't asked her in, and she hadn't volunteered to join him during a brief visit to his uncle.

Shivering with nerves, she rang the door bell on the third floor. Nobody answered, and she rang it again. Perhaps he wasn't home. Perhaps he'd seen her get out of the cab, recognized her, and didn't want to see her. Perhaps . . .

The door opened, and a hard, rocky-looking face peered at her. "Yeah?"

She swallowed. "Uncle Michael?" she asked in a tone half the strength it usually was.

The tall man stared at her levelly with eyes as black as Marc's. He was built like a boxer, though not as tall as his nephew. Had she done a stupid thing by coming here? He looked much more formidable than she'd imagined, and perhaps Marc had already turned him against her.

He looked her up and down, taking in the neat gray dress with its high collar, the sleek chignon her hair was pulled into, the grace and poise of her carriage.

"I saw you at Joe's funeral," he said simply.

Yes, he had seen her at the funeral. And only now did she recognize him; the silver-haired, handsome old man in the blue pin-striped suit who'd been standing by himself, behind Marc. There had been several people she didn't know at the cemetery, and she hadn't paid particular attention to them.

"Yes," she said quietly, without backing down, which was what she really felt like doing. This man's reputation gave her cold chills.

"You're the one Marcus was yelling his head off

about, aren't you?" he continued, his voice cold and emotionless.

Her long nails bit into her clutch purse. "Yes," she confessed, and her green eyes challenged him to do his worst.

His wide lips pursed, then drew into a faint smile. "Well, you've got guts, I'll say that for you," he muttered. "Took one hell of a lot of nerve to come here."

"More than you know, I think," she said with what was left of that nerve. She shifted her stance, glad she'd worn low-heeled shoes. She might stand here a long time. That was what she did mostly these days, stand and wait for one of the Stephanos to listen to her.

"You want to come in?" he asked, cocking his head. For a moment she thought his dark eyes were laughing at her. "Might be dangerous, all alone with a shady character like me."

She sighed wearily. "Mr. Stephano, I'm in so much trouble, anything you might do to me would be a favor."

The sound of his deep, soft laughter startled her. He chuckled and stood to one side. "Come on in here, doll," he invited. "And I thought I was 'Uncle Michael,' not 'Mr. Stephano.' "

"That was what Joe and Marc always called you," she said sheepishly, moving into the apartment past him. Surprisingly it had been furnished with exquisite taste and obvious money.

He closed the door and walked into the green-and-white decor of the living room. He was wearing slacks and an open-throated white shirt. He was in his stocking feet, and Gaby thought he might have been taking a nap because his thick, straight silver hair was mussed.

"I hope I didn't disturb you," she began apologetically, and sat down on the very edge of the sofa.

"I saw a princess on television one time," he remarked as he dropped into a big armchair across from her. "She wasn't one bit more elegant than you look." He leaned back and lit a big cigar and reached out to tug an ashtray closer on the table beside the chair. "So you're Gaby," he mused quietly.

"I'm Gaby," she confirmed. She stared at him expectantly, seeing more of Marc than Joe in that rugged face.

"I remember hearing about you years ago," he said surprisingly. "I thought you had wings and flew in the clouds from the way Marc described you." He drew in a slow breath. "Too bad you broke up. He never was the same after that. And the next thing I know, it's about ten years later and you're going around with Joseph. You must like the Stephano family."

" 'Like' was the right word," she told him sadly. "Unfortunately Joe wanted it to be more. I couldn't give him what he wanted. But I didn't help to kill him. And that's why I came. I know something terrible about Joe's death, and Marc won't listen to me. He blames me for everything. I can't get near him."

"Like a snarling wolf, isn't he?" he asked knowingly. He tapped ashes into the ashtray. "Spill it. What do you know?"

She told him, quietly and concisely, what she suspected and why. "The clincher was when Bob Donalds left town with bruises all over him. He wouldn't tell me a single thing, but his face told me a lot. I'm almost sure David Smith has something to do with this. I just can't get anybody to listen to me."

He watched her like an old hawk, and he didn't blink. She could imagine him backing down a thug with just that level, threatening stare. It gave her goose bumps.

"Why don't you think Joseph was taking drugs?" he asked.

"Because he never did. I was with him a lot of the time during the last few weeks. I would have recognized the symptoms." She laughed bitterly. "I've seen enough addiction and near addiction to know."

"Yeah, me too. Stupid habit." He drew in a puff of smoke and let it out, stared at his cigar's glowing tip. "That doesn't sound like Joseph, what you described him doing that last night. No, that doesn't sound like Joseph to me. He was quiet, even when he was hitting the booze."

"Yes, I know. I've seen him drunk. He just passed out eventually. This was different." She studied her long fingernails with their pale pink polish. "He'd been changing lately. Losing weight, brooding. He looked really bad. I hated to cut our friendship off," she said in anguish, lifting her eyes to his, "but I felt it would be worse to lead him on, to let him get his hopes up. I swear, it was nothing more than friendship on my part from the beginning. I told him so and kept telling him so. But he wouldn't listen. He told Marc some terrible lies about me. I don't understand it. He seemed out of his head completely. I remember wondering if it could be pressure or alcohol doing it to him, because it was so unlike Joe. We were friends, but he was never obsessed with me, or at least he never seemed to be."

"Men keep a lot to themselves, Gaby," he said. "Too much, sometimes. Joseph didn't talk to me like Marcus did. But Marcus mentioned that his brother was really crazy about you. It bothered him. He knew you didn't feel the same way. He was sure you were trying to get to him through Joseph."

"I know. But I wasn't. I liked Joe. I often thought that if his life had been a little different, if he'd joined the service or gone out on his own, he might have adjusted better."

He stared at her hard. "You think Marcus protected him too much."

"Yes," she said bluntly.

He laughed shortly. "Yeah. Me, too, but Marcus never listened to me. He used to think I was a bad influence on the boy, so he kept him away from me. Pity. Marcus loved him, you know. He just felt too much responsibility for the boy."

"Just the two of them, I guess so," she agreed. She studied the older man. "Why didn't they live with you when they were younger?"

"With me? God forbid I should have kids

around, living like I do!" He got up and went to the window, staring down at traffic. "How much you know about me?"

She gulped. "Just a few things."

He glanced at her with a rueful smile. "Yeah. Well, most of them are true."

"Is their mother still alive?" she asked to change the subject and also because Marc had seldom spoken of her.

"I don't know," he said curtly. "I don't want to know. Neither did they. She was a real jewel. She was the kind of woman who could give motherhood a bad name. She never took care of the boys, and even when they were small, they had to fend for themselves."

Gaby shuddered, thinking about how terrible it must have been for two children. No wonder they'd grown up so tough.

"What did you do?" she asked, drawn into the story.

"I wasn't in a position to do much. I helped them whenever I could, but even then Marcus was as independent as they come. Somehow they managed to survive. They were tough little cusses!" He took another draw from the cigar. "By the time Marcus was fifteen, he was a real streetwise kid with a mean right hook. He didn't talk about his mother. He just let me believe she was with them. Then mother was away with one boyfriend or another as often as she was home with the kids. They were mostly on their own. Marcus got a job at that garage and supported himself and Joseph, and by the time I realized that they had to fend for themselves most of the time, he had everything well in hand. Hell of a boy, Marcus. And look where he got to. His own company. An empire. All legit. Makes me sick with jealousy."

She didn't mention that it was the five thousand dollars her parents had given Marc to drop her that had made the difference. He'd paid it all back. The only victim in that transaction had been herself, and what did that matter now? Marc would never be able to forget how Joe had died or her part in it, however small. There was nothing she could do about that. All she could hope for was to clear Joe's name and help find his killer. Perhaps that would make Marc feel a little less hatred for her.

"But what matters now is that Smith creep," he said, and when he turned, his eyes were narrow with menace.

"Tell me what to do," she said quietly.

He pursed his lips. "I'll bet that's a switch," he said, chuckling. "Marcus used to say you had a lot of spirit."

"It's rather bent at the moment," she confessed. "But I'll bounce back one of these days. Right now I just want to make sure that big rat doesn't get away with what he did to Joe."

"You're sure it's him?"

"I'm sure," she said without a second thought. "I'd bet on it."

"Bad girl," he clucked, pointing a finger at her. "Gambling is not a nice pastime."

"I'll remember," she promised. "What do we do?"

172

"You do nothing," he returned. "I'll start asking a few innocent questions and see what I come up with. You keep your mouth shut. I don't want you to get yourself in trouble before I get answers."

"I don't want that, either," she said fervently. She got up. "Thanks for hearing me out. I ran out of people to confide in. I don't have any close friends. Except Joe," she said with a wobbly smile.

"Hey," he chided, "cut that out. He wouldn't want his friend crying over him, would he?"

She swallowed down the lump in her throat. "Nope. Guess not. He was a nice guy, that's all." She went to the door, opening it before he could. "Should I give you my phone number or get yours?" she asked, turning.

"It's better if we keep our association on the QT," he replied. "You don't want to be connected with a bad man like me."

"Bull," she shot back. "The only bad men I know are disguised as well fed executives."

"Yeah, that sounds familiar, all right. But we don't want anybody to suspect that I know about all this. And you look over your shoulder," he added firmly. "Gossip gets around. That roommate of Joseph's might have said too much already."

"I'll look out for myself. You will let me know if you find out anything?"

"Sure. In ways you'd least expect. You live alone?" he asked with a hard frown.

"No. With my father, at his house."

"You'll be safe there. Don't go out at night alone."

She stared at him and shook her head. "You're a bossy man."

"Yeah. I should have had ten kids to boss around, but my girl died, and I never wanted anybody else," he said. His eyes roved over her hair. "She had auburn hair. Big blue eyes. Freckles. Hell of a pretty girl."

"What happened to her?" she asked.

He lifted the cigar to his mouth. "She got pneumonia," he said simply. "Damned twentieth century. Television, movies, men on the moon. But she got pneumonia, and all the drugs they had wouldn't save her. She was twenty-four," he recalled, "and I was thirty. I'd have died for her." His shoulders rose and fell. "She was the only human being who ever loved me just the way I was."

She bit her lower lip because there were tears in his eyes and she couldn't stand to see them. She turned away. "I'd better go," she said gently. She didn't say she was sorry because that was too trite. He was a nice old man with a horrible reputation that terrified people. But he didn't terrify Gaby anymore. She liked him. "Good night, Uncle Michael."

"Good night, Gaby. Take care."

"You too." She smiled over her shoulder as she went out into the hall and heard him close the door softly behind her.

She went back home, feeling a little more confident about the whole situation. If Uncle Michael could probe gently into Motocraft, Inc., and check up on David Smith, he might well come away with some tangible evidence as well. The auditors were a logical contact, but Gaby was no private detective, and snooping could be dangerous. Even if she hired a detective, she might be discovered. The thought made her uneasy.

She wondered if Uncle Michael would talk to Marc. Probably not, she decided. He seemed the kind of man who wouldn't confide secrets unless it became necessary. But perhaps she could make one more effort to get through to Marc, to make him listen to her.

She picked up the phone and dialed his apartment. It was late, and probably Lana would be there, but that wouldn't be so shocking. She knew they were lovers, so why get upset all over again? She gripped the receiver and held her breath while the phone rang once, twice, three times.

On the fourth ring, just as she was starting to loosen her grip, there was a click followed by Marc's deep, "Stephano."

She hesitated. Would he slam the phone down in her ear? What could she say that would force him to listen?

"Hello?" he demanded impatiently.

"If you'd only listen," she said wearily, "I know you won't. But if you'd just hear me out one time."

There was a pause. "What do you want to tell me, Gaby? I already know more than I ever wanted to."

"Somebody gave Joe drugs," she said quietly. "Somebody doped him. Listen, Marc, was Joe the kind of man who'd stand on a street corner screaming at the top of his lungs for half an hour, even if he was dead drunk?"

There was another pause. "You ran with a crowd where drugs were easy to get," he scoffed, but at least he was listening.

"No. And Joe and I weren't having an affair. And I didn't slip him anything. But somebody did. Check your books, Marc, before it's too late! Smith and Joe were into something over their heads. Smith was—"

"Not again," he said harshly. "Aren't you tired of that story? Dave says it's a bald-faced lie, and if you repeat it, he's going to sue you."

Her blood ran cold. "You told David Smith what I said?" she asked in a ghostly whisper.

"Of course I told him!" He sounded impatient, fed up. "He's been with me for ten years. He's the nearest thing to a friend I've got. Yeah, I told him. He had a right to know you were making wild accusations about him."

She felt the fear like an icy finger drawing a cutting line across her throat. "And it never occurred to you, did it, that if I'm right, he'll come after me next?" she asked.

"Stop it, Gaby," he said curtly. "Haven't you had enough mileage out of your lies? Joe might not have been on drugs, but he was sure out of his head over you. If you hadn't led him on and dropped him, he'd still be alive. Look, I'm tired. I loved my brother, Gaby. I raised him, just me. Leave it, will you? I want to get over it. If you want to make up excuses, fine, but don't tell them to me. I don't want to talk to you. I don't want any part of you ever again." And he hung up.

Her eyes closed. He didn't realize what he'd

done. And now she knew that she shouldn't have told him anything. He'd told Smith, and Smith was going to have to do something. Uncle Michael hadn't been far off the mark with his advice to look over her shoulder. She was going to do that, all right. And she was going straight to the police, first thing in the morning. She was going to make sure they knew what was going on, just in case she did have an unfortunate accident. Even if Smith killed her, she was going to make sure somebody knew about him.

She made sure the doors and windows were locked before she went to bed. She hardly slept, though, because Smith knew about her. He knew that she'd figured it out. He knew how much he stood to lose if she talked. He wasn't going to let her get away with it; he couldn't afford to. She was sure that he'd make a move, and it wouldn't be long.

It wasn't. The phone rang early the next morning. With trembling fingers she lifted the receiver.

"Hello?" she said, trying to sound calm.

"Miss Bennett?" a strange voice asked.

She wondered who it was. "Yes?"

"I hear you've been asking some questions about Joe Stephano's death. Better keep your mouth shut or you may wind up in trouble. You got that?"

She sat up in bed, wild-eyed. "Who is this?"

"Never mind who this is. Lay off."

"I won't," she shot back without thinking. "I'll go to the police!"

The line went dead. She jumped out of bed and

dressed quickly. There was no time like the present for getting down to the nearest police station and telling everything she knew. She felt like her life might depend on it at this stage of the game.

She tugged on pink slacks and a floral top and sandals, barely taking time to fix her face and brush her long hair. *Thanks a lot, Marc,* she thought furiously. *Now you can come to my funeral too.*

With haste borne of fear she grabbed her clutch purse and ran downstairs. She opened the door and quickly locked it behind her and went down to the curb to hail a cab. But just as she spotted one and lifted a hand to hail it, a car came around the corner, out of nowhere, and ran up onto the sidewalk, missing her by inches.

She dived behind a telephone pole as the car, dark-colored and ordinary, screeched back onto the street and around another corner, leaving her shaking and out of breath.

"Hey, lady, you okay?" a pedestrian asked, touching her shoulder in concern.

"Did you see that?" a heavyset woman asked her elderly companion. "That car tried to hit her!"

Yes, Gaby knew that. It was a warning.

She hesitated, standing on the street corner trembling. What was she to do now? If she went to the police, just what was she going to tell them? That David Smith had given a drug to Joe and caused the wreck that killed him? That Smith was a thief? Where was her proof? What could the police do on that kind of charge? And if they confronted Smith, he could very well turn the tables and sue her for character assassination, couldn't he? And unless she had evidence, unless she could prove those allegations, she'd be in hot water.

Great, she thought, walking on shaking legs back to the house. She fumbled the key into the lock and got inside. She closed and locked the door, just as the phone rang.

She stared at it, afraid to pick it up and hoping it might stop. But it didn't. And before she finally picked up the receiver, holding it with both hands because she was trembling so, she knew who it was.

"Close call," the strange voice she'd heard earlier drawled in a deceptively gentle tone. "Next time you might not be so lucky."

And there was a click.

She sat down heavily on the staircase. That was a threat. He'd threatened her life. Smith had sent somebody after her! But she had no proof. It would be his word against hers. And even Marc would stand up in court and swear that she was lying, that David Smith wouldn't harm a leaf on a tree. She laughed at the irony of it, that the man she loved most in all the world was the only one who wouldn't listen to her or believe her when she told him the truth. As her tears began to fall, she wondered if he'd believe it if Smith succeeded? Would he believe it then and come and apologize to her corpse?

She laid her head on the steps and cried brokenly. If only her father were home, if only she had someone to run to. In the old days Marc would have been there. Marc would have held out his arms and comforted her. But Marc wouldn't help her these days. The only real friend she had, or thought she had, was Uncle Michael. And could she really trust him? After all, he was a Stephano. Perhaps he would turn against her too.

This was too much, she thought. Too much. Now she was getting paranoid. She staggered to her feet and brushed back the hair that had blown into her eyes as she ran. What a mess her life had become. What an irony that it was Marc who'd betrayed her again. But this time he might have cost her far more than her pride or her heart. This time he might yet cost her her life.

CHAPTER ELEVEN

It took Gaby the rest of the day to get over what had happened. She brooded about it until she realized that she couldn't just let it drop. It was bad enough that Smith had killed Joe, but now he was intimidating her, trying to frighten her into hiding what she knew. He had too much to lose to let anyone expose him. In addition to theft there was every possibility that he could be held responsible for Joe's death if he had, indeed, been drugging Joe.

She weighed the consequences of her own actions and decided that she couldn't live with herself if she took the coward's way out. Joe had been her friend. How could she let his murderer get away scot-free? In addition to that she had to clear her name with Marc. If he hated her for old grudges, that was one thing. But she couldn't bear to have him go on thinking that she'd led Joe to his death. The contempt in Marc's deep voice, the hatred in his eyes when he looked at her, haunted her. She remembered his voice on the phone, what he'd said during that last conversation. It was almost beyond bearing. *Marc, how could you believe that of me?* she wondered miserably. He didn't even trust her enough to take her word. And, of course, he didn't love her. How could he and believe that she'd do such a thing?

The only problem with this decision was the fact that it exposed her to danger. But if she was careful and planned her every move, she might just trap Smith.

She phoned the family attorney and asked him to suggest a reputable private detective. She then called Jack Harrolds, the detective, for an appointment and was able to get one that very afternoon.

Instead of going directly to the address, in case she was being watched herself, she switched cabs three times, careful to first go inside various buildings and out the back way. Eventually she arrived at the Harrolds Agency and was quickly shown in to see the detective.

He was nothing like she'd pictured him. His office was neat, and he looked like an ordinary businessman. He wasn't young and single and debonaire. He was middle-aged, balding, and had photographs of a woman and three teenaged boys on his desk. There went all her illusions.

"Miss Bennett?" he greeted her pleasantly, rising to shake hands and offer her a comfortable chair in front of his big laminated desk.

"Thank you for seeing me so quickly," she told

him. She put her purse in her lap, smoothed her gray skirt, and leaned back with a weary sigh. "Mr. Harrolds, someone is trying to kill me."

He had to smother a grin. "I'm sorry, but that line . . ." he offered.

She smiled back, despite the gravity of the situation. "Yes, I understand. Nevertheless it's quite true. And this is why."

As precisely as she could, she gave him a sketchy account of what had happened to Joe. She told him about Smith, what she suspected, and why. And then she told him about the telephone call and the runaway car.

"Have you been to the police?" he asked then.

"I can't," she said miserably. "Joe Stephano's brother told Smith I'd made that accusation, and he's threatened to take me to court and sue me if I say anything. Then, too, there's the car that almost hit me to 'suggest' that it would help me stay alive if I kept my mouth shut." She leaned forward, her green eyes wide. "And if I went to the police, what could I tell them? There's been nothing to link Smith with the attempt on my life. I didn't recognize the voice. And Joe was in an accident. They found evidence that he'd been using drugs, but that doesn't prove anything, either. They could say that he did it voluntarily. All I have is a lot of suspicions. Not one hard fact. They'd laugh me out of the building if I took them this."

He smiled gently. "I hardly think so."

"Nevertheless I have grown accustomed to living," she replied. "I do not want to become another statistic, like Joe did. I know something is going on. I want proof."

"Let me understand this," Mr. Harrolds said, and folded his immaculate hands on the desk over his blotter. "You want me to investigate a possible theft at Motocraft, Inc."

"That's right." Her eyes pleaded with him. "Can you, without anyone finding out?"

He chuckled. "It's possible, Miss Bennett. I can probably get what you need."

"Thank God," she breathed, sitting back.

"It will be expensive," he added honestly, and quoted his rates.

She didn't even flinch. "My life is worth that much, I think," she told him, and smiled. "Thank you so much."

"I hope we can find something that will help you," he said. "It's quite possible that we won't, you understand."

She grimaced. "Maybe I have a guardian angel," she said hopefully. "I could certainly use one about now."

All the way back home she thought about what he'd said. What if he didn't turn up anything? And worse, what if, despite his discretion, he was found out? What would Smith do to her if he knew she wasn't going to drop it?

It was frightening to think about being a target. She'd led such a sheltered life; she'd never even been treated roughly. And now she could be a victim, could be killed by someone who didn't even know her. By a stranger. And the attack could come from any direction.

The first thing she had to do, she thought, was to get out of her home while the investigation was going on. This was the obvious place for an attacker to come looking for her. So she'd go to a hotel and register under an assumed name. She smiled to herself. That would throw whoever was after her off the track.

She called her modeling agency and told them that she was under the weather—well, that was true enough, her spirits certainly were—and that she couldn't accept any more assignments for at least a week. Then she started getting her things together. Mr. Harrolds had said that he'd put one of his employees right on the case and start looking for evidence. That meant possibly today. She had to move fast.

Just as she was about to leave the house the phone rang. She froze, staring at it. Could it be her father? She didn't dare not answer it, even if it was the would be assassin on the other end of the line.

With damp palms she lifted the receiver gently and held it to her ear. "Hello?" she said hesitantly, her voice weak and strained.

"Why in hell did you go to see my uncle?" Marc demanded hotly, his deep voice laced with fury. "What's wrong with you? Why won't you leave my family alone?"

Her heart leapt, just to hear his voice. Even though he was angry, he seemed somehow comforting. Her fingers caressed the receiver. What a dear voice. She might never see him again or hear him. If Smith got wind of what she'd initiated today, he might kill her.

"I like Uncle Michael," she said quietly. "He didn't know me from Adam, but he believed me."

He breathed slowly, deliberately. She could hear him trying to keep his temper. "He's a little shady, you know."

"He's a nice old man," she shot back. "And right now he's the only friend I've got in the whole world, Marcus!"

"Gaby . . ."

She felt her eyes burn with threatening tears. It had been a horrible few days, and most of it was his fault. "Somebody tried to run me down yesterday morning," she told him bluntly. "I got a phone call telling me to stop asking questions about Joe's death, and when I went out the door, a car came right up on the curb and tried to run me down. And then, before I stopped shaking, the phone rang, and he said that it had been a warning, that I wouldn't walk away the next time."

There was an indrawn breath and a long silence on the other end of the line.

"You told me to drop dead, didn't you?" she said curtly. "Well, you almost got your wish!"

"Oh, Gaby," he ground out. "Gaby, I didn't mean it!"

"Didn't you?" she asked. She let out a weary sigh. What did it matter now? There was so little left to lose. She might never hear his voice again, and here she was picking fights.

"Look," she said gently, changing tactics, "I've got to go. I'm moving out of the house for a while. I'm sorry about everything, Marc. Most of all about

Joe. He was my best friend. I wouldn't ever have hurt him."

"I was crazy that day. Hurting and half mad with guilt for all the ways I'd failed him." There was another pause. "Gaby, come out with me. We'll talk."

For an instant she was thrilled and wanted to rush to him, but then she realized that might put Marc in danger. She couldn't bear it if anything ever happened to him.

"No," she said gently. "I can't do that. Being seen with me would make you a target too."

"What the hell does that matter?" he demanded. "Look, I'm not going to stand by and let you get yourself hurt! Okay, so maybe I'm having a hard time believing you. Convince me. Talk to me!"

She clutched the receiver and pressed a warm, soft kiss against the mouthpiece as tears threatened to run down her cheeks. She did love him so. Despite everything, she loved him terribly! "Good-bye, Marc," she whispered huskily. "I'm sorry about everything. None of what happened was your fault. The only thing you were ever guilty of was loving your brother."

"And ruining your life?" he muttered shortly. "I did, didn't I? I never considered what it would do to you when I took that money. I underestimated what you felt for me, didn't I, honey?"

"That was a long time ago," she said wistfully.

"What we did together on that beach in the Hamptons wasn't so long ago," he replied. "I can't forget it."

"Sex doesn't last," she told him. "It was just what you said: an attraction that we never got out of our systems, a loose thread in the fabric of our lives."

"My, my, aren't we poetical?" he shot at her. "Sex, hell. We had a lot more going for us than that nine years ago, and you know it. We knew each other inside out."

"We've changed!"

"Not basically," he retorted. "You're still the same little overgenerous, self-sacrificing fool you were then. You're blind about men, or you'd never have wanted anything to do with a half educated, opinionated grease monkey like me."

"You left out reckless and trusting," she said.

"Yeah. Which one of us?" he asked, his voice almost teasing, so soft and tender that it made her heart ache for what might have been.

"Both of us, I guess," she managed in a tight little voice.

"We were always passionate people," he reminded her. "Never half measures in anything. We had so much going for us. And I threw it all away. You'll never know how it hurt me to do that."

"No. I never will," she said in a resigned tone. She clutched the receiver tighter and nuzzled it. Soon he'd be gone. She'd never talk to him again. "Why haven't you ever married? You used to talk about a home and children and roots."

"I never wanted children with anyone but you," he said quietly, with blunt honesty. "Time got away from me. I was so busy looking after Joe and my company that all I had time for was an affair here and there. Like Lana."

"How is Lana?" she asked mundanely.

"I don't know," he said after a pause. "I lost track of her after Joe's funeral. I think she finally got the message and went off after that Arab prince she met in the Hamptons."

"I'm sorry," she murmured.

"Are you? Why?"

"You cared about her," she replied dully.

"Honey, I care about Italian sausages, too, but a man can get sick of them after a while. Listen, Gaby, she numbed the ache, that's all. Nobody ever cured it. There was this skinny little rich girl, you see," he said in a deep, seductive tone, "and I used to take her around my neighborhood and watch her enchant my buddies. And I'd lie with her on a blanket in Central Park on lazy spring days and dream about having kids with her. I never quite got over her."

The tears overflowed now, hot and wet, stinging down her cheeks. "I never quite got over that greasy Italian mechanic," she confessed brokenly. "But I guess fate had other plans for us both. There you are a tycoon, and here I am a model, and we're both rich enough that we'd never have to work another day. I just want you to know that I never cared that you weren't rich, and I never wanted anything you couldn't have given me. Because the things I wanted from you couldn't be bought with money."

"Oh, stop, you'll have me bawling," he ground out, but it sounded so close to the truth that it stung. He drew a ragged breath. "Look, maybe you need to know it all. Maybe it would help if you knew the truth. Maybe we could start over."

"No," she whispered with a trembly smile. "It's too late for that. I just . . . I just hope you'll realize someday that I was telling you the truth about Joe. That I never hurt him or led him on. That I loved him like a brother and told him so. That I didn't help to kill him."

"Let me come and get you," he said. "We'll talk."

"I'm sorry, but I have to go now. It isn't safe to stay here," she replied. "Good-bye, darling."

"Gaby!"

She thought that as long as she lived she'd hear his voice, hear the agony in it as he called her name, and she hung up on him.

"I'm sorry, Marc," she whispered as she disconnected the phone. "I love you, but I can't put you at risk too. One of us is enough."

She took one last look around at the house she'd lived in all her life, went out, and locked the door behind her.

With her carryall firmly in hand, containing the few things she treasured and one or two changes of clothing, she started walking down the street. She hailed a cab and told the driver to take her to a huge luxury hotel about six blocks away from her home. After she'd checked in Gaby wondered if someone could have followed her. She hadn't bothered to change cabs or tried to conceal her tracks. Oh, well, she thought. She shouldn't be in too much danger in a crowded hotel. She lay down on the double bed in her room with a sigh of utter relief. The building was watched over by a doorman, and she felt safe.

After she'd had room service send up a meal, the first she'd enjoyed in two days, she went to bed and had an early night.

The next day she sweated it out until early afternoon and phoned Mr. Harrolds. Since he didn't know where she was, he could hardly call her to report anything.

"Have you found out anything at all," she asked immediately when the secretary connected her with the private detective, "or is it too soon?"

He hesitated. "Miss Bennett, I'm sorry to tell you that we've found nothing of any use to you in the way of evidence. Mr. Smith does have large outstanding debts, and there is a little more money in his accounts than his salary would provide. But you have to understand that it would be pretty stupid of him to stick money he embezzled in a bank where it could be discovered. He could have it in banks out of the country. He also could have it under assumed names. There are hundreds of ways to disguise illegal money."

"What about Motocraft?" she asked, feeling hope dwindle.

"On a preliminary check, nothing there, either." He sighed. "We'll continue to investigate, of course, but the longer it takes, the higher the bill. That can't be helped."

"I don't care how much it costs," she said fervently. "Mr. Harrolds, no one suspected what you were doing?" she added.

"I don't think so." He hesitated. "Miss Bennett, are you at your home?"

"No, sir. I checked into a hotel, just in case."

"I was going to suggest that," he said. "I don't want to alarm you, but my man thinks he may have been spotted. He's sorry, but that won't help you. My recommendation is that you go to the police, regardless of your lack of proof, and tell them everything you know."

"You think I'm in danger?" She had to know.

He paused. "Yes, Miss Bennett. I checked with the coroner who did the autopsy on Joe Stephano, as you asked me to."

"And . . . ?" she asked, prodding. It hurt to think about Joe's thin body being impersonally probed and inspected by people who didn't even know him.

"The coroner's assistant had some suspicions about the way Mr. Stephano died. He said it appeared to be a cut-and-dried case. But there was some doubt as to whether drugs or the impact of the crash was actually responsible for Mr. Stephano's death. You see, they had no reason to suspect foul play."

"Yes, I understand."

"That could be cause for investigation by the police," he suggested. "You might think about it. Because, if it was murder, and this suspect of yours has so much to lose, he wouldn't think anything of putting out a contract on you. And, Miss Bennett . . . professional killers don't miss. I urge you to go to the police."

"Thank you for your advice," she said calmly,

although she felt anything but calm. "I'll sleep on it," she added, and hung up.

She didn't sleep. She paced the floor, wondering what to do. She looked out the window, past the fire escape, and at the city spread out in a dazzling display of jeweled lights and wondered how many other people in that beautiful expanse were as troubled as she was. She was only twenty-six years old. She was frightened and alone, and she couldn't even go to Marc for help, although she wondered now if he wouldn't give it to her. He seemed much less furious with her, much more reasonable. She wanted so badly to go to see him, to be held and comforted by him, to let him take care of her. But that wasn't possible. Now that she had only herself to rely on, she'd better decide what to do.

As if there was really any choice, she thought miserably. Of course, she'd go to the police, as she should have in the first place. They could conduct as discreet an investigation as a private detective. They wouldn't storm into Motocraft, Inc., without evidence and start threatening Smith. Besides, what Harrolds had said had frightened her deeply. Yes, if Smith had killed once, he wouldn't hesitate to kill again. Now he had nothing to lose.

With her mind made up she went back to the bed, leaving on the ruffled white lacy peignoir that covered her matching long negligee. She couldn't seem to get the air conditioning adjusted properly and felt chilled. She lay down, closing her eyes, and memories flooded into her mind, memories of how it had been between her and Marc years ago.

Memories of more recent times, of his ardent, early-morning passion on the beach in the Hamptons. Later memories—of his contempt and fury at Joe's funeral. And now the hauntingly sweet memory of that last phone conversation with him. She'd live on that. No matter what happened, at least she knew that he didn't hate her anymore. That was enough. Almost enough.

She seemed to sleep, but a noise awoke her in the early hours before dawn. She imagined she was hearing things, that it was just nerves. But when she heard it again, she knew someone was at her door. A feeling of sheer terror hit her, and Gaby jumped from her bed.

Afterward she didn't remember how she'd gotten out onto the fire escape, it seemed to have been a frantic fumble through the curtains. She screamed, drawing attention from other rooms. And that might have been all that saved her. She scrambled down the steps, nearly falling as she went.

She heard a loud noise, like a firecracker, and it frightened her so much that she tripped as she was going down the last few steps. She fell roughly and felt a sharp pain in her shoulder. She didn't even look up or behind her; she didn't waste the time. She dragged herself upright, panting from exertion and nervousness, and started running again. There was something wet on her arm. She touched it and saw a red film on her fingers. The terror magnified. It was a nightmare, and she was actually on her feet and participating in it!

She ran around the building to the street, where

traffic was coming and going, and she knew that the presence of other people would offer protection. She rushed for the telephone booth. There wasn't a policeman in sight, but passersby stared. She fumbled with the receiver. She didn't have a quarter, but she did remember her telephone credit card number. Please, God, let the operator accept it.

She punched the operator button and gave her credit card number from memory and only then, after she'd given the number she wanted, did she realize how instinct had taken over from logic.

The phone rang twice before a deep, calming voice came over the line. "Stephano."

"Marc," she said, weeping. "Marc . . . someone's after me."

He cursed furiously. "Where are you? Quick, where are you?"

She licked her lips. She was feeling terribly sick, she told him hesitantly.

"I'll be there in five minutes. Stay put! Are there people around?"

"Yes."

"Thank God."

The phone went dead, but she didn't hang it up. Standing on the street in her nightgown might look odd, but it was her only hope of survival. Whoever was after her might still be around. She couldn't risk fainting. She had to stay right where she was until Marc came.

It seemed to take forever. She hung on to the telephone cord, oblivious to the slight wound in her shoulder reciting rhymes in her mind, pretending to talk into the receiver while she held the phone so that it was actually dead. She didn't know what to do. She was terrified now, really terrified, and certain that whoever had been at her door wanted to kill her. Her eyes closed. Please don't let anyone hurt Marc, she prayed. Please don't.

She didn't even understand why she'd called Marc. The logical call would have been to the police, but she hadn't thought logically. She had only reacted out of fear and need.

Several minutes later a screeching of tires caught her attention, and her heart leapt as she whirled, not sure what to expect, not sure it might not be the killer.

But that tall, hard physique was unmistakable, that confident stride. He was in slacks and a red knit pullover shirt, his hair disheveled, his eyes bloodshot.

"Marc!" she cried. She started toward him and almost collapsed into his hard, warm arms. "Oh, Marc!" He smelled of cologne, and she wanted to stay in his arms forever.

"It's all right," he said tautly. "It's all right. I've got you now. You're safe."

His face was grim, pale, when he saw the blood on her arm. He ushered her toward his car, and lifting her as if she were a child, he put her gently into the front seat. "Are you sure you're all right?" he asked in a voice deep with emotion. He whipped out his handkerchief and pressed it against the wound and tied it gently around her arm. Passersby were now taking a belated interest.

He was close, very close, and then she realized just how upset he was. His face was rigid with control, his eyes black and narrow with pain.

"Hey," she whispered, touching that hard face gently with her fingertips, "I'm all right."

He swallowed, but he didn't say anything. "Stay still. I'll get you to the hospital, then we'll call the police."

"But, Marc—"

"No buts!" he said curtly, and softened the impact by brushing a tender kiss across her mouth. "I'm taking care of you from now on, like I should have in the beginning. You'll be all right now. You'll be fine. If he comes near you again, I swear I'll kill him with my bare hands!"

He went around and got in under the wheel, glancing at her to make sure she was all right. "Here." He fastened her seat belt, arranging the shoulder harness so that it didn't touch her wounded shoulder. "Okay?" he whispered softly, searching her pained green eyes.

"Yes," she replied. She wasn't, but it was heaven being near him.

"Just relax. It's all right now, I'll get you to a doctor."

He cranked the car and drove quickly away from the hotel, weaving in and out of traffic with expert precision. She turned her head on the back of the seat, watching the way he drove, eyes straight ahead, glancing only occasionally in the rearview mirror or the side mirror. He was single-minded in this, as he was in everything. Even when he made love . . .

197

Her face colored. He slowed for a turn and glanced at her. "Embarrassing thoughts?" he asked with faint humor.

"Yes," she confessed. "I was just thinking how single-minded you are about things. You drive very professionally."

"I used to race cars," he said. "You didn't know that, did you? It was after I . . . after we broke up," he said, correcting himself. "You mind if I smoke, honey?"

"No."

He jerked out a cigarette and fumbled with the lighter, laughing bitterly at his own lack of grace. "I'm a little shook up," he confessed. "I didn't know what I'd find when I got to you. It's a miracle there weren't six cops on my tail when I got to the hotel."

"I'm sorry I involved you," she said quietly. "I was so scared. I should have called the police, but your number was the only thing I could think of."

"I'm glad you called me," he said tautly, staring straight ahead. "So stop apologizing, will you? Don't you think I know it's my fault? If I hadn't mistrusted you, if I hadn't opened my big mouth and spilled everything to Smith, you wouldn't be in this mess."

So that was it. That was the root of his concern. Guilt. Just as he'd felt guilty for Joe, he felt guilty for bringing this on Gaby. She closed her eyes, and as her wound began to throb under the blood-stained handkerchief, she wondered if they ever would be free of guilt.

CHAPTER TWELVE

The hospital emergency room was crowded, but Marc bulldozed right through red tape and got her quickly into a cubicle. A young resident physician treated the wound while Marc borrowed a phone and called the local police precinct. By the time Gaby was cleaned up, stitched, and bandaged, a weary-looking detective sergeant was sharing the cubicle with her.

"Hard night, huh, little lady?" the sergeant asked without a trace of a smile. He was dark like Marc, short, and a little overweight, and he looked like a man who was used to scenes like this. "I'm Sergeant Bonaro," he said, introducing himself. "Hell of a time to do this, but I need you to answer a few questions for me."

"I'll tell you anything I can," Gaby promised. She smiled. "But please don't expect me to be too lucid. He gave me two shots, I'm not quite sure of what."

"One was tetanus," Marc volunteered, hands deep in his pockets as he leaned against a wall. "The other was for pain."

"No wonder I feel disoriented." Gaby sighed. "I get knocked out by an aspirin tablet."

"Do you know who shot you, Miss Bennett?" Bonaro asked, holding a small pad and pen in his hands.

"No, sir. I never got a look at him. I woke up just as he was pushing the door open, and then I just panicked and ran down the fire escape."

"Lucky for you," Bonaro said ruefully. "For the guy to get past the doorman and into your room, it looks very much like we're dealing with a pro. Do you have enemies, Miss Bennett?"

"I'm afraid so," she confided. And with an apologetic glance at Marc she poured out the whole story.

When she finished, Bonaro sat back in his chair with a rough sigh. "This looks as if it could get sticky. Well, you can have police protection, for what it's worth, but I have to tell you in all honesty that you may still be in a lot of danger—"

"Thanks a hell of a lot," Marc said, interrupting curtly and glaring at the shorter man.

"I'm telling you the odds," Bonaro said. "I happen to think it's better to face facts. The lady needs to know how serious the situation is. She can protect herself a lot better that way."

"What protecting needs doing, I'll do," Marc

said, his face hard and imperturbable. "If it takes an army to guard her, I'll hire one."

The sergeant stared at him curiously. "Stephano, that your name? You related to this Joe Stephano who died?"

"My brother," Marc said gruffly.

The sergeant pursed his lips and scowled. "Any kin to Michael Stephano?"

"That's Uncle Michael," Gaby volunteered.

Bonaro cocked his head. "Your uncle?"

"No. Marc's. But everybody calls him Uncle Michael," Gaby offered drowsily.

"There are lots of other things people call him, lady," Bonaro said sarcastically, "but Uncle isn't one of them."

She smiled at him. "He believed me," she said. "Long before anybody else would listen, he believed me."

"I'm lost," Bonaro confessed. He leaned forward. "Suppose you explain that."

"About David Smith," she said, "and something to do with theft at Motocraft, Inc."

"Which I own," Marc volunteered.

Bonaro ran a hand through his curly dark hair. "I must need more sleep," he mumbled. "Okay. It's your company," he said, staring at Marc. "And your brother was stealing from it?"

Marc shrugged. His dark hair fell onto his broad forehead, and his eyes were heavily shadowed. He looked as if he hadn't slept much, either.

"I loved my brother, Sergeant, but I wasn't stupid or blind. Joe was in trouble most of his life. Usually it was from hanging out with the wrong people. He liked easy money, and he hated the fact that I was worth more than he was financially. Sure, he'd steal from me. And he wouldn't really feel that guilty about it. After all, can you really steal from family?"

"We could debate that for hours, if I had more time," Bonaro said disinterestedly. He scribbled something down. "This private detective you hired," he said to Gaby, "you say he didn't come up with anything you could use, from checking out the books at Motocraft, Inc."

"That's right," Gaby confessed. "He did advise me to contact the police," she added. "I'd planned to do that in the morning."

He scribbled something else. "Give me the name of that detective agency again, will you?"

She told him, and he wrote that down too.

"Okay, I think that's all I need for now. Where can you be reached, Miss Bennett?"

She started to give him the name of the hotel, but Marc interrupted her abruptly and gave his own address.

"No!" she burst out angrily, her auburn hair like fire where the light caught it.

"Yes," he returned curtly. "Look, I got you into this mess. The least I can do is help you out of it!"

"I don't need your help!"

"Like hell you don't need it!"

Sergeant Bonaro sighed. "Could we dispense with hostilities long enough to verify this address?"

"Sure," Marc said. "It's verified. Now come on, honey, before I toss you over my shoulder and carry you out of here. Think how undignified that would look," he added with a gleam in his black eyes.

She felt like exploding. He was worse than a brick wall, once he made up his mind. Stubborn, hardheaded . . . With a sigh she gave in. She was tired and still frightened, and his strength was comforting.

"Okay," she said weakly.

"We'll be in touch," Bonaro said. "Good evening."

He left. Marc paid the hospital clerk and escorted Gaby out into the darkness. Light was just glowing on the horizon, heralding a new dawn. She took a deep breath and almost fainted, she was so drowsy from the shot.

"I feel woozy, Marc," she said numbly.

"Yeah, you look it too." His black eyes scanned her bloodstained white gown and negligee. "You sure look interesting right now."

"I didn't really have the time to change my clothes before I left," she reminded him haughtily.

He let out a heavy breath. "It was a close call, wasn't it?" he asked quietly.

"It was just pure luck that I woke up when I did," she confessed, "and that there were people on the streets. I think one of the theaters had just let out. There were people all over the place."

"And not one of them stopped to help."

"What a risk to take," she said gently. "Marc, it's hard to ask a stranger to lay his life on the line for you, to risk his future and his family's future to get involved in someone else's problems. I know of one woman who interfered in a family quarrel to try to stop a man from killing his wife, and she was killed as well. I don't blame anyone for not interfering, and neither should you."

He caught her fingers in his and held them gently. "That's one of the qualities in you I always loved," he said softly, looking down at her lined face. "You always looked for the best in people. I never got past the worst."

"We had different upbringings," she reminded him. "It's easy to look for the best when it's all you've ever seen."

"I guess so. I had it pretty bad. The rough edges still show, too, don't they?" he asked with a rueful smile.

"I never even noticed them," she said honestly, looking up at him with soft, adoring eyes.

His cheekbones had a ruddy look, and he glanced quickly away. "We'd better get you into bed."

"Shame on you," she chided. "I'm in no condition to be seduced."

"I didn't mean that," he ground out. "You know it, too, so stop insinuating things."

"Don't you want to take me to bed?" she asked dizzily, laughing up at him as he put her into the front seat of the car.

"I always have. Probably I will when you're ninety and sagging all over, but this isn't the time or the place," he said.

"Spoilsport. And it's such a plush place too," she added, glancing at the soft velour. Then she noticed the dark bloodstains and touched them with regretful fingers. "Oh, Marc, I'm so sorry."

"I'll have it reupholstered," he said tautly as he got in beside her and started the car. "Don't worry about the car. It's you that concerns me."

"I'm okay," she said.

"For now." He pulled into traffic, his face hard and worried. "It's later that bothers me. If Dave floated a contract on you and some back alley hood bought it, it might be too late to do any canceling. We can nail Smith, but what if he can't call off his hit man?"

That thought hadn't occurred to Gaby. It occurred to her now, and she felt a cold film of sweat covering her body. "Oh, boy," she said with a sigh.

"Oh, boy, is right. I'm going to get a bodyguard for you, and you'll live with me until we put an end to this, one way or the other. No arguing," he shot at her when she tried to open her mouth. "Or I'll sic Uncle Michael on you," he added with a faint grin.

"I remember hearing you and Joe talk about him years ago," she recalled, leaning back against the plush seat. "I thought he must have two heads. He turned out to be nothing like I expected."

"I guess he's not too bad a guy, after all, if you like him," he replied. He glanced at her. "But I could have tanned your bottom when he told me you'd been to see him."

"I didn't know what else to do. Dad's out of the country, and I have no close friends. I was desperate."

"Yes. I should have listened. I'm sorry I didn't,

Gaby. It isn't going to be easy to live with that." His hands clenched the steering wheel. "It's damned hard to swallow that Joe was murdered. And by Dave, of all people. I thought I could trust him with my life!"

"As much as I hate to say it, there's still no real proof," she began hesitantly.

"Your word is all the proof I need," he replied harshly. He glanced at her. "From now on, honey, if you say black is white, I'll buy it."

"Thanks for the vote of confidence." She hesitated a moment. "Marc, you don't have to do this. You don't have to involve yourself."

"Shut up. How can I drive with you interrupting?" he grumbled.

She shook her head and smiled softly. "Incorrigible man."

"I always was, so don't pretend you didn't know. Close your eyes. We'll be home soon."

His apartment felt familiar and safe, but she couldn't help remembering that night she'd come here with Joe. She shivered a little, as if a ghost might be in residence. But she was tired and numb from fear, and she went where Marc led her with no resistance at all.

He took her into the bathroom and ran a tub of water. "This will help," he said. "Then you can sleep."

"I may sleep in the tub," she murmured drowsily.

"Not likely." He filled the tub and added some kind of fragrant suds that she didn't want to know the source of. Probably Lana's, she thought miserably.

"Okay, honey, in you go." He started easing the peignoir off her shoulders, careful not to jar the injured one.

"Marc, you can't!" she whispered frantically.

"Yes, I can. I know what you look like, baby," he said softly, and continued with his task. "It won't shock me to see you, and it shouldn't shock you to let me look. Except for a trick of fate, I'd have made love to you twice already."

"I know. But . . ."

"Shhh," he said softly, and he touched her mouth with his fingers. "Not another word, little one."

She stared up into his black, black eyes as he eased the gown over her shoulders, too, and let it fall to the floor. He looked at her then, at the firm, high perfection of her breasts, her small waist, her gently curved hips, and the long, sleek line of her legs. Then he bent and lifted her and eased her down into the water, smiling as she caught her breath at the strength it betrayed.

"You'll break your neck," she whispered.

"Not on a tiny little wisp like you," he replied. "Here."

He got a washcloth from the vanity drawer, put soap on it, and began to bathe her tenderly, ignoring her efforts to take the cloth and do it herself.

"Sit still now, so I don't miss any spots." He chuckled wickedly. She flushed, and he continued with his task, savoring her body as he drew the cloth over it. By the time he finished, she felt as if he'd made love to her with his hands.

"Stand up," he whispered when he was through, and held out a heated towel for her.

She got out of the tub like a sleepwalker, standing tall and proud while he dried her slowly, inch by inch, pausing now and again to touch her with tender, possessive fingers, to learn her body by sight and feel.

"I'd like to have bathed with you," he whispered, searching her eyes. "We could have made love in the bathtub."

She swallowed because his voice was as seductive as his hands. "I . . . don't want that."

"Yes, you do," he said gently, and brushed his lips softly against hers, the touch as light as a butterfly's wings. "But we won't do it until your shoulder is better. I don't want to risk tearing the stitches."

"We won't do it at all," she said, faltering.

"Gaby," he whispered, dropping the towel, "don't you want me?" And he drew her slowly against his body, looking down into her eyes with an expression that defied interpretation. He cupped her face in his hands and bent to her mouth. "Don't you, Gaby?" he asked as his mouth hovered over hers.

She couldn't answer. She could only watch in fascination. He breathed, and his mouth opened hers with exquisite patience, feeling it tremble, hearing the soft gasp of her breath as his tongue intruded into the soft, dark womb of her mouth and teased the tip of her own tongue.

She felt her body shudder at the contact, felt his heart slamming against her bare breasts. "Marc," she whimpered under the crush of his mouth.

"Forgive me," he whispered, lifting his head as his hands moved up to take the soft weight of her breasts. "Forgive me, but I came so close to losing you tonight, so close. I want to feel you, to touch you, to have the warmth of your body as proof that you're still alive and close to me."

"Don't," she protested nervously as his thumbs edged out toward the hard tips of her breasts and rubbed them tenderly, causing her to jerk with the sudden rush of pleasure it caused.

"You like having me know that you want me," he said, taunting her softly. "You like me to see the desire you feel for me. Don't you want to feel mine for you, Gaby?"

And as he spoke one big hand went to her hips, drawing her slowly against him so that she could feel the changing contours of his body. He looked into her eyes as it happened to him and smiled even through his hunger and need, and her pupils widened until her eyes looked almost black.

"Yes, you like that. You like knowing you have that power over me," he breathed. "You like feeling the proof of my desire against you."

Her lips felt as dry as bone as she searched his smiling face. "I've never . . . felt that . . . with another man. Any other man. It . . . it disgusted me in other men. But it was always so natural with you. It was never shocking or embarrassing."

"Part of life," he agreed softly. "I taught you that, Gaby. I taught you that desire was natural and beautiful, something for lovers to share with each other without shame or fear. I'm glad you remembered it that way."

She felt reckless with him, abandoned. It had always been that way, despite her anger and humiliation and sense of betrayal. She moved away a little and brought his hands back to her breasts, watching them touch the high, smooth curves.

"God, it excites me when you do that," he whispered, his voice harsh and shaky.

"I like . . . watching you do it," she whispered back, her eyes glazed with hunger as she looked up into his face. "I like seeing your hands touching me."

His eyes closed and he shuddered. "Gaby . . ."

"I'm sorry." She moved away from him, bending to pick up the towel and wrap it slowly around her. She grimaced because the movement hurt her shoulder, and she touched it as she gave him a wry smile. "It's your temperament, isn't it?" she asked as he went pale and strained to breathe properly. "All that Latin fire that smolders when a woman comes too close. I didn't mean to make you ache."

"Yes, you did, and I wanted it just as much, Gaby," he confessed, though his voice was a little less firm than usual. He straightened and smiled ruefully. "We'd better cut that out until you're in better health. What I have in mind for us will require both a big bed and a lot of strength."

She blushed in spite of her training and quickly turned away. "Oh, Marc, I have no clothes!" she said suddenly, looking back at him, wide-eyed.

"You can have one of my pajama tops. I usually sleep in the raw, but I keep a pair or two for emergencies." He went into the bedroom and retrieved a pair from his drawer. "For the sake of modesty I'll wear the bottoms. But I've only got the one bed, and I'm not leaving you in it alone. Not after what happened tonight."

She didn't even protest. Marc was the lesser of the two evils right now.

She took the pajama top and got into it while he went to have a shower. When he came back, she was tucked up under the covers because his air conditioning was on too.

He looked so delightfully masculine in the low-slung black pajama trousers that her heart went wild. His broad, bronzed chest had a triangle of thick hair that went down his flat belly and disappeared under the black fabric. He was still perfect, big and muscular and fit. She looked at him and wanted him, just as she always had.

"No staring," he cautioned. "I want you pretty bad, too, and you're in no shape for it tonight. I'll let you sleep in my arms if you want, but no playing with my chest. Got that?"

She faltered, flushed, and blustered. "I wouldn't think of it!" she finally managed to say.

He only laughed as he went to lock up. "Like fudge," he muttered. "I'll be lucky if I'm not raped in my sleep."

"You'd be lucky if you were!" she shot back.

He went around to check the doors and windows and turn out the lights. When he came back, her head was under the pillow. He flicked off the light, and she felt his formidable weight as he sank into the mattress beside her.

He laid back, his hands folded under his head. "Don't you want to snuggle up?" he said, taunting her once again.

She did feel lonely on her side of the enormous bed. It had been a hard night. A hard few weeks. She still grieved for Joe, as he must also. And she wondered, when this was all over, if she'd be alive to remember this night.

"You can't seduce me if I do," she told him, moving out from under the pillow.

"Okay."

"Promise?"

"Cross my heart," he agreed, crossing it in the semi-darkness. She could see the white flash of his teeth too.

"You wicked man," she said with a sigh. But she went close and felt his big arm enfolding her, strong and warm and comforting. Nothing could hurt her. She was afraid of nothing when Marc had her in his arms.

She cuddled closer with a long, tired sigh, and he kissed her disheveled auburn hair lightly.

"Go to sleep," he whispered. "I'll be here if you need me. I'll always be here. Go to sleep."

"I'm so tired," she said sleepily. "I was really scared, Marc. . . ."

"Yes. So was I. Go to sleep."

And all at once she did, as the medication and the fear and relief all coaxed her body into a deep and dreamless oblivion with Marc's arms holding her tenderly in the darkness.

CHAPTER THIRTEEN

When Gaby woke up the next morning, she felt warm and comfortable and safe. And only when her eyes opened and she saw a smiling Marc looking down at her did the night before come flooding back. The horror came first, along with the ache in her shoulder. And then came the beauty, the knowledge, that Marc didn't hate her anymore. That he was her friend again. She didn't dare hope for more than that, but perhaps it would be enough. If only she could be sure that it wasn't just guilt motivating him.

He looked at her sleepy face, smiling softly. "What a dish," he said. "Just the way you looked in the Hamptons that morning when I came to wake you. You look gorgeous first thing in the morning, Gaby."

"Thank you. You're not bad, either," she said drowsily.

He wasn't, either. He needed a shave, but it only added to his allure. He looked very masculine with his bare chest and dark, seductive eyes. Very Italian, she thought. Delicious.

"I wonder if I could get into *The Guinness Book of World Records,*" he said thoughtfully as he looked at her, "for the most unsuccessful attempts at seduction with one woman over a period of nine years."

"You only tried twice," she reminded him.

"In my mind," he breathed, "I tried every day." He brushed the hair away from her eyes and watched her solemnly, seeing the color in her cheeks. "You'll never know what it was like, having you in my arms all night and knowing that only two thin pieces of fabric separated your body from mine. It was all I could do not to undress you and take you in your sleep."

She stared at him, feeling strangely embarrassed. "I wouldn't have enjoyed it like that," she whispered.

He smiled. "Don't worry, Gaby. When the time comes, I'll be as gentle as can be. I wouldn't hurt my little virgin."

She searched the dark eyes above hers. "I thought you didn't believe I was still a virgin?"

He smiled ruefully and toyed with her hair. "So I was jealous." He shrugged. "I thought Joe had had you."

"I guess he was pretty convincing," she said, sighing. "He must have been out of his mind with drugs at the end."

"And not by choice, I'm beginning to realize.

He and I, we always competed. He never seemed to be satisfied. He stretched his salary beyond its reach and then came to me to bail him out." He grimaced. "Bailing him out was like my life's work. But when he started seeing you . . . oh, *bella mia*, that tore at my heart. That hit me where it hurt the most. And all the time I could never be sure what you really felt or thought."

"I thought he was a nice man," she said genuinely. "And I loved him like a brother. That was the truth."

"Hindsight is a great thing." He sighed. He searched her eyes quietly. "I'm sorry for every cutting thing I said to you. The way I behaved at the funeral, the accusations I made, the way I ignored you after. I was torn up."

"I knew that," she said softly. "I understood."

"Yeah, well, that doesn't help my conscience a hell of a lot. I never quite felt like I was in your class, you know," he added, smiling faintly at her surprise. "I've still got a lot of rough edges, and I'll probably never lose them. I came up hard with no frills. That leaves scars."

"I imagine so. But you were always in a class of your own, Marc," she replied genuinely. "And I wouldn't have been ashamed to go anywhere with you."

He tugged at her hair. "Gaby, in the Hamptons, that night at the club . . . did you really think I was trying to get you away from Joe by pretending to be interested in you?"

"Honestly?" she asked hesitantly.

"Honestly."

She lowered her eyes to his square jaw. "Yes. I couldn't quite trust you."

"That makes more sense now than it did then," he confessed. "But it wasn't that. I really thought maybe we could start again. From scratch. I . . . hoped you wanted to."

She looked back up at him searchingly. "I did," she whispered softly. "But I was afraid of being . . . that you might . . ."

He sighed heavily. "That I might betray you again. I'll have to work on gaining your trust back, little one. I think I'll work very hard at that, though," he added with a gentle smile. His eyes went over her relaxed body, and his chest rose and fell more heavily. *"Bella,"* he whispered in Italian. *"Che bella."*

Her lips parted because he was telling her she was beautiful. She stretched, wincing a little with the movement of her shoulder but feeling voluptuous and ardent with the silence of early morning around them and the warmth of his eyes on her face. It was like that morning in the Hamptons all over again, only this time they were totally alone and there was no one to interrupt them. She felt the impact of wanting him all the way to her toes. She wanted to feel his hands on her cool, soft skin. She wanted to touch him, as she had that day.

"Undress me," she whispered weakly. "Look at me."

His jaw clenched. "And take you? Because I would." He moved the cover aside. "Look."

Her eyes sought him, awed by him. "I feel that way too," she whispered, unembarrassed as she

216

looked up again. "I want you all the time. But, Marc, I can't. What if I got pregnant? That hit man—"

His big hands went to the buttons of the pajama top and lingered there while he made decisions. His breathing sounded ragged, and he hesitated.

"Don't," he ground out, anguished. He drew her up against him, holding her close, rocking her. "Don't even think it! He isn't going to get you, I promise. Do you hear me, Gaby, I promise!"

"Life doesn't come with guarantees," she whispered at his ear. Her good arm clung to his neck, loving the strength of the powerful, warm body against hers. "Don't you see, if anything happened, it would be such a sweet memory, Marc. So sweet, the memory of lying with you, being loved by you. My body aches all over."

"So does mine, but I can't," he said achingly. "I can't. Not like this. I don't want it to be an act of desperation, don't you see? We're neither of us rational enough to make a decision like that right now."

"I don't want to be rational. I want to be made love to."

"So do I," he whispered fervently. "I want your body twisting under mine. I want to take you in a way you'll never forget. But not this way."

"Why?" she whispered, and her green eyes pleaded with his dark ones.

He touched her cheek gently, although his fingers were unsteady. "I don't want to be a temporary comfort."

"Is that all you think I want?" she asked quietly.

"Yes. And you're looking at me and thinking that I'm doing this because I misjudged you. Aren't you?" he persisted.

She couldn't deny it. "Yes," he said with a sigh. "And those aren't the right reasons for something as momentous as what we'd do to each other in this bed. If I take your virginity, it has to be for the right reasons, don't you see? Such a precious gift has to be given in love. Not out of gratitude or guilt."

"You used to be less noble," she reminded him. Her body felt hot, burning, and she wanted him, not excuses, even though she realized that he was right.

"I used to be more stupid," he returned. "I made some bad decisions and they hurt you. I don't want to take any more risks. I've got a second chance now. I'm not about to blow it."

He rolled away with those enigmatic words, and while she was puzzling them, he pulled out underwear from a drawer and went to the closet for a shirt and tie and suit.

"Where are you going?" she asked.

He took off his pajama trousers and turned to smile at her fascinated, fixed expression. "I'm going to work, if not to the office. I have to find a big, mean bodyguard for you, Gaby. One who knows it all and isn't afraid to use it."

"You are . . . so magnificent," she whispered softly, only half hearing the words.

He chuckled. "I'm glad I appeal to you. You look pretty good yourself in a similar condition."

Her lips parted as his body began to react to that stare. She flushed, and he burst out laughing.

"It's so easy for you, isn't it?" she charged, tearing her eyes away.

"I accept life for what it is, that's all," he countered. He tugged on his clothing, leaving his shirt unbuttoned as he went to sit quietly beside her on the edge of the bed. "Does it embarrass you, seeing me like that?" he asked softly, turning her face to his.

"A . . . a little," she said, faltering.

"You'll see more than that when I take you for the first time," he said, his voice deep and low and gentle. "You're just beginning to understand the intimacy, aren't you?"

Her eyes sought his. "I feel so silly to have reached my advanced spinsterhood and be so unenlightened," she tried to explain.

"Oh, your unenlightenedness delights me, little rich girl," he said with a slow smile. "I look forward to shocking the wits out of you at some future time."

"If what you usually do to me is any kind of indication," she whispered softly, "I don't think I'll have enough wits to be shocked. You make me go crazy when you start loving me."

"I'd like to love you," he whispered back. He bent and brushed his mouth slowly over the pajama top he'd lent her, lingering on a hardness that the thin fabric did nothing to hide.

She moaned softly and laughed, and her hands brought his mouth even closer.

"Does that please?" he whispered mischievously.

"It pleases very much," she replied, nuzzling her face against his hair. "It always did, even when I was too young to understand why it made me feel hot all over."

"I was your first man in that respect, wasn't I?" he said teasingly, lifting his dark head. "The very first one."

"Nobody else liked me that way. Boys thought I was too skinny and shy."

"Fools," he muttered, letting his eyes tell her what he thought of her.

"I hardly even had breasts when you and I met," she reminded him.

'Sure you did," he countered, brushing them lightly with both hands. "Small but perfect, and I loved touching them. Delicate little breasts."

"Touch me," she coaxed, her fingers going helplessly to the buttons of the top. "Marc, touch me," she pleaded huskily.

"Unbutton it, then," he said quietly. "Show yourself to me."

And she did, without embarrassment or hesitation, because he was the love of her life, the only man with whom this had ever happened or would ever happen. She belonged to him.

She tugged the edges away from her high, taut breasts, and he helped her, easing it down her arms so that she was bare to his eyes from the waist up.

She arched, twisting a little on the cool sheets because she felt burning all over.

"Are you hot, little one?" he asked as he stared down at her.

"Burning," she confessed, trembling a little with it.

His hands caught her waist, slid up her rib cage, teasing her body until it stiffened. "All right, Gaby, I won't make you suffer," he whispered. He lifted her in an arch, right up to his mouth, and at the first touch of his moist, warm lips on one taut breast, she cried out.

He murmured something that she didn't hear, and the pressure of his mouth increased, taking her right inside that moistness with a delicate suction that drove her wild. She caught his thick, cool hair in her hands and tried to pull him closer, but all at once he tore himself away from her and got to his feet.

He stood with his back to her, shuddering visibly, his breath coming hard and fast. He ran a hand through his hair and went to the mirror to fumble with his shirt and tie while she lay helplessly on the bed watching him, her heart shaking her with its pounding.

"That," he said ruefully, "was a near thing. You get more seductive than ever with age. I find it incredible that you can still be a virgin."

"You're the only man I ever wanted," she said quietly. She drew the pajama top back on, trembling a little, and she grimaced with pain as she tugged it over her bandaged shoulder.

"Yes, I know. It makes me feel humble," he said surprisingly. "Want something for pain? That doctor in the emergency room gave me some pills for you."

"I'd like one if you're going to be around," she added nervously. "I go out like a light from medication of any kind."

"I'll be around, all right," he said darkly. "I won't leave you until this is resolved. What I need to do, I can do on the phone. I'll get your capsule."

She watched his broad back as he walked into the living room, straightening his tie. Her eyes adored him, but she lowered them before he came back with the capsule. She couldn't let him know how desperately she loved him. After all, it was only guilt, she reminded herself. Only guilt and leftover desire. She had to remember that, despite his tenderness. Otherwise it was going to be pure hell when it was all over and she was alone again. And this time the loneliness would last all her life. Joe had been her only link with Marc. With Joe gone there would never be another thread to connect her life to his. She would drift forever alone, without hope. She closed her eyes because she couldn't face that, not just yet. Besides, she had more traumatic concerns. Like how she was going to stay alive with a professional killer after her.

CHAPTER FOURTEEN

Gaby had no clothes with her, but Marc produced a pair of jeans that had obviously belonged to a smaller man—such as Joe—and a white T-shirt. She had to roll up the jeans, and the T-shirt was revealing enough to have bothered her if she hadn't been a model for so long. She borrowed his comb and got most of the tangles out of her hair and went to see about making breakfast.

"Not bad," Marc remarked when she joined him in the spacious kitchen. "You look a lot better in that T-shirt than I do."

She glanced down with a dry smile. "I don't suppose you'd happen to have a bra . . . ?"

"I never wear one myself," he returned. His black eyes twinkled as he stirred something in a frying pan. "Hungry?"

"I could eat. May I help?"

"Make some toast. I've got bacon and eggs under control."

"You can cook?" she exclaimed.

"I'm handy in the kitchen," he told her. He dished up the scrambled eggs onto a platter beside a tray of crisp bacon while she buttered bread and put it in the oven to toast. "I had to be, you know. Back in the old days I fed Joe and me out of a single frying pan with a hot plate for a stove. I learned to create." He glanced at her. "How do you feel about baked beans on mackerel?" he asked with a wicked grin.

"Yuch!" she said emphatically, shivering visibly as she took out the toast and put it on a saucer.

"Well, it filled empty space at the time." He pulled out a chair for her and brought a pot of coffee to the table. Then he sat down too. "Help yourself." He poured coffee into two thick white mugs. "How's the shoulder?"

"It aches a little, but it's not so bad. I still can hardly believe it happened." She looked up at him uneasily. "What do we do now?"

"We wait," he said quietly. "My uncle is digging up a witness."

"Uncle Michael found somebody who can link David Smith with theft?" she burst out.

"He thinks so." He smiled faintly as he reached for toast. "Uncle Michael has some interesting, if unconventional, ways of extracting information."

She remembered the craggy old man and felt her skin chill. She could imagine exactly what Marc meant.

She nibbled at her toast and sipped coffee. Life

had slowed for her, become precious as she realized how close she'd come last night to losing hers.

"Don't brood," Marc said quietly. "We'll get him."

"Yes, I believe that. The question is, will we get him in time?" She leaned back in her chair with a sigh, and her worried green eyes met his. "I never thought about dying. Not until the past two days. Now I've discovered that I'm not indestructible after all, and I'm afraid."

"Death comes for us all, one by one," he returned. "But as long as there's breath in my body, nobody hurts you."

Her eyes searched his hard, determined face, and she smiled. "I'm sorry I involved you. I tried not to. I wasn't going to tell you any of it. Then this happened"—she touched her shoulder gently—"and I lost my sense of reason."

"You'll never know how I felt when you told me you were leaving your house and hung up on me," he said. He sipped his coffee and put the mug down and stared at it. "I think that was when I started believing you, Gaby." He looked up, dark-eyed, wickedly attractive. "That was when I realized that I could lose you."

"Would it have mattered, losing me?" she asked, avoiding his gaze.

"Now what do you think?" he returned. His black eyes narrowed on her face. "Are you that blind?"

"You've never made any secret of wanting me," she replied.

"And you think wanting is all it is."

"You said it was."

He ran a hand through his thick, shaggy hair and glared at her. "Women," he grumbled. "They forget all the good things and go wild remembering the bad ones. Eat, will you? You're curdling my cream."

"Excuse me," she said, chiding. "Heaven forbid that I should curdle your cream." She sipped her own coffee. "Were you serious about a bodyguard?"

"Until about ten minutes ago I was," he said thoughtfully. He studied one big, darkly tanned hand. "I've got a better idea."

"Why do I have this terrible feeling that I'm not going to like whatever it is?"

"That's a fact," he said. He stood up with a weary sigh and stretched, pulling the white shirt half out of his trousers. Under it bronzed muscles rippled, and Gaby's fingers itched to smooth over them as she had earlier.

He glanced down, saw her expression, and laughed. "Want to touch me? Come on. Here I am. Come get me."

He held his arms wide, daring her, challenging her, his white teeth flashing against his dark tan.

"You're a wicked man." She laughed.

"Wicked. And hardheaded. And hotblooded as all hell, just like you. Come on. Come here and make a little love with me."

Her body tingled. She glanced up at him and then down again, demurely. "No. I'm a good girl."

"Is that a fact?"

"Besides, you have to go to work, don't you?" she asked.

"How can I work and leave you here alone?" he replied, sobering.

"You can't follow me around for the rest of my life and ward off trouble," she said, lifting her face. "Nobody can."

"I'm going to call that police sergeant and see what's going on," he said abruptly.

"Now?" she burst out. "But it's barely morning!"

"So what?" He jerked up the phone and dialed the precinct, his fingers idly fumbling for a cigarette.

Gaby cleared the table and went to wash up the breakfast dishes, her ear attuned to Marc's deep, curt tones in the living room as she walked back and forth between the kitchen and dining rooms. It was several minutes before he broke off the connection and hung up.

"Oh, boy," he said in a weary undertone. "Oh, boy, oh, boy."

It was obvious that he wasn't celebrating. His face had new lines and his eyes were stormy as they searched hers.

"Bad news?" she asked hesitantly.

"Worse than bad. That witness I told you Uncle Michael was working on? They picked him up early this morning and he spilled his guts. Apparently what he said was enough to convince the district attorney that he had probable cause for a case against David Smith. They picked up David about a half hour ago. The sergeant was just about to call and tell me."

"But that's wonderful!" she burst out. Her face flushed with color from relief and joy. "Oh, Marc, it's over! It's over!"

She ran flying into his arms, buried her face against his chest, and clung. "I was so worried and all for nothing. I'm going to buy Sergeant Bonaro a cigar, a big fat black one and—"

"It's not over," Marc said quietly, pulling her away from him.

"But I don't understand," she said, searching his troubled face. "You said they arrested Smith."

"It wasn't Dave who was after you, baby," he said. "Sit down. No. Here, on my lap."

He sank down into a big armchair and pulled her down with him, easing her head back against his arm while he smoked his cigarette.

"Gaby, Dave broke down when he realized that he'd been found out. He confessed to all of it, to stealing from the company and selling parts on the side with Joe's help. He even admitted that he gave drugs to Joe, damn him, to try to damage his credibility in case Joe said anything about the illegal goings-on. Apparently he never meant to kill him. It just happened. But he also admitted to the attempts on your life."

"I'll have to testify," she said. She understood that.

"He admitted to advertising a contract for your life," Marc continued in a voice as dark as night. "The required amount of money was put into a numbered account out of the country, and the contract man was given a photograph of you and as much information as Dave had at the time."

"Then they can pick up the killer," she ventured.

His arm drew her closer and he sighed. "Gaby, Smith doesn't know who the killer is. He's never seen him. He doesn't know his name. He can't call him off. The contract man has been paid. He'll fulfill the contract."

She could feel the blood draining out of her face as she stared up at him, horrified.

"I'm sorry," he said, pulling her closer, so that her hot face was buried in his throat. "I'm sorry. The sergeant says Dave is half crazy with fear, because he knows that if anything happens to you, he'll be tried for first-degree murder. His whole plot backfired."

"Why did he do it?" she asked miserably.

"Money. His wife liked living high. He was in love with her. Men do crazy things when they're in love. I know." He brushed his lips over her disheveled hair. "She was threatening to leave him, so he had to get some extra cash. At first it was just a few parts here and there, for some spare spending money. Then she got more demanding, and he doctored the books and got a little more. It snowballed. Eventually he was in too deep to quit. Joe found out"—he paused, his voice deepening when he continued—"and demanded to be cut in for a share. They made a pact. Everything went fine until I brought in outside auditors. I didn't really suspect anything. It was just a routine kind of thing, to make sure of my figures for the IRS. But Joe thought I was on to him. He threatened to talk, to tell me, because he knew I'd pull him out of the fire, like I always did. But Smith had no such guarantee and he panicked."

"And poor Joe got in the way." She touched his shirtfront lightly, staring at it with eyes that weren't really seeing anything. "All he really wanted out of life was to be you, did you know?" she said with a soft smile. "He worshiped you, despite all the arguments and plotting. You were his hero."

"He did a fair amount of worshiping you as well," he told her. "He always wanted you. That's why he lied to me. He knew I wanted you too."

"I didn't want to hurt him."

"Yes. I know that now. I'm sorry I didn't trust you, Gaby. It had been me and Joe against the world for too long. Losing him hurt like hell."

She nestled closer, feeling his comforting arms around her as hers wound around his neck, and she held him, rocking with him. "I wanted to come to you when it happened," she whispered. "And at the funeral, but I couldn't. I was afraid you'd hate me for the rest of your life."

It was a long minute before he spoke. "I thought I would too. Until you came to see me and kept calling me, battering away at my conscience. Last night, when you called that last time and told me someone was after you, I wouldn't have cared what you'd done. I'd still have come running to see about you."

She smiled into his collar. "Thanks, pal," she whispered.

"Oh, I think maybe we're a little more than pals, aren't we?" he asked at her ear. "After last night?"

"What about last night?" she asked contentedly.

"You tried to give me this delicious body," he replied, smoothing down her breasts and waist and hips with his big hands. "And I said no."

"You said it had to be for the right reasons," she corrected, gasping as he found the tips of her breasts and cupped them in his warm palms through the thin shirt.

"I said a lot of stupid things," he replied. He lifted his head and looked at her with black, reckless eyes. He didn't say another word, but his hands became insistent, and he watched her face color, her eyes dilate. He let his gaze fall to the T-shirt, and slowly his hands bunched it, lifting the hem with devastating slowness until her taut breasts slowly became visible.

"Don't look so shocked," he said softly. "You wanted me to do this this morning."

"What are you doing?" she whispered shakenly as he eased it over her head and moved his hands to the waist of her borrowed jeans.

"You know what I'm doing," he said in a voice as seductive as perfume. His breath came quickly, but still he smiled. His hands tugged at the zipper and eased the jeans off, tossing them roughly to one side so that she was lying in his arms without a stitch of clothing on her body.

"Oh, yes," he said in a rough, gravelly tone, smiling triumphantly as his eyes and his hands smoothed down her body and felt the silken warmth under his rough fingers. "That's much better. Here."

He lifted her hands to his tie and helped her

fumble it off, along with his shirt. Her fingers hesitated at his belt, but he coaxed her into unfastening it, into helping him get the rest of the fabric from between them. Then he lifted her, so that she was facing him, and pulled her against the aroused contours of his body and stared into her eyes as his hands smoothed her breasts and flat stomach against his warm, hair-roughened skin.

"That's right, you don't have to be in a bed or on a sandy beach," he whispered. He brushed his mouth over hers, feeling its soft trembling as his hands touched her with sudden, devastating intimacy. She shuddered and gasped.

"Marc—" her voice broke on his name, her nails scratched lightly, helplessly, against his broad shoulders as his hands dragged her body slowly, roughly, against his.

"You and I are going to do it sitting up, Gaby," he breathed, holding her eyes with his. "Right here. Right now. And I am going to watch you every step of the way, and you're going to watch me."

"But . . . we . . . can't," she managed. His hands touched her again, and she lifted right up, moaning in exquisite pleasure.

"Shhhh," he breathed. He kissed her eyelids while his hands touched her where no other man's ever had. He smiled at her sobbing gasps, loved the way her nails bit into his chest as she arched and shuddered when he found the most sensitive areas.

"Please, please." She was whispering it, her teeth nipping helplessly at his mouth as it hovered over hers, his hands tormenting so sweetly that she had to have him, had to have more than this delicious teasing. "Please, please, Marc, please, darling. . . ."

His nose rubbed against hers. His own breath was rustling now, his chest pulsating like the rest of his taut body. "Now?" he whispered. "Are you ready for me so soon?"

"Yes!" Her hips moved involuntarily against his, rotating slowly, pleading, like her soft voice.

His big hands took her hips and lifted them, positioned her. "Open your eyes and let me watch," he whispered as he moved her, watched her green eyes dilate as he searched for and found the softness, the warmth. "Yes, now, like this, be one with me. Take me softly, Gaby."

She enveloped him easily enough. He felt her body opening, like a stream absorbing a stone, so that there was no wild struggle, no trauma.

She gasped. Her eyes came back up to his, wide and uncertain and still a little frightened.

"Listen," he whispered urgently. "Gaby, listen. Show me where. Show me where and how. Here." He took one of her hands and moved it to his hip.

She didn't understand at first, until he told her with feverish whispers what he meant, and she went beet-red.

"No," he chided through the building pleasure. "Don't be ashamed to show me. Let me give you pleasure. Let me make it happen for you this time, the first time. I can if you'll show me! Only hurry. Hurry, Gaby, hurry . . . !"

His face was contorting, and her hand hesitated

only a minute before it moved, before her body shifted, and she cried out when his hips lifted.

They were both sweating. His skin was slick and wet against her lips as she buried her mouth against his shoulder. Under her she felt the power and strength of his body like a wall; she felt her body joined so closely to his, felt him as part of her, and cried out in sheer joy at the exquisite intimacy of the union. Two becoming one. Bodies locking. Surging together like whitecaps. Crashing now, frantic, slamming and grinding and pushing toward something not even tangible. She heard his gasping breaths through the thunder of her own heartbeat, felt the pressure building until it was deliciously unbearable, a tension that strung her out like a thin thread. She arched backward, crying, her hands on his hips now, holding him there, her body pleading for release, for an end to the tension that was tearing it apart.

Her voice broke into a thousand shrill pieces as the end came unexpectedly with shocking pleasure, an ecstasy that all her wild dreaming hadn't prepared her for. She felt the shudders racking her, and her mind seemed to be somewhere else, watching the body it inhabited writhing and convulsing, the face contorted as if in unbearable pain.

And it passed so quickly. So quickly that she felt the life drain from her. She was aware of shudders in the body under hers, of a voice crying out roughly, hoarsely, of hands making bruises on her thighs as they clung to the pleasured heat of her own. And more slowly than she, he began to relax, the powerful body trembling helplessly, his mouth pressed into her wet throat, against her sweat-drenched hair, his arms enfolding her, comforting her, as they came down from the ceiling.

"I don't ever want to let you go," he whispered in a voice drained of passion, deep like velvet now as his mouth touched her throat, her ear. "I want to sit here like this and hold you to me and never move."

She sighed with delicious fatigue. "People would stare."

"What people? We'll never leave the apartment again."

"I'd like that," she whispered. She nuzzled closer, feeling him shudder again at the movement.

"Want to do it again?" he whispered. His hands moved her insinuatingly against his still taut body. "I can if you can."

"Not sated yet?" she taunted softly.

"Not at all, honey. Just momentarily satisfied. I want you again. Now."

Her mouth brushed his. "Then take me."

"You aren't uncomfortable?" he asked, lifting his dark head to stare intently into her lazy, passion-filled eyes.

"No."

He smiled. "No regrets?"

She sighed slowly. "No. Not even one." She looked into his eyes with adoration. "I used to dream about doing that with you," she whispered. "And I'd wake up crying, because it never happened."

"And now?" he asked softly. He brushed the tangled hair from her face.

"If it all ended today," she whispered softly, "I wouldn't have a single regret. I wanted more than anything in life to belong to you, even if it was only one time."

His eyes closed, and he buried his face in her throat. "You make me feel humble. I wasn't even going to do this. I wasn't going to let it happen. Things were so complicated already. But I wanted what we just had together. So much, Gaby. So much! You weren't the only one who dreamed."

She smoothed his thick black hair, nuzzling his cheek. "I'm still not taking anything."

He lifted his eyes to hers. "I know." He touched her cheek. "I'd like to have a child with you," he said, as if the thought dazed him. "I'd like to live with you, Gaby."

Her heart leapt, and she started to speak, but he covered her mouth with his. "I love you," he breathed into it. "I always have."

His voice splintered as he began to move against her again. He was slower this time, more thorough, and long before it happened, she was moaning softly at the unbearable pleasure he was making in her untried body. At the last second she opened her eyes and looked straight into his. And as long as she lived she knew she'd never forget what happened then or how it felt to see the love in his eyes as well as feel it in his powerful, hard-muscled body.

They collapsed together in the chair when the trembling finally stopped, and she curled up nude in his arms and slept. It was a long time before he awoke and carried her into the bathroom, climbing into the whirlpool tub with her to ease their aching muscles. Then, lazily, they dressed.

CHAPTER FIFTEEN

"Why?" Gaby asked later when they were sipping coffee on the big sofa in the living room, sitting as close as Siamese twins.

"Why, what?" he asked with a warm smile, and bent to brush a kiss over her still swollen lips.

"You wouldn't touch me in the Hamptons," she reminded him. Her eyes searched his quietly. "Especially when you knew I wasn't taking precautions."

"The situation isn't the same now," he said softly. "We've changed. Everything has, including my priorities. I've decided that I'm tired of playing it safe. I never grew up putting my feet carefully one in front of the other, and I'll be damned if I'll do it now." He kissed her eyelids closed. "Listen, honey, I'm a hungry man, and you're the sweetest taste I've ever known. Tomorrow can take care of itself. From now on we're going to be together, no matter what."

Odd how much that sounded like a proposal, but she was afraid to ask him if he meant it that way. The relationship between them was so new, so fragile, that she didn't want to risk tearing it in any way.

She stared up at him quietly, loving the strength of his face, the darkness of his eyes, the firmness of the mouth hers had clung to so hungrily.

"What a look." He laughed, the sound a little unsteady. "You always did have the most seductive eyes. You could look at me and make me go hot all over."

"Really?" She grinned.

"Really." He pulled her closer with a long sigh. "Gaby," he breathed, burying his face in her hair, "what we did together was so profound, so beautiful. There was a reverence to it that made it much more than sex. It may sound trite, but I've never known that with a woman," he confessed quietly. "What you give me is exquisite, Gaby. Loving you makes me feel whole."

Her body trembled a little at his words. She moved closer to him, absorbing the warm strength of his big, husky body. Her hand pressed close against his chest, feeling the steady heartbeat. He was her world. A child would be heaven. But did she have the right to help create a life that might only be sacrificed if the contract man made his hit?

"Don't worry," he told her. "I'll take care of you. Uncle Michael is on his way over."

She lifted her head. "You called him too?"

"Yes. When I finished with the sergeant. He said it would be a couple of hours. Thank God it was." He laughed softly, watching her blush as the memories came flooding back and heated her skin. "In a chair. It was good, wasn't it, Gaby? I heard you cry out, and I hoped it wasn't because I was hurting you, but I was half crazy with passion. I could barely breathe."

"You never hurt me."

"A little," he said, correcting her and smiling as she flushed. "You tried to get away, but I wouldn't let you. It passed quickly, though, yes?"

"Yes."

His mouth brushed hers warmly, then her nose, her eyes. "We'll do it again tonight, Gaby. In the bed this time, so we have room to move around together."

Her face had to be beet-red, but he didn't laugh at her this time. He cupped her face in his big hand and looked at her as if he'd die trying to see her enough.

"You could have stopped me," he said softly. "You knew that? That I wouldn't force you?"

"Yes, I knew," she replied. She adored him now, more than ever, with the hope of some kind of future with him, but at the same time she felt shy with him, even after what had happened between them. "Marc, after we broke up, did you ever wonder about me?"

"All the time," he said without hesitation. "All the time. I used to burn all over, thinking about how it had been. You made an indelible impression, little one. The light went out of me when I let you go."

How odd, that phrasing. He hadn't let her go, he had thrown her out. She felt chilled as the anguish of it penetrated and the old fears came back.

He sensed that and tilted her face up to his. "I'll never let you get away again," he said huskily. "Even if it means making you pregnant and keeping you pregnant, you'll never be free of me as long as you live."

"Marc . . ."

"Hush. Kiss me," he whispered, and bent to her warm, parted lips. She soon forgot every question she wanted to ask as the aching pleasure of it made her go limp and cling to him.

"If Uncle Michael wasn't due," he breathed, "we could have each other again. I don't know how I'm going to live until tonight."

"But it was twice," she said innocently, searching his face, wide-eyed.

"I'm hungry for you," he whispered. "Insatiable. I look at you and get aroused. It's always been like that, since the very first time I saw you. It's never dulled or dimmed, that passion. It grows as I grow."

She realized that and was puzzled by it. Passion died eventually, they said, but his had lasted well over nine years. Like hers. And hers was prompted by love. Was there a chance, even a small one, that his emotions were truly involved as much as hers?

He looked down into her eyes and made a rough sound. His arms arched her up to his mouth just as the door bell pealed loudly, making her jump with its unexpectedness.

She laughed. "I guess I'm nervous."

"Sure," he said knowingly. He caught her lower lip in his teeth and tugged on it gently. "Later you and I are going to set my bed on fire."

Her body trembled at the deep, husky suggestion. Her eyes searched his. "Are we?"

His head nodded slowly. "For a long time too. I want to teach you how to satisfy me." He smiled at her curious expression. "No, you haven't yet, not completely. I'll show you how. Think about that while we get through this day."

And he got up to let Uncle Michael inside the apartment. Michael was smoking like a furnace, his big black cigar sticking out one side of his mouth, his face stormy.

"Well, I've used up contacts I hardly remember having," he grumbled, pausing to greet Gaby with a faint smile. "And I can't find out a thing. I'm hoping somebody will remember something. If they don't—" He broke off. "Have you got anything to drink in this joint? I'm burning up!"

"How about a beer?" Marc asked.

"Sure. Anything." He dropped down into an armchair and stared at Gaby. "You okay?" he asked, nodding toward her bandaged shoulder.

She touched it lightly. "I'll live. It was the experience of a lifetime," she said with faint humor.

"I've been shot at and hit a few times myself," he confessed. "Hurts, doesn't it?"

She nodded. She sat down on the sofa and studied the husky man in the blue pin-striped suit.

"Did Marc tell you that they've arrested David Smith?"

"Yeah." He sighed. "He told me everything."

The look on his face wasn't comforting. Marc came back and handed him a bottle of beer. He took a swig of it before he lit a cigar, then sat smoking it quietly while Marc sat down with Gaby.

"You haven't heard anything?" Marc asked him.

Michael shook his head. "I must be getting old, boy. I can't seem to pry information out of people like I used to. All that's out on the streets is that this guy is an import, not local talent. And that makes him a hell of a lot harder to finger."

"Can't we trap him?" Gaby asked. She got up, folding her arms across her breasts in the T-shirt. Both men gaped at her. "Well, I'm not crazy," she said. "I'm just desperate. Why sit and wait for him to come to me? We could set a trap, pick a spot for him to take another shot at me. . . ."

"You watch too much television," Uncle Michael said with gentle humor. "People get killed like that."

"It looks like I may get killed, anyway," she replied matter-of-factly. "So why can't I choose the way I want to go?"

"Because it's stupid!" Michael said harshly.

"And foolhardy," Marc added in the same biting tone.

She glared at both of them. "Well, look who's got cold feet," she said, chiding. "And what would you do if he was after you?" she asked Michael belligerently.

He shifted restlessly. "I'd bait a trap and lure him into it," he replied honestly.

"Turncoat!" Marc yelled at him.

Michael threw up his hands. "What do you want me to do, lie?"

"Yes!"

Gaby laughed in spite of herself. They were so much alike, so volatile.

"I hate to say it, but she's right," Michael replied in a calmer tone. "Can you think of a better way to get him out in the open?"

Marc hesitated. His black eyes wandered over Gaby with soft possession, and his jaw tightened. "No, I can't. But to put her at risk like that . . ."

"They've already come after me once," Gaby reminded him. "And it's a miracle that I escaped. Next time I won't, Marc."

His face paled. "I—"

"What's that cop's name?" Uncle Michael asked. "The one who talked to you at the hospital?"

"Bonaro. Sergeant Bonaro."

Michael got up and dialed the police precinct number, apparently from memory, and Gaby wondered how many times he'd been there. She had to smother a grin. She remembered the sergeant asking if Marc was related to Uncle Michael and wondered if the veteran policeman would pass out when he knew who was calling him.

Michael was connected and quickly handed the phone to Marc. "Ask him to come over," he said under his breath. He sat back down while Marc spoke to the man, winking at Gaby. "I didn't want

244

to give him indigestion," he whispered. "Bonaro and I go way back."

"Not the best of friends?" she said teasingly.

"I could put it better."

Marc said something else and hung up while they were talking. "He's on his way over." He pursed his lips and stared at his uncle. "You aren't carrying a gun?"

Michael glared at him, sighed, and with resignation lifted a wicked-looking pistol out of his belt and handed it to his nephew.

"You can have it back after he leaves," Marc said, hiding it in a drawer. "You aren't supposed to be carrying firearms."

The older man glared at him. "So I'm breaking the law! Big deal!"

Marc glared back.

Gaby got up quickly. "Marc, want some coffee?" she asked to break the tension.

His big shoulders shifted. "Yes. I guess so."

"I'll get it!" She rushed into the kitchen, relieved to be out of the line of fire. *Volatile* really wasn't the word for them.

Tense minutes later Sergeant Bonaro arrived, looking tired and out of sorts. He nodded at Gaby, shook hands with Marc, and stopped dead when he saw the man on the couch.

"Well, don't go for your gun," Uncle Michael muttered, scowling at the policeman. He opened his jacket. "I'm not armed."

"Sure," Bonaro said. "And the pope isn't Catholic."

"I never discuss religion," Uncle Michael said imperturbably. "It's a dangerous subject."

"We want to talk to you about something," Marc said. He gestured Bonaro toward the sofa, and after he accepted the coffee Gaby had brought him, he sat back sipping the rich black liquid and listened while Marc outlined what the three of them had argued.

When he finished, Bonaro eyed Gaby quietly. "You realize what could happen?" he asked.

"Look what already did," she replied.

He shrugged. "I agree. It's probably a good idea. But even with the best will in the world I can't guarantee that it would work out the way you planned. Something could go terribly wrong, and you could wind up in big trouble."

"The alternative," Gaby reminded him, "is that I can wait for him to choose his own time and place."

Bonaro grimaced. He leaned forward, folding his hands. "Yeah."

"Isn't it a fairly good guess that he knows where I am right now?" Gaby asked. "That I'm here, that Marc is with me. And isn't he probably watching the apartment?"

"I would say, yes," Bonaro agreed.

Gaby drew in a deep breath, watching Marc's hard, uncompromising face as she spoke. "Then suppose Marc goes to work in the morning as usual and leaves me here alone."

"No!" Marc said curtly. "No, I don't like it." He got up, sticking his hands in his pockets. "There has to be some other way. We could leave the city. . . ."

"He'll go along," Uncle Michael said. "He'll enjoy himself, trailing along behind you until he picks his shot. Boy, you've got a lot to learn about contract men. Part of the glamor is the hunt."

"You should know," Bonaro muttered.

"I never hired out my services," Uncle Michael corrected. "I may know the business, but I don't indulge."

"Yeah, I guess you were more inclined toward other less violent means of getting what you wanted."

"Living people pay better," Uncle Michael said, and grinned irrepressibly.

Gaby shuddered, and Bonaro glared at the old man.

"I still don't like the idea of making you a target," Marc told Gaby, uneasiness in his deep voice.

"I don't, either," she said, agreeing, "but I can't live on the run. I want him caught. That means I have to do my part to help catch him."

"Well," Bonaro said with a sigh, "I've got a marksman in my department. I'll put him around the building, along with a couple of plainclothes detectives. Tomorrow morning?"

"Yes, sir," Gaby said.

He got up. "Okay. I'll be in touch. And don't say anything over the phone, huh? You can't be too careful," he added. He touched the brim of his hat and stared at Uncle Michael. "And if you want to break arms, don't do it on my shift, okay?"

Uncle Michael grinned. "Wouldn't dream of it, old pal."

"Old pal? That will be the day!" Bonaro turned to leave. He stopped, turned back. "You keep out of this," he cautioned Michael with a long finger. "You're not as young as you used to be."

Michael spread his arms. "I'm unarmed," he protested.

"Only until I leave or I miss my guess," Bonaro said doggedly. "I mean it. If you fire one shot, you're up on charges. Got that?"

Michael sighed angrily. "Yeah, I got it."

Bonaro pursed his lips. "Black-and-white stripes wouldn't suit you," he said. "No class."

Michael shrugged. "Well . . ."

"Why don't you take up a nice quiet occupation, like raising pigeons or something?" Bonaro suggested. "Retirement is nice."

"Retirement is for dead people," the old man replied. "And I'm not doing anything illegal!" he added hotly.

Bonaro's shoulders lifted and fell heavily. "If you say so. But big brother will be watching."

"Yeah, well he'd better wear telescopic glasses," Michael returned.

Bonaro actually grinned. He nodded at Marc and Gaby and went out the door.

"He's talking about me retiring?" Michael burst out when he'd gone. "He's at least as old as I am!"

"Yeah, he probably lied about his age, just like you do," Marc said, chiding.

Michael got up. "If all you can think to do is

248

insult your poor old uncle, I'm leaving." He put
out his cigar. "Give me back my gun."

"Only if you promise to give me the bullets,"
Marc said doggedly.

"What good is the gun without ammunition?"

"You could pretend it's a boomerang," Marc said
imperturbably. He retrieved the gun from the
drawer where he'd placed it, unloaded the clip,
and handed it to the older man. "There you go.
And thanks for your help," he added with a grin.

Michael made a face at him. He looked at Gaby
as he put the gun back in his belt. "Watch yourself.
I've gotten used to you. I don't like losing people I
get used to."

"You do the same," she replied with a smile. "I
don't have any uncles except you."

He grinned. He clapped Marc on the shoulder
as he left. "Stay out of trouble with the law," he
advised from the doorway.

"Such wisdom!" Marc said tauntingly. "Take
your own advice."

Michael said something in Italian, threw up a
hand, and closed the door behind him.

"You and your uncle are a lot alike," Gaby told
Marc.

He made a rough sound. "I'm no hood," he said
curtly. "Although," he confessed, rejoining her on
the sofa, "maybe I came close a time or two. Joe
and I, we had a rough life."

She touched his face, tracing the hard lines.
"Yes, I know. Uncle Michael told me."

"Did he?" He caught her hand and pressed the
palm to his chiseled lips. "He would have looked

249

out for us, but my mother wouldn't let him. She was a real loser. She'd love us one day and act as if we didn't exist the next. In between there were men, all kinds of men. I got so sick of it. Finally I got sick enough to take Joe and run for it."

"That must have been hard, trying to support both of you. You were young, yourself."

"Not that young, honey," he said with a chuckle. "I got by. I was never afraid of hard work. That helped."

With loving eyes she studied his broad, dark face. She understood him better now than she ever had. He had so many good qualities, so much compassion. He didn't seem the kind of man who'd take a bribe to give up a girl he loved. That was the only remaining doubt she had. It was the one thing that kept her from telling him exactly how she felt about him. He'd betrayed her for money. But now it made sense. She could understand how badly he'd needed it. He'd had full responsibility for Joe, and they'd had a horrible life. Perhaps he'd been so desperate . . .

"What big eyes," he said, noticing her stare.

"You fascinate me," she said softly. "I never get tired of looking at you."

His breath caught. "Yeah, you're not bad to look at, either, with clothes or without."

"I could use something to wear," she said with a smile.

"You look fine the way you are. And we're not going to be socializing for the next couple of days," he added darkly. He searched her troubled eyes.

"Gaby, are you sure you want to go through with this?"

"I have to," she said simply. "Marc, I can't live in terror, never knowing when it's going to happen. I'd rather have all the fear at once than spread it around. I think that if it were you, you'd feel the same way."

"It might as well be me," he said, his voice deep and soft, his eyes possessive. "Do you think I could stay alive without you?"

She smiled shakily. "You managed very well for nine years."

"I knew you were okay," he said. He touched her lips gently. "I knew you were alive, in the same city with me. I knew when you became a model, who you worked for, what you were doing."

"You didn't want me working for you," she recalled.

"Because Joe set it up," he told her honestly. "I knew he was crazy about you. I kept trying to warn you off because I was so afraid that you might revenge yourself on me through him. Or worse, that you might come to care for him. Either way, I couldn't stand having you around with the past between us." He laughed bitterly. "I tried to keep my hands off you, Gaby, I swear I did. But that morning in the Hamptons I came in to see about you, there you lay in that little wisp of a nightgown, and I went crazy."

"But you stopped in time, then," she whispered, tingling as she became aware of the tension between them, the sweet tension of remembered intimacy.

"That was then," he said. "There were too many complications at the time. Now," he added, drawing her to him, "there's only you and me." He looked into her eyes so deeply and for so long that she felt heat smothering her. "I love you so much."

"Oh, Marc," she whispered in a shaken tone.

"Tell me you love me, too, Gaby," he whispered back. "Tell me you want that future we planned so many years ago and never got."

"I do want it," she said miserably. Her eyes dropped to his mouth. "But, Marc, there are so many problems. . . ."

"They'll be over soon," he said. "We'll have nothing but time."

But would they? Her worried eyes sought his. "You want me now," she said. "But what about later? What about when the newness wears off?"

"And the past," he added, reading the look on her face with precision. "Yes, and the past. You still think I betrayed you for money."

She bit her lower lip. "I . . . I'm not sure anymore," she began.

He actually smiled. Slowly. Like the sun coming out. "Come here."

She let him draw her close, and she curled against his big body as he sought her mouth warmly with his. The kiss went on and on, but it wasn't wildly passionate or even sexual. It was healing. Soft and tender and exquisitely fulfilling in and of itself. It was more a promise than a sensual caress.

Her breath caught in her throat when he lifted his head, and she touched his thick, shaggy hair with wonder. "You've never kissed me like that," she whispered.

"I used to," he reminded her with a smile. "All the time. You'd just turned eighteen and had blossomed. And I thought about marrying you and having babies and growing old together. Yes, Gaby, I kissed you like that. And you kissed me the same way. It was always more than just sex, although that's sweeter with you than I ever dreamed it could be. It's the most exquisite pleasure I've ever had with a woman."

She dropped her eyes to his collar. "Were there a lot of women?"

"Some. I couldn't be completely celibate, Gaby," he said, his voice earnest. "I'm a man. And, too, I thought there never could be anything between us again. You hated me."

"I suppose I did. I really did at first. Losing you was the most horrible thing that ever happened to me."

"Yes, I know that now. I'm sorry. When this is over, I'll tell you the truth."

"Will it be over?" she asked gently.

"Yes." He bent and kissed her softly. "How about some television? Or a movie?" he asked.

She hesitated. Her eyes searched his, and he grinned knowingly.

"Yes, I want that too," he whispered. "But let's save it for tonight. The anticipation will make it so much better."

She flushed, but she didn't argue. He turned on

the VCR and they watched some movies. Eventually she fixed supper, and then it was dark. And she sat beside him on the sofa and worried and worried about the next morning, when it would all come to a head, when she would live or die, depending on the skill of her protection and the random whim of a hit man.

It was late before he turned to her, and she read what was in his eyes with devastating pleasure.

"Now," he whispered, touching her neck, "do you want to watch the news or would you rather make love?"

"Oh, the latter, definitely," she whispered back, smiling softly at him. "In bed, didn't you say, where we had more room to . . . move around?"

"That's right," he said huskily. "And you'll need it this time, because I feel pretty amorous. I feel more like a man than I ever did in my life."

She lifted her arms around his neck and felt him rise with her cradled against his chest. He carried her into the bedroom, closed the door, and dumped her on the bed.

"Now"—he laughed, throwing himself down on top of her—"let's see what kind of fires we can make, huh? Let's see if we can make it even hotter than it was last time."

Her body moved softly under his, and she laughed at the groan it dragged from his lips. "Burn me up," she whispered, lifting her mouth to his. "And I'll put out your fire, Mr. Stephano."

"Better have a tanker truck," he murmured against her mouth. "You're going to need it!"

He wasn't gentle this time. As if he knew, now

that she was safely over the hurdle of initiation, that he could show her passion without frightening her. He stripped her with deft, sure hands and kissed her soft body slowly and warmly with every inch he exposed. By the time she was lying nude in the king-size bed with its creamy coverlet, she was trembling all over with the hungers he'd aroused.

He stood up, removing his own clothing, smiling down at her with a purely masculine appreciation in his black eyes as she watched him. "It's going to be a little rough this time," he said, half under his breath. "And you're going to love it."

"I want you," she said in a voice she hardly recognized.

"Yes, I know, I can see it and feel it. And this time you'll cry when it's over because I'm not going to give you what you want until you're screaming for it."

He slid down against her, his hands catching her hips, dragging her to him so that he was kneeling between her silky legs. He pulled her up and pressed his mouth down hard against her stomach, feeling the instant reaction of her body, the gasp that passed her lips. Her hands clenched beside the pillow as his mouth opened. His tongue traced her hips, her belly. His teeth drew across it, to her hips, down her thighs. Then he shifted her and his mouth, and heard her cry out.

It was so unexpected that she began to sob with mingled fear and excitement. She tried to get away, but he held her there, and in seconds she was shuddering with a pleasure beyond bearing. It went on and on, and the sounds she was making startled her.

He moved again. She felt his mouth on the soft inner skin of her legs, and he turned her, the rough hair on his body abrasive as he slid against her while his mouth discovered her back, his hands smoothing over her like rough silk, her breathing as rough and shaken as his own.

"Don't make me do it all," he whispered roughly. "Come here."

He rolled over on his back, shifting her, showing her what he wanted. She was so shaken with pleasure that she obeyed him without a single question or hesitation, feeling his body shudder as she touched him and watched the helpless reaction of his body to her soft stroking, to the hesitant touch of her mouth.

He laughed through the staggering pleasure, his body arching, his eyes closed. "Oh, do that again," he said, groaning. "Do it again. Yes, like that, like that! Gaby, love, *bella mia,* you make me feel such a man!"

Her long hair drew against his skin, tickling it, as her head moved. She slid alongside him, moving her body softly against his, until she could reach his mouth. She opened her own, easing her tongue into that warm darkness, her breasts taut on his chest where they rested, her body trembling with a horrible, consuming need for fulfillment.

He held her hips in his and moved her against him. "Is your need as sweetly aching as mine?" he whispered into her mouth. "Are you dying for me?"

"Yes—" Her voice broke because the ache was staggering.

He moved abruptly, throwing her back on the cover. His eyes were black, his big, hair-roughened body looming above her. She'd never seen him look like that, so formidable and dominating.

He knelt and caught her thighs, dragging her up in an arch to him. "I want to see you," he whispered. "I want to see you this way. . . ."

His hands contracted, and she gasped as his body suddenly, sharply merged with hers. His fingers pressed into her hips, and he laughed roughly as he jerked them even closer in rhythmic surges that caused unexpected sensations to rip at her body.

"Marc!" she cried out, gripping the pillow with both hands, her eyes wild and dilated and shocked with the sweeping fever of passion.

He made a sound deep in his throat and laughed again, and all at once he came down on her with the full weight of his body, his hips invading, his mouth crushing hers.

It was like nothing she'd ever dreamed. She whispered things she'd never believed she could say to a man; her hands touched, pleaded; her eyes opened and looked up into his. She needed, wanted, had to have that inexpressible intimacy of knowing when it happened for him.

And he let her watch. He let her see it begin, in soft shudders, in the dilation of his black pupils, in the anguished contortion of his face and the pulsating tension in his throat, and in the cry he bit off as his head was flung back in tormented ecstasy.

She felt the tension that arched his powerful body down into hers, felt his body ripple with helpless convulsions. And even as she watched him, she felt that silvery ecstasy pulse through her own body. Her eyes closed, and she bit her lip as the involuntary movement of her hips and the writhing of her body suddenly intensified, became a hot wave of deliciously unbearable pleasure. She cried out in a pitiful, high-pitched whimper that she couldn't control and clung to him, burying her face in his hot, damp throat as it went on and on and on . . . and it wasn't enough, she needed more, more!

"What a sweet, wild little sound," he whispered at her ear as her body shuddered. His hands smoothed back her hair. "Shhhh. Let me see you."

He lifted his head and looked into her tormented eyes, and he smiled tenderly and soothed her, even as the shudders grew worse. "Gaby," he whispered. "How beautiful you are in passion."

"I can't . . . bear it," she whispered in an agony of pleasure.

He moved slowly against her. "Soon. Almost now," he breathed, studying her face, seeing the soft contortion. "Soon. Lie still."

"Marc!"

His movements intensified as he heard her gasping cries, felt her body jerking, writhing beneath him. "Here," he whispered, drawing her hands to his hips. "Hold on to me now. Hold on while I make it happen for you. Now. Now!"

Her body seemed to explode in silken flames. She thought she would never survive it, live through it. His face blurred, became an outline in a red mist, and her nails must have hurt him as she arched up, crying in great, gasping sobs as something incredible happened to her, controlled her, beat the breath and life out of her with its crashing ecstasy, its unbearably sweet fulfillment. She felt the shudders and couldn't control them. And for a second, for a bare instant, she flew among the rainbows, became one with the sun. And with Marc.

She wept for a long time afterward, and he held her cradled against his sweat-damp body, soothed her with his big, loving hands. His mouth touched over her flushed face in soft, tender kisses that were comforting, adoring, almost reverent.

"The little death," he whispered in her ear. "Now you understand, don't you, Gaby?"

She licked suddenly dry lips. "It was . . . it was . . . unbelievable."

"Yes. For me too. We fulfilled each other completely." His arms drew her closer. "Oh, Gaby, I hope you don't want a big wedding. I just want to put a ring on your finger and keep you with me day and night for all my life."

Her face lifted. "Married?" she burst out. "You want to marry me?"

"Well, what did you think I meant? In case you haven't noticed," he added, brushing a tender kiss over her mouth, "I'm trying very hard to make you pregnant so you'll have to stay with me."

"You didn't say you wanted to get married."

"But I do," he said fervently, searching her eyes. "Don't you?"

She could hardly manage a smile through the tears. "Yes."

He laughed, bending to kiss her eyes, her nose, her soft mouth. "Yes. Mrs. Marcus Stephano. It sounds good."

"It sounds wonderful." She clung to him. "Oh, Marc, I . . ." She almost said it. She wanted to say it. *I love you.* But she couldn't. He might not want that. He might not feel that way. He could want her without loving her.

"You what?" he asked, lifting his dark head. He smiled. "Can't you say it?"

She cleared her throat. "I need a drink of water."

He hesitated, as if he wanted to say something. Then he ruffled her disheveled hair. "Okay. How about champagne? What we just gave each other calls for a celebration, don't you think?"

"Yes, I do," she agreed fervently, and he laughed as he got out of bed and went to fetch glasses and a bottle of champagne.

They drank it thirstily and then showered, bathing each other with lazy, sated pleasure. Then they slept in each other's arms without a shred of cover, and Gaby thought that she'd never in her life been so deliriously happy. Perhaps he didn't love her now. But she could hope. And perhaps he'd learn to love her as she loved him. She'd work so hard at it.

If she had time, her mind kept prodding. If the killer missed. If they trapped him. The fear, forgotten for a little while, came back with shattering force. Tears threatening, she pressed close against Marc's sleeping body. *Please,* she prayed silently. *Please don't let me lose this now, not after so many years of anguish. Please let me stay with him just for a little longer. Just a little longer.* And as she prayed, the weariness caught up with her. And she slept.

CHAPTER SIXTEEN

The morning came all too soon. Marc was already awake and fixing his tie in place when she opened her eyes. She lay quietly in the bed, her gaze wandering over him as he tucked the tie into his vest and took a comb to his thick, shaggy hair. He really needed a haircut, she thought lovingly. The thought was such a wifely one, she couldn't help but smile. She felt a warm glow all the way to the tip of her toes.

"Good morning," she murmured drowsily, and smiled when he came back to the bed and leaned over to kiss her.

"Good morning," he replied, smiling back. "How are you?"

"I ache in places I didn't even know I had," she said with a wicked look. "And I feel better than I ever felt. How about you?"

"I could go you one better on that ache," he

262

replied, chuckling as he loomed over her, "but mine isn't the same kind."

Her eyebrows arched, and he leaned over and whispered, "It's worse for men early in the morning."

"After last night?"

He burst out laughing. "Ah, Gaby, that was last night. And I've been hungry for you a long time."

She blushed prettily. "Well, I'll keep that in mind when you come back home this evening."

His face sobered abruptly, as did hers. They stared at each other for a long moment, with the specter of the day between them, with the fear that there might not be a joyful homecoming. Because there were, as the police sergeant had said, no guarantees.

He sat down beside her and touched her face with just the tips of his fingers. His eyes were protective, worried. "Gaby, fate couldn't be so cruel to us," he said softly. "Not after what we've been through. We'll be together. I promise you, we'll be together." He bent and kissed her with aching, thorough tenderness. "Together. Even if the worst happens." His voice caught in his throat, and she saw him swallow. "Because I can't live if something happens to you. I can't!"

"Marc!" She wrapped her arms around him, tears stinging her eyes as she pressed against him, feeling the wetness on her face as it smeared against his warm throat. "Oh, Marc, I couldn't live without you, either, not now. I wouldn't want to. I . . . need you so," she whispered, amending what she meant to say, what she wanted to say.

He lifted his head and looked into her eyes. "Only need?" he asked deeply. "I don't think so." He kissed her eyelids closed, and his fingers were delightfully loving on her face as he traced it. "I want to stay with you so much, *bella mia*. I want nothing in life less than to leave you now, with danger so close." His arms tightened, pulling her closer. He sighed raggedly at her ear, and she thought the warmth of his concern would last her through any trouble.

"I'll be all right," she whispered. "Really I will, Marc."

"I'll pray. And I mean that, just exactly the way it sounds." He lifted his dark head and stared at her for a long, silent moment. *"Amore mia,"* he whispered. "There will never be another woman. Not for the rest of my life. I swear that."

She leaned forward and kissed him tenderly, and then more forcefully, loving the strength of him, the warm, muscular huskiness of his big body so close to her. If only she could stay like this and not have to go through with setting a trap for a killer who might be lurking somewhere nearby. But there would never be a future for her if it didn't end now.

She drew away finally and ruffled his dark, disheveled hair. "You'll have to comb it again," she said teasingly.

"It was worth it." He got up and went back to the mirror, watching her as she climbed out of bed and dressed. "Isn't it intimate, watching each other dress?" he asked softly. "I like that. It feels like being married."

"I want to be married to you," she replied, shaking back her hair when she was wearing the jeans and T-shirt again. She grinned at him. "So don't think you'll escape this time."

"I won't," he said. "I promise." He glanced once more at his reflection and pocketed the comb. "Well, I'm as ready as I'll ever be. You?"

"Me too," she replied, folding her hands in front of her. "Want me to cook you some breakfast?"

He shook his head. "Not even coffee. Let's get it over."

"My thoughts exactly."

She held his big hand as they walked to the front door and tried not to think that this might be the last time she saw him in this life. There was a twinge in her shoulder as the stitches pulled when she reached up to hold him as he opened the door, and it reminded her of how desperate the situation was.

"See you later, big man," she said loudly, in case the killer was within hearing. "Don't work too hard."

"Yeah. You too. See you." He kissed her with apparent carelessness, and with eyes full of black torment, he forced a smile and turned and walked away toward the elevator.

Gaby went back inside, closing the door. She started to lock it. No, she thought. That would make it too hard. She'd appear to be careless.

She stared around the apartment. Which way would he come? she wondered. Where would he be? Would he come through the front door? Or

. . . there was the fire escape outside the bedroom. Would he come through it?

She twisted her fingers. It was nerve-racking, the waiting, the not knowing. It might not even be today. He might not fall for the bait. He might lie low and wait for days or weeks or months. Her eyes closed on a wave of pain. It could go on forever!

And just as she opened her eyes again they widened with horror. Because there was a noise in the bedroom. She instinctively went to the doorway to look, and there he was.

He was blond. Short, not impressive-looking at all, except for the small pistol in his hand. He didn't seem to be very dangerous; he didn't even look like a hoodlum. On the street she might have mistaken him for a businessman.

"Sorry," he said with a faint smile. "Now you won't have to be afraid anymore. It's over."

She wanted to break and run, but she couldn't even move. She prayed as she'd never prayed that their marksman was somewhere watching. Please, she thought. Please.

She could see the certainty of death in the small man's eyes. He held the pistol at his waist, and she knew that he would press the trigger any minute. He wasn't kidding. It was no joke. This was it.

Well, she thought fatalistically, if it happened, it happened. But the darkness would be so terrible without Marc. . . .

Tears welled up in her eyes as she closed them and tensed, waiting for the inevitable. Her body poised, like a dancer's, on the edge of infinity.

CHAPTER SEVENTEEN

Gaby waited for the pain. Go ahead, she thought, please go ahead. Get it over with!

And as if in answer to that bitter prayer, the sound echoed like a firecracker as a gun suddenly fired.

But no impact came. Her eyes opened, her sight blurred a little as she stood there, frozen. And as she watched, the light went out of the gunman's eyes. The pistol fell from his hands. He pitched forward onto the carpet.

She bit her lip. She knew as long as she lived that she'd never forget. She'd never forget. . . .

"That was close!" Uncle Michael said from the open window as he climbed in with his pistol out. "You okay, honey?" he asked quickly.

Her mouth fell open. "The police!"

"They're on the way up."

Seconds later the front door flew open, and policemen piled in, followed by Sergeant Bonaro and a panting, white-faced Marc.

"Gaby!" Marc yelled.

He brushed past the policemen, grabbed her up in his arms, and held her and kissed her as if the world were ending. She clung, sobbing, loving the feel of his mouth on her cheeks, her lips, her nose.

"I'll never stop shaking!" Marc groaned. "I heard the shot, and I thought, did he do it, did he hurt her, and I wanted to die!"

"I-I'm all right," she said brokenly. "I'm all right."

Uncle Michael handed his pistol to Sergeant Bonaro. "He ducked around to the side and went up the fire escape like a monkey!"

"We lost him inside," Bonaro said ruefully, with an apologetic glance at Gaby. "So you shot him?" he added with a hard glare at Uncle Michael's gun. "With your record, even under the circumstances, it's going to be pretty rough on you."

"But he saved my life," Gaby burst out defensively.

Uncle Michael threw up his hands with a faint smile. "Hey, you got it wrong," he told Bonaro. "I never fired that gun you're holding."

Bonaro frowned. He unloaded the clip and lifted the muzzle to his nose. "Hell! It hasn't been fired!"

"It must have been your guy in the apartment across the way." Uncle Michael grinned. "I saw his rifle barrel glint in the sun. Lucky he was there. I wouldn't have gotten up those steps in time. One of the problems with my age," he added with a grimace. "Maybe there's something to retirement, after all."

Bonaro was letting out a slow breath. "Don't scare me like that!" he burst out. "I had visions of a departmental shake-up if it got out that a retired mobster saved the girl while the police took the wrong elevator! Not to mention that it would most likely have landed you back in the slammer again," he said, emphasizing the point.

Uncle Michael laughed. "Yeah. Lucky I didn't shoot the turkey, wasn't it?" he murmured.

"Yeah. Here," Bonaro said curtly, handing back the pistol minus the clip. "Hide that somewhere and don't let me catch you carrying it again!"

"Okay. Whatever you say." He went to pat Gaby on the back. She smiled at him past Marc's broad shoulder. "Take it easy," he said gently. "You're safe now. I'll be in touch."

"Thanks," she said softly.

He winked at her, gave Marc an oddly smug look, and walked out the door. Minutes later, after the body was removed and the police were through asking questions for the record, Bonaro smoked a cigarette and frowned.

"Something wrong?" Marc asked as he sat beside Gaby with his arm still close and protective around her shoulders.

"I talked to my men, and none of them fired that shot," he said unexpectedly. He turned and caught the surprise on their faces. "And it wasn't the marksman, either. Of all the times to have to make a trip to the john, he had to go apparently just as the hit man was climbing up the fire escape.

Just one of those things. But you sure have a guardian angel somewhere, Miss Bennett." He sighed. "This is going to be hard to explain to my superiors."

"You're sure it wasn't my uncle?" Marc asked.

"How? His gun hadn't been fired. I checked."

"Well, whoever did it, I'm just thankful," Gaby said softly. "I didn't want to die."

"Who does?" Bonaro asked kindly. "I'll let you know what we find out. But as far as we're concerned, this was the contract killer. It's just that the way he was dealt with is going to give me a few problems."

"I'm sorry," Gaby said. "But thank you so much for all you've done."

"I wish it could have been more," the sergeant said sincerely. "Good day."

Marc walked him out. When he came back, his face was faintly amused, and Gaby stared at him curiously.

"What do you know that I don't?" she asked politely.

"That Uncle Michael carries a spare pistol," he replied. "But I couldn't testify to that in court. And why should I arouse suspicion?"

Her face brightened, and she laughed softly. "Dear old Uncle Michael, and he didn't even take credit for it."

"He didn't dare, honey. Not with his record."

"But the man with the rifle, he would have seen him, wouldn't he?"

He grimaced. "The policeman with the rifle was in the john, remember. Those necessary trips do happen, you know, despite police dramas that show the dedicated cop never leaving his post. But thank God Uncle Michael was around. When I think how it could have come out, despite all our plans . . ."

"Oh, Lord," she whispered, "it was a near thing."

"All too near," he replied. His dark eyes searched hers, but she turned away abruptly.

So now it was over at last. And his conscience was clear. She had a horrible feeling that all of it, his protectiveness and his tender loving and the words he'd whispered to her, all of it, was just out of misplaced guilt. She couldn't believe that he'd actually meant it.

"I'm glad we got at the truth," she said. She folded her arms across her breasts defensively. "I don't think Joe would have rested easy otherwise."

He took a cigarette from his case and lit it quietly, watching her, as if he could see the doubts and fears and uncertainty written all over her.

"It's too bad I didn't listen to you in the beginning, Gaby," he said. "It would have saved a lot of grief."

"You didn't know," she said simply. She turned. "Marc, I'd like to get my things from the hotel and go back to my house. Dad's been away a long time. He may have called, and I'd hate for him to worry."

He studied the tip of his cigarette. "You're sure you want to go?" he asked.

"I'm sure," she lied. She forced a smile. "Thanks

for your hospitality. And for the loan of the clothes."

"Gaby," he began, as if he weren't quite sure of what to say or how to say it.

"Could we go?" she persisted, her eyes wide and very green and threatening tears. "Please!"

"I wish you'd stay a little longer," he said tightly. "You look bad."

"Of course I look bad. Someone just tried to kill me!"

"That's not what I meant!"

She threw up her hands. "If you won't drive me, I'll walk," she said, fuming. Her mind was made up, and he wasn't changing it. Her soft heart and even softer head had landed her in this mess in the first place. She wasn't going to compound it by becoming his mistress. She didn't even believe the marriage proposal anymore. She didn't believe anything. Shock and stress and misery were warping her whole outlook.

With a muttered curse he followed her out the door.

They went to her hotel and got her purse and the few clothes she'd left there, and then they went to her house. He walked into the dark, cool hall with her, watching as she went to the phone, and rewound the message tape. She listened for a long time, smiling faintly as she heard her father's voice, calling to tell her that he was on his way home at last and would be there in another day.

"Dad's coming home," she said quietly. "I'm glad he wasn't here while it was all going on. I try to protect him, you know. He's not made of very sturdy stuff. Mother used to lead him around by the nose."

"And now you do, huh?" he said, gently teasing.

She shrugged. "Now I do." She forced herself to look up at him. "Thank you for all you did. And . . . and thank Uncle Michael again too. I owe him my life."

"He won't want it," he said with a grin. "He doesn't like being responsible for saving people. It embarrasses him."

She smiled back. "Yes."

"Anyway, you're safe now. God works in mysterious ways." He bent to crush out the cigarette in an ashtray. Then he moved just in front of Gaby, his face somber as he caught her arms and pulled her gently to him. "So now, suppose we get married and live happily ever after. Okay?"

She searched his dark eyes. "You don't have to marry me. . . ."

"Of course I have to," he grumbled, and glared down at her. "Don't you know how I feel?"

She shook her head, feeling shivery pleasure in her spine, because the look in his black eyes made her knees go weak. "No, I really don't," she confessed. "I thought . . . I thought maybe it was guilt."

"Guilt?" He laughed bitterly. "Well, yeah, maybe it was a little. But there's more than that. Much, much more." He touched her hair lightly. "Okay, I'm going to tell you the truth this time," he said, his voice deep with emotion. He took one of her hands in his and smoothed over its slender back. "That money your parents gave me was to pay back some very expensive vandalism that Joe and one of his buddies had done to an apartment on the East Side during a robbery attempt. The people said they wouldn't prosecute if Joe would pay back the money. Your parents found out about it. They said if I'd drop you and let you think they'd bought me off, they'd give me the money to clear Joe and keep him out of jail."

She burst into tears. She should have known, she thought miserably. She should have known it had to be something like that. Marc wouldn't have taken money, not the way he'd felt about her, unless it had been a desperate situation. All this time she'd fed her hatred, misunderstood his overtures, turned away from him. And for nothing!

"Yeah, I figured you'd take it like that." He sighed and wrapped her up in his big arms and rocked her while she cried. "Now, now, they thought they were protecting you. They didn't want you to ruin your life by getting married to a grease monkey with no future. They wanted something better for you."

"How could they?" she cried. "How could they? And I thought . . . Forgive me!"

"There's nothing to forgive except my own stupidity," he said at her ear, cuddling her closer. "I should have told you the truth long ago. I gave my word, Gaby, that I'd never tell you. But under the circumstances, the way things are now, I felt justified. Before we can have any future, we have to sort out the past."

"But you paid the money back," she said, searching his black eyes. "You gave it all back.

How did you do all you've done? The parts and transmission business . . . ?"

He smiled ruefully. "I guess I had a better brain than I realized, Gaby," he replied. He kissed her nose. "And a lot of incentive. In the back of my mind I kept thinking that if I got rich, I could fit into your world. And maybe if I could teach you to forgive me, I could make you want me back."

She bit her lower lip. Although he was smiling, it was no joke. He meant it.

"Didn't you know that I never cared what you had?" she asked in a whisper. "Or what you were? I'd have married you and lived over the garage and learned how to help you fix cars. I loved you," she breathed fervently. "I loved everything about you. Money never would have mattered to me if I'd had you."

His eyes glazed over, and he bent to bury his face in her throat, his arms faintly tremulous as they crushed her against his big body. "Forgive me," he whispered unsteadily. "I loved my brother. I had to put him first. As it was, I put him first one time too many. I smothered him. It's been hell, knowing that. I guess that's why I was so cruel to you. I was taking out my guilt on you."

"I forgave you long ago," she said, snuggling closer. Her arms caressed his back under his jacket, against the thin shirt. "Marc, do you still care a little?" she whispered, and stood very still while she waited for the answer.

"A little." He laughed softly. "Oh, Gaby, you're so blind. Everybody who saw us together knew how much I cared. Lana knew. She walked out on me because of it. Joe knew. We had fights over you like you wouldn't believe. Even Smith knew. And yet you can look at me and not see it or feel it or sense it."

She drew away and looked up. Then she felt as if she were drowning in the warmth of his black eyes.

"Amore mia," he whispered, "means 'my love.' You are. You always were. You always will be, until I die. Forever." He bent and kissed her with slow, sweet reverence, tasting the tears that fell from her eyes. "I love you."

"I love you too," she whispered brokenly. "I never stopped, I never will . . . oh, Marc! Marc, dreams come true, they really happen!"

"I know. Now I know." He bent and kissed her warmly for a long, long time, feeling the throb of her body and the heavy beat of his own pulse at his ribs. He smiled against her eager lips as he pulled her even closer. "Didn't you even realize at the country club that night what I was trying to tell you? I was trying to work up enough nerve to tell you I loved you, that I wanted to marry you. Cutting Joe out never entered my mind. I was burning up after what we'd shared on the beach. I have all these sweet dreams of starting over. I was so sure . . . and then you wouldn't believe me."

"I couldn't. I was afraid to trust my heart again," she confessed miserably. She looked up at him with love all over her face. "I'm so sorry about Joe," she began.

"Me too. I'm sorry we didn't find out in time to save him. He was a pretty good boy." He drew in a steadying breath. "Gaby," he whispered, "what if we name our first son Joseph? How does that strike you?"

"Like lightning," she murmured on a tremulous smile. She touched his face with a tender hand, loving the freedom she had now to touch him, to be possessive. "Can we really live together?"

"Sure. But we'll get married first," he told her. "And soon. Just in case," he added with a wicked grin, and touched her stomach, "when does your father come back?"

"Dad!" She drew away, gasping. "I forgot all about him!"

"That's no way to treat our son's future grandfather," he said, chiding.

"He'll have so much to hear about," she said with a smile. "And so much to be thankful for. I think he hated what Mother cooked up. He never would say a bad word about you in recent weeks."

"I'm glad. I'll try to set his mind at rest. I promise you that. Now. Suppose you make us some coffee?" he murmured, brushing a kiss across her mouth, "and we'll talk about the ceremony."

"What a delicious idea." She laughed. She locked her fingers into his and led him into the big kitchen, her face bright and smiling, her hand curling lovingly into his. It was the most beautiful morning of her life. It was the beginning. A belated beginning, and all the nightmares were laid to rest at last. Joe would be pleased, she thought as Marc smiled down at her. Joe would be pleased.

CHAPTER EIGHTEEN

A year had passed since the gunman had come after Gaby in Marc's apartment. They'd been married in a quiet ceremony barely a month later with Gaby's father and Uncle Michael as witnesses. Her father had accepted the news of the engagement with obvious relief, and his halting explanation to his future son-in-law had been cut short by a beaming Marc, who was too happy to hold grudges.

Uncle Michael had consistently denied his part in saving Gaby from the gunman, but she knew, of course, because of what Marc had told her, that the old man was just denying it to stay out of prison. Nevertheless she'd promised that he could be their children's godfather, and he'd accepted that role with evident relish. Gaby only hoped that he wouldn't take his duties too seriously. She didn't really want her children schooled in subjects like the protection business.

She was almost through cleaning the white sidewalls on Marc's 1956 Chevy, which they'd repainted the same bright red it had been in the old days. Marc didn't know what she was doing; he'd told her to stay out of the sun. It was hot, and she was tiring easily these days. But it was a labor of love. They'd gone on their honeymoon to the Hamptons in the Chevy, and she had a special affection for the antique car.

"Where are you, babe?" Marc called from the house.

She glanced up, gnawing her bottom lip. "Uh-oh," she said under her breath. She pushed a sweaty strand of long hair out of her eyes and stood up, touching a hand to her aching back. He was going to be difficult when he realized what she'd been doing, she just knew it.

She smoothed her gaily colored smock top down over the soft bulge of their first child and smiled guiltily as he bounded down the steps. This house was just minutes from the city, a lovely old stone house that had a history as charming as its setting on Long Island Sound. Gaby had loved it at first sight, and Marc had immediately given the real estate agent a down payment. It was perfect for a young family, and it had an enormous garage to house their cars.

"What do you think you're doing, may I ask?" he burst out when he saw her. Sweaty hair, greasy hands, spotted maternity blouse, wet spots on her slacks. He threw up his hands. "What am I going to do with you?"

She wiped her nose, leaving another spot, and walked toward him with the water pail in her hand. "Well, the white sidewalls were dirty," she mumbled.

"And you're nuts!" he shot back. He looked formidable that way, hands on his lean hips, sexy as all get-out in his khaki slacks and white T-shirt. He looked bigger than life sometimes, very dark and muscular. She liked running her hands over his big body and watching him tremble softly. The passion they shared hadn't diminished one bit, and the camaraderie had grown and grown. Gaby thought she'd never been so happy in her life. And now, with the promise of a child to complete it, she felt as if she had the world.

"Now, darling," she said, sliding her body up against his to kiss his firm chin, "no fussing. You'll upset the baby."

"I'll upset the baby," he mimicked, still scowling at her with narrow black eyes. "What about the baby's daddy, huh? What about—"

"Shhhh," she whispered against his firm mouth, smiling as the anger drained suddenly out of him, and he wrapped her up in warm, protective arms. His kiss grew deeper, more intimate.

"Drop that pail," he breathed huskily, talking against her mouth, "and let's lie down and discuss this."

"If we lie down together, we won't discuss anything," she whispered back. "And Uncle Michael is due here any minute for lunch, remember?"

He muttered something about Uncle Michael, and she laughed again.

"Later," she whispered. "I promise."

He let her go with a sigh. "Why do we have to have company?" he asked miserably.

"Because Uncle Michael has just come back from Italy, and we haven't seen him for two months," she said. "And because I owe him my life."

He studied her for a long moment. "Yeah," he said hesitantly. "I guess so."

"He did shoot the gunman. You said so."

"Actually, what I said was that he had a pistol," he said, hedging. He looked uncomfortable. "Never mind, let's eat. . . ."

"Wait just one minute," she said, touching his muscular arm. "Would you mind explaining that?"

"Gaby . . ."

"Suppose you tell her the truth, boy?" came a deep, amused voice from just above them.

Uncle Michael was standing on the deck, leaning over it with his forearms crossed and a big black cigar in one finger.

"Hi!" Gaby called. "Welcome home!"

"Thanks! I had a great time seeing the family, but it's nice to be back. Marcus, your grandma and your uncle send their love. They want you and Gaby to come and see them after the baby's born."

"We'll do that," Marc promised. He looked down at Gaby with mingled adoration and concern. "After the baby's born," he added.

Gaby went up the steps and sank into one of the

chaise lounges, closing her eyes briefly as the cool, salty sea breeze tangled her hair. Beyond the deck seabirds called to each other above the crashing of the surf. "I love it here! Sit down, tell us all about Italy," she told Uncle Michael.

"In a minute," he promised. He straightened, staring at Marcus. "Tell her. It's time she knew the truth."

Marc drew in a deep, short breath. "I don't know. . . ."

"He fired the shot that dropped the hit man," Uncle Michael said bluntly.

"He what?" Gaby burst out. She sat up, staring at Marc. "You shot him?"

Marc stuck his hands in his pockets and glared at his uncle. "Well, I was afraid the police wouldn't be watching the right place," he muttered. "I was waiting outside the building with Uncle Michael. We spotted the hit man, but Uncle Michael couldn't get up the steps quick enough. I could. And I used to be pretty good with a gun." He shrugged. "I got up the steps just in the nick of time."

"But why did you let me think it was Uncle Michael?" she demanded.

"The gun wasn't registered," Marc said quietly. "If the police had found out it was his, he'd have been in trouble. I dropped the killer, dashed back down the steps, and then got back upstairs just after the police did. Uncle Michael came in the window and told the gospel truth. He hadn't fired the gun he was carrying."

"I couldn't admit it in front of the police," Michael shrugged. "Later I thought Marcus had told you the truth. Not that I wouldn't have pulled the trigger on that guy," he added, "but I hate taking credit I don't deserve. He saved your life. I was just along for the ride." He grinned suddenly. "Bonaro suspected, though. He came to see me a couple weeks later. We had a hypothetical discussion. He's not a bad guy, for a cop. We played a game of chess after. That was when I retired for sure."

"Retirement suits you," Marc told him. "You look more relaxed."

"I'm bored to death. But I'm too old to do time, so I guess it's all for the best. Maybe there's something to being law-abiding. And, besides, I can tell your kids all the things they shouldn't do."

"Which will be a blessing. Just don't teach them how to break arms, okay?" Marc said, taunting him.

"Who, me? I'll be a model uncle," he returned. "What's to eat? I'm starved!"

"Ask Carla for something. She's working on lunch right now," Marc told him.

"I cook better than she does," Uncle Michael said, insulted. He got up. "Maybe I should go in and give her a hand."

"Oh, Lord," Gaby muttered, hands at her mouth when he went inside, "Carla will kill him!"

Marc simply laughed.

"You saved my life and you never told me," she said softly. She touched his face. "Why?"

He smiled. "It's a dumb reason," he said, confiding in her. He toyed with her smock top. "I wanted you to want just me. Not to agree to marry me out of gratitude."

"I loved you," she said. "It was only that. Always that."

"Yeah. I wanted to be sure, that's all," he said. He searched her eyes for a long moment, and she felt his heartbeat against her fingertips as he held her close. "I do love you so, Gaby," he breathed fervently. "You and this little one."

She reached up, brushing her mouth tenderly over his. "They say if you save a life, you're responsible for it from then on."

He chuckled. "That will be a pleasure." His mouth brushed against hers, caressing it softly, warmly. He lifted her closer, deepening the kiss, so that they were both trembling and breathing raggedly when the sound of fierce arguing erupted from the kitchen.

"Do you suppose we ought to separate them before they kill each other?" Gaby asked.

"If we want lunch, maybe so." He grinned.

There were louder noises from the kitchen and a metallic crash, followed by unprintable words in a deep, angry voice.

"And we'd better hurry," Gaby said.

He touched her hair with a possessive hand, smoothing it down. "No rush," he said. "We have time now. All the time in the world."

She looked up at him. Well, that being the case, she wound her arms around him and lifted a radiant face to be kissed. He laughed tenderly as he bent his head.

Inside the house, loud English had changed to louder Italian. And it sounded as if lunch would be just a little late.

NAN RYAN

"Nan Ryan is one of Passion's leading ladies." —ROMANTIC TIMES

☐ 20603-0 **SUN GOD** $4.50

☐ 11306-7 **CLOUDCASTLE** $3.95

☐ 20337-6 **SAVAGE HEAT** $4.50

☐ 20464-X **SILKEN BONDAGE** $3.95